the Boss

Andrew O'Keeffe

Roundtable Press

Published by Roundtable Press
PO Box 415
Bellingen NSW 2454
Australia
Phone: +61 (0)412 616 047
Email: info@hardwiredhumans.com

Cover and text design by Sheila Parr (sheilaparr.com)
The epigraph is reprinted from *HRMonthly*, March 2005.

Publisher's Cataloging-in-Publication Data
(Prepared by The Donohue Group, Inc.)

O'Keeffe, Andrew.
The Boss : a novel : based on true stories about bosses at work / Andrew O'Keeffe.—2nd ed.
p. ; cm.
Originally published: Royal Exchange, NSW : Great Bosses, 2006.
ISBN-13: 978-1-929774-89-0
ISBN-10: 1-929774-89-3

1. Supervisors—Fiction. 2. Clerks—Fiction.
3. Office politics—Fiction. I. Title.
PR9619.3.O5 B67 2009
823/.993/44
2008941990

First published in 2006 by Great Bosses Pty Limited

Second Edition

"... my key task is to keep sane people sane in insane places."

Professor Manfred F.R. Kets de Vries

Why I Wrote This Book

AFTER OUR IMMEDIATE FAMILY MEMBERS, the next most important person in our life for most of us is our manager! If we work for someone, then this person, this boss, has a major impact on our life-journey because of his or her impact on our energy—energy for work and the energy we have for outside of work.

A range of studies reveals a disturbing picture. A Human Synergistics study found that ninety percent of people work in a negative culture of blame, indecision, or conformity. A range of other studies shows a similar, alarming picture. In most workplaces, less than fifty percent of employees believe their senior executive is worthy of their trust. If they could, thirty percent of people would sack their boss. Of people who choose to change jobs, some eighty percent do so because of their manager. In a Corporate Leadership Council study, when people were asked what aspect of work was most important to them, a "quality manager" was at the top of the list. The behavior of many managers and the nature of many workplaces create a dilemma shared by numerous people in today's society; Is corporate life for me? And if so, how do I cope?

This book exposes the true behavior of many managers. It is neither a textbook nor a book of theories. It's a novel about what really happens in many workplaces.

As I talked to people about this book, overwhelmingly people instantly recalled an event about a bad manager. Generally, the event was still emotionally raw to the person, and even though it may have happened years before, the person shared the story as though it had happened yesterday. The emotion of the experience—the fear, hurt, despair, melancholy, or joy—was still vivid.

While this novel is based on true stories, the organization and the characters are fictitious. Any resemblance to persons living or dead, or to any organization, is purely coincidental.

In writing this novel, and in exposing what really happens for many people at work, I hope to improve the standard of management. Managers who read this book will make quiet resolutions to be better managers. HR staff and leadership trainers and coaches will use the book to demonstrate the emotional impact managers have on people's spirit. Young leaders can gain from observing the impact they have on their staff and how that impact varies when they model themselves after poor role models versus good role models. Ultimately, excellent managers will be the norm rather than the exception. Hopefully, this story provides insight into the management practices to avoid and those to adopt.

At the end of the book we provide ideas and question guides to help organizations use this book in developing managers.

And this book is very much written for staff members. If you have ever felt diminished at work, there is a high probability that this was due to a poor relationship with your boss. I am hoping that as you read this book, you are comforted that the "problem" was most likely not you—more than likely the problem was the situation you were in and the behavioral choices of your boss.

Whether you are someone who manages or someone who is managed, I hope you are moved by this book. I enjoyed writing it, motivated by the desire to share what's happening in many workplaces and to do something to improve the situation. No doubt you will be able to associate with many of the people, situations, and emotions expressed in this story.

Andrew O'Keeffe
April 2009

1
The Dog in the Manger

DEADLY DI. THAT'S WHAT WE CALLED HER—the boss from hell. The boss who burns you or crushes you, take your pick. Today she passed the point of no return; she outdid even the worst version of herself.

I had planned my day so that I could prepare for an important meeting I was chairing at noon. At about ten o'clock I received an email from Deadly Di, sent from her BlackBerry. She was in an executive meeting, and she wanted a presentation prepared for her to present to the executive team at two o'clock. There was no "please." There was no context and not much detail in her email. True to form, she left me to guess what she wanted.

To do what I assumed she needed would take me about three hours. If I took that long to do *her* job, I'd have to postpone my own meeting. I'd have to contact internal and external people to reschedule. And my project would be delayed. Shit. What should I do? Then I remembered the advice that Di was always giving me.

"Lauren, don't strive for perfection," she is always telling me.

"Lauren, drop your standards," she says.

"Lauren, you only need to do an eighty percent job," she warns me. "The return on the remaining twenty percent is not worth the effort."

So, okay, I would do an eighty percent job—near enough to be good enough. An eighty percent job would take me about an hour, and I could then rush to be ready for my own meeting.

I finished the presentation for Di around eleven-thirty and emailed it to her. I then did what I could to get ready for my meeting.

About mid-afternoon, Di caught me in the corridor outside my office. I had my back to her, so I didn't realize she was there, about ten yards away. I jumped out of my skin when she shouted at me, "Lauren, that presentation you did for me was crap." I froze. Turning, I glanced around to see who was listening. People either had their heads down or were disappearing into their offices.

"It's typical of your shoddy work," she sneered loudly, waving a stack of papers I assumed was the presentation. "I was embarrassed to present this analysis as the work of our team. In fact, I had to apologize to the whole executive team that the work was yours. Have you got no sense of pride—if not for yourself at least for your colleagues?"

Not yet done, she added, "Really, Lauren, eighty percent is not good enough."

I sought refuge in my office, embarrassed to be humiliated in front of my colleagues. She followed me.

She slammed the presentation on my desk. "If you dare give me one more shoddy piece of work, you'll be looking for another job."

She stormed out. I shut the door and just stood there, shaking.

Thank goodness I was now heading home. The drizzle outside matched my miserable mood. I turned out of the parking lot and merged into rush hour traffic. I ran through a red light and the camera flashed. Now the bitch had cost me a fine! Concentrate, Lauren, I told myself.

I couldn't get Deadly Di out of my mind. Deadly Di was Di Ashman. What a horrible eight months since she became my manager. She was cruel. She was selfish and insensitive. She humiliated everybody under her—except her few favorites. She was constantly negative, always complaining. The words "thank you" never forced their way out of her mouth. To Di, life was a competition that she had to win. And when she won, she didn't know how to stop.

I felt angry most of the time. Angry that she had ruined a job I loved, a job I had been doing well. Angry that she made me feel inadequate. Angry that my eleven-year career with the company was now derailed. Angry with the amount of work she piled on us. Angry that I was so drained and had little energy left for my family.

I slowed down and watched my speed. At least the drizzle had stopped.

I parked in the driveway, still fuming from being humiliated—humiliated in front of my colleagues and with the executive team. Annie and Harry, my beautiful kids, ran out of the house to meet me. I hugged them, trying to hide my frustration.

Walking in the front door, I almost tripped over Harry's toys. I bit my lip to stop myself from snapping at him and stormed into the bedroom. I threw off my shoes and sat on the bed. By the time Paul came into the bedroom, I had changed into my jeans and T-shirt and felt better for peeling off my corporate life.

"Should I ask about your day?" he said, sitting on the bed. I sat down as well.

"I've had it with her!" I couldn't keep it in.

He slid along the bed and put his arm around me. He knew I was talking about Deadly Di.

Tears started to roll down my cheeks. "I just can't believe she's so cruel. Why am I putting up with this?"

"And the answer is?" Paul tried to smile. "You can't keep going like this—we can't keep going like this," he pleaded. He was right. I had to put a stop to it.

"I'll tell you what," I spoke louder now and sat up. "I don't need to be a victim. She can humiliate me. She can even hurt me. But I have a choice too. I can leave!"

"Thank you, Lord!" shouted Paul. "You've finally got there." He'd been at me for weeks to do something.

Even though I was still angry, Paul's sudden happiness made me realize how much I had put him and the kids through, taking my anger and frustration out on them day after day, all because of Di Ashman.

He hugged me, this man who always supported me.

"So, will you change divisions?"

"No, I'm over it. I'm leaving!" I couldn't believe how good it felt to say that. "Anyway, I need experience elsewhere, so now is a good time to go."

Paul held his hands out to pull me up from the bed. "Well, start looking tomorrow. You've had a miserable eight months. We all have!"

I let him pull me to my feet. He hugged me again. I felt stronger from his warm embrace. Annie came into the room.

"Who are you talking about?" she asked.

"My boss," I forced a smile. Annie screwed up her face. Paul and I exchanged grins.

"Okay," Paul clapped his hands, "I'll cook dinner. Annie, you and Harry get ready for your bath. Mom will be there in a minute."

By the time we sat down to eat, my dark mood had lifted.

Later that night, when I tucked Annie into bed, she asked me to read her a fable. Annie had taken to Aesop's fables recently after a friend at Girl Scouts had gotten her interested. Paul had laughed about that. His mom had raised him on Aesop. She thought it would help prepare him for adult life. But fables were fairly new to me. Last week, Paul had gone hunting for his old Aesop book and found it hiding in a dusty box somewhere in the attic.

I flicked open the book and read a few pages to Annie. The last one was a fable called "The Dog in the Manger."

> A dog was lying in a manger on the hay, which had been put there for the cattle, and when they came and tried to eat, the dog growled and snapped at them and wouldn't let them get at their food. "What a selfish beast," said one of the cows to her companions. "He can't eat it himself, and yet he won't let those eat who can."

Annie's blue eyes were getting heavy, and her blonde head was sinking into the pillow. I kissed her cheek. As I turned out the light, she murmured, "Your boss sounds like the dog in the fable."

She was right! Di Ashman was the dog, keeping everyone else from satisfaction with her mean and nasty attitude. And even a seven-year-old could see it. It sealed my plans.

I slept well that night and woke the next morning, eager to find my new job.

2

The Search

FINDING A NEW JOB wasn't as easy as I'd hoped. I'd expected a better response from the recruitment agencies. I thought my resume was impressive enough—good qualifications and a track record of steady promotions that had taken me to my current role as strategic marketing manager of a major corporation. I had been on a fast-track career as a "high potential." Apparently, that wasn't enough.

I decided to contact Chester Osborne at the recruitment agency Radcliffe and Richards—a firm of so-called headhunters. I had met Chester some months before at a Marketing Institute breakfast. Chester had enthusiastically introduced himself to everyone at the table, swapping business cards and making comments about each of our industries. At the time, he had seemed interested in my company and in me. Of course, now that I was looking for a job, all I got back from him was a polite "thanks, but no thanks" letter that I received two weeks later.

I tried a few other top-tier headhunting firms and got the same response: "Thanks. We'll be in contact."

For the next three months, I combed the Internet for jobs. I sent my resume to a number of recruitment agencies and posted my resume on various Web sites. There were plenty of jobs coming through, but nothing was right for me.

I struggled on with Deadly Di in the face of her vicious attacks on me and everyone else. As time dragged on, I got more and more frustrated.

I was miserable at work and depressed at home. My mood was foul and I snapped at Paul and the kids. Paul pushed me to pay more attention to Annie and Harry. Each morning, I grew more anxious as I headed off to work. I clung to the hope that I would soon escape. Maybe I needed to take a step backward to get away. I started to look at lower-level jobs, which did nothing for my self-esteem. I was at my lowest point when suddenly everything changed for the better.

Without telling me, the market research team at my firm had nominated me for the Excellence in Product Strategy category of the Marketing Excellence Awards. What an honor it was to be presented with the award at a gala dinner of the Marketing Institute. And what a difference receiving an industry award made in my job search! I received three invitations—from the same firms who had previously ignored me—to exclusive boardroom lunches with "a select group of experts in their field." Of course, I accepted all three invitations.

The day after the awards night, I thanked Di Ashman for signing the nomination form for my award.

"My pleasure," said Di, promptly turning her attention back to her computer screen and ignoring my excitement. Dog in the manger. It was during the celebration drinks with the market research team that I learned why she was so dismissive.

"No way!" my friend Michelle exclaimed with a shocked look. "When I first mentioned to Di that we were nominating you for the award, she *laughed*. We had to really hound her to sign the form. She said the nomination was premature because this was only your first strategy project. She said you didn't have a track record yet and it was too early to back you. We kept at her until she finally gave in."

Deadly Di progressed from mean to psychopathic. She fired more attacks at me. She gave me projects to complete, but then, at crucial times, she changed the rules. She deliberately withheld information from me. She criticized my output. She gave me urgent jobs late in the day. She shouted at me in front of others.

But winning the award had given me a huge boost of confidence, and Deadly Di's attempts to crush me didn't succeed. Now that I had been recognized as a capable professional with plenty to offer, it was surely only a matter of time before the right job came along.

In fact, it was exactly one month after the awards night when I received a call from Chester Osborne.

"Lauren, no doubt you remember me from a Marketing Institute breakfast several months back. I was in the audience at the recent awards dinner. Congratulations, by the way. Do you have a moment to talk?"

"Sure," I said, "good to hear from you, Chester."

"I have a role I'm researching that may interest you. We've been asked by a major corporation to fill a key position—strategic marketing manager. The company has ambitious growth plans with new product and service directions they want to pursue. They would like to talk with you. Are you interested?"

"Well, Chester," I said playing coy, "I may be interested." I was desperately hoping this would be my ticket to escape the evil Deadly Di.

Chester continued, "You should know that one of the senior executives at the company has specifically asked for you to be part of this process."

"Really! Who?"

"It's a little difficult for me to say—this is a confidential assignment. Why don't you come to my office and we can discuss it further?"

"Okay, Chester, I'll do that. Thank you for calling."

We made plans to meet the following week. I hung up, excited that this could be the job I'd been waiting for. At least it gave me hope.

Five days later, I knocked on the imposing wood-paneled door of Radcliffe and Richards's office and entered. The young, smartly dressed receptionist quickly and discreetly ushered me into a private room. I sat and waited nervously. I hadn't been in an interview since graduating from college eleven years before. I was out of practice.

Chester got to the point quickly, though. After covering the normal pleasantries, he explained the job was at a company called Harlow Kane, a global developer and distributor of business software and a provider of business consulting services. Outside China and India, the business was mainly a sales and service organization.

"Please treat this information as confidential," he said sternly. I nodded. "Meg Montgomery from Harlow Kane has asked that you be considered for the role. She said she's met you a couple of times."

My heart beat with excitement. The opportunity to work with Meg Montgomery definitely hit the target. She was a shining light in the local marketing conference circuits, smart, savvy, renowned for her ability to get right to the heart of the problem, and from what I'd seen, a kind and generous person as well. An opportunity to work with Meg was a dream come true.

At the end of the interview, Chester and I agreed that I would meet with Meg to discuss the role.

My interview with Meg was scheduled for three days later. I let Deadly Di know that I had a personal commitment that afternoon. An hour before I was to leave, Di asked me for an urgent report. That's all I needed—an unreasonable deadline to stress me out. I did her stupid report—which would probably sit in her tray for a day—and raced to the car.

About ten minutes later, I had the horrible feeling I was lost. If only Di hadn't slowed me down. Trying to stay calm, I called Paul, but he was with a patient. "Damn!"

What a disaster—being late for the interview for my dream job.

I stopped the car. Shit. I wondered if I should ring Harlow Kanc and let them know I'd be late, but I decided to hold off on that until the last moment. I grabbed the map and tried to work out where I was. Yes, I remembered passing that road a few minutes earlier. That might just do it. I did a U-turn and hit the accelerator.

Thank goodness. With a few minutes to spare, I made it to the Harlow Kane parking lot.

I had only a moment to compose myself. I locked the car and looked around, taking in three deep breaths. Harlow Kane shared a modern business park a fifteen-minute drive from the central business district. Ten or so other companies were also located in the park, with Harlow Kane occupying the prime space and the largest building—a modern multistory complex.

I reported to the receptionist and waited for Meg. I sat in the plush leather lounge chair and took in the spacious surroundings and the aroma from the ground-floor coffee shop. I had only just sat down when I saw Meg approach, smiling at the people she passed. She strode toward me, waving hello from a distance. She looked sharp—blonde hair, a navy suit, and a gold necklace. We shook hands warmly and she thanked me for being interested in talking about the job opening.

We caught the elevator to the nineteenth floor, one floor lower than the top. She invited me to sit at the end of a large table, then moved her chair so we were sitting almost side by side. She looked me in the eye.

"I assume we both have the same objective here," she said, "that at the end of your visit today we'll both know whether we're interested in continuing the discussion about working together." She made it a shared objective instead of a question of her assessing me. This was great. She was treating me like a professional. I was already sure I wanted to work with her!

Meg sat upright, leaning slightly forward. She briefly and confidently spoke about Harlow Kane's business direction and the responsibilities of the role. She described the job: to lead the strategic marketing for the firm, reporting directly to her. What an opportunity! It was exactly the role I wanted, and even more important, I would be working for someone I really admired.

She congratulated me on my award, asked me about my background and experience, and politely probed me on my abilities and track record.

"And in your current role," she asked, "what is the achievement you are most proud of?"

"Definitely the review of the company's product strategy," I answered. We talked about the situation that led to the review. She asked about the key challenges of the review and what obstacles I had overcome. She asked me how I engaged other people in the process. And she probed me on the outcomes of the review and what impact there had been. We talked for probably thirty minutes just on this topic. By then, she knew almost as much as I did about the review and had gained good insight into the way I worked.

Meg asked me why I was thinking about leaving my current job. I didn't want to say it was because of a nasty manager. That wouldn't have been professional. Instead, I told her that after eleven years with the same company, I needed a career change.

"But that wouldn't be a reason in itself," she observed. "Presumably, there's a specific reason for looking around right now. Are you not enjoying your current role?"

I still hesitated to talk negatively about my current manager or company. "Well, I had a call from Chester, and so I met with him. This opportunity seems exciting and challenging and really worth exploring. It's come at a good time in my career."

She wasn't shifting. "What is it that this role provides you that your current role doesn't?"

"Two things. First, the opportunity to work on a total marketing review that impacts the whole positioning of the business, and second, the chance to work with a manager from whom I can learn and grow."

"Who do you work for now?"

"The marketing director."

"What's the marketing director's name?"

"Di Ashman," I answered. Meg smiled, perhaps knowingly. She didn't push the point any further.

Meg then invited me to ask her questions. She answered openly and was completely unguarded in the way she spoke—how refreshing. I asked her more specifically about the project of reviewing the firm's marketing strategy. She stressed the importance of the initiative. It was to be a major review of the company's product and services strategy and its branding. Meg explained that she had good experience in marketing strategy, but she couldn't spend enough time on the subject. She needed someone devoted to the project to make sure it got done.

"I can't emphasize enough how extensive this review will need to be," she explained. "And it's so critical that it be done thoroughly. I anticipate it will take about two years to complete the whole review, to get it to a point of sign-off and implementation."

She explained the two-year time frame. "We can discuss in detail the key steps of the project if and when you join us. But to give you an idea, I'm thinking there might be several stages. Stage one would be a review of where we are currently with our products and services. We then need to compare our performance against the performance of our competitors and develop a gap analysis. Also at this stage would be an assessment of our sales capability, our channel strategy, and our product development capability. After that, we would need to conduct research of customer needs and motivators. And then the final stage might be the ultimate recommendations and implementation plan. That's my current thinking, and it's only a guide. You and I would work out the actual project plan when you joined us."

By now, I was jumping out of my skin with excitement. I was also slightly scared at the responsibility of leading such a review. This must have shown on my face.

"You won't be on your own with all this," Meg smiled. "I will be here to mentor you, and I know a good consultant in this field—Sally Morton—who could work with us as well."

"It all sounds fantastic, Meg," I said enthusiastically. "I would so much love to be offered this role."

"That's great, Lauren. Anyway, you can see why I think the project will take at least eighteen months, more likely two years, to complete."

"And of course," Meg added, "the outcomes from the project will impact the business for at least the next decade, so we can't afford to rush it—we don't want to get it wrong."

I was so pleased to hear this. The time frame sounded realistic and it meant that I could do a quality job.

Meg then turned to the subject of references. She asked for two or three names and added, "You might also want to do a reference check on me." I thought she was joking. "Just as I want to check on you, you might want to do a check on what it's like working for me. I'll give you the names of three contacts."

I was surprised, and for a few seconds I didn't know what to say. "Sorry, Meg," I said, "I'm a bit thrown by that. I've never heard of anyone doing that before, but I greatly appreciate it. Yes, I'll call them."

"You should!" she smiled. "I'll email you the names and phone numbers after I call them first."

Again, I appreciated her making this a joint process and was delighted at how different she was from most bosses I'd known. I liked her!

We had talked for about an hour and a half when she concluded by saying, "Well, Lauren, I have really enjoyed our discussion. Your expertise and style are very well suited to us. I would like to keep exploring the possibility of you working with us. Would you?"

I confirmed I was, restraining myself ever so slightly. Good-bye, Deadly Di, I thought, you're about to lose me! And how happy I will be to be away from you!

Meg then said she'd like me to meet the Chief Executive Officer, John Squires. That was a good sign. She phoned John and invited him to join us. He promptly knocked on the conference room door and entered. Meg introduced us as I stood and offered him my hand. He was much taller than me, partly because he was taller than average and partly because I am shorter than average. He was sincere and friendly—a gentle giant. I immediately warmed to him. Meg said good-bye and that she'd call me later.

"Lauren," John said as we sat down, "we would really like you to consider being part of our company and our growth. We have ambitious plans for new products and services. We're in a tight struggle with our competitors, and we want someone with your credentials to help us in this journey. If you want a challenge in your career, this is the opportunity."

We talked for an hour, covering his background, the changes he had experienced over his twenty-six years with the company, and his last five years as CEO. He spoke of the quality of his management team and his pride in the organization.

"We are very proud of our culture," he said. "Our values are very important to us. We don't play games, we don't have hidden agendas, and we support each other. Our culture is the foundation of our success."

This really pleased me. I desperately wanted to have a challenging job, working for a great boss in a good company. It impressed me that the CEO placed an emphasis on culture and seemed to be comfortable talking about it.

He was also interested in my background and asked about my early experiences. I started to explain my decision to study business at college.

"No," he smiled, "go back to the beginning! Where did you grow up? What were the forces that shaped you?"

I was thrilled he wanted to know about me as a total person. "Well," I began, "I grew up in the country, in a small town called Marlow." It wasn't far away; he knew the town. "I am one of four children. I enjoyed school and sports and—"

"What was your proudest achievement at school?" he interrupted, smiling.

I thought for a moment. "I was vice president of my class my senior year in high school."

"Congratulations," he smiled, "that's a great honor. How about sports? What was your biggest accomplishment?"

"I didn't have too many great achievements in sports. I really liked swimming and basketball. It was more the team camaraderie that was satisfying than any great victories."

"Okay," said John, "you were telling me about going to college. Why did you decide to study business?"

"We had a good family friend who was in marketing. Whenever she stayed with us, or we visited her, she talked about her career and business travels. It sounded so challenging and exciting. I decided at a young age that that was what I wanted to do. And I've always been happy with my career choice."

I told him about some of my college experiences and the roles I had filled since. He asked about my aspirations, and he talked about Meg's capability and the high regard in which she was held.

I was a little surprised, however, about what John didn't talk about. He didn't talk at any length about the company's direction, market position, or priorities. I started to wonder if he enjoyed the position of CEO more than the responsibilities of the job itself.

As we were leaving the meeting room, John introduced me to another senior manager.

"Nicholas!" he called to a short younger man who was rushing down an imposing staircase from the top floor. "Nicholas Strange, Chief Operations Officer, I'd like you to meet Lauren Johnson." He shook my hand in a dominant style, clamping down and trapping my hand in his grip. John explained the purpose of my visit. Nicholas appeared to be more interested in making eye contact with the other people walking by. After a few awkward minutes, he said he had to go.

John rode with me in the elevator to the reception area and bid me farewell from the front door. Saying good-bye to him was like saying good-bye to my grandfather.

I called Paul from the car to tell him about the fantastic interview, and he wondered if it was too early to open a celebratory bottle of wine.

Meg called as soon as I hung up with Paul. She said she enjoyed meeting with me and hoped I enjoyed my visit and talk with John. We agreed that he was a gentleman. She asked whether I was interested in the job.

"Absolutely!" I said. "Meg, I can't believe my good fortune to be considered for this role. This job would be a dream come true!"

She said they would be talking to two other candidates and she would call me the following week.

Home seemed different now. Harry's toys everywhere didn't bother me as much. The mess in the kitchen didn't seem so important. How desperate I was to be offered this job. Desperate to work for a good boss. Someone I respected, someone who added energy to others, someone I could trust. Someone unlike Deadly Di Ashman.

3

The Call

THE FOLLOWING WEEK, I spoke with two of Meg's references. Both people spoke enthusiastically of Meg's skills, her personality, and her leadership ability. They both commented on how well she developed her people and said she had a talent for forming strong teams. She sounded like a dream boss.

Chester reported that Harlow Kane was impressed with me.

I anxiously waited for Meg to get in contact with me once more. What relief when she called and asked me to visit her office again. She said that I was the top candidate, and she wanted me to meet two members of her team.

As I drove to Harlow Kane a few days later, I could hardly contain my excitement. I already felt I was working with Meg. I already felt at home! This time, I knew my way. And I had made the meeting early in the morning to make sure I wouldn't be delayed by Deadly Di.

When I arrived, Meg introduced me to Sandra Pearson and Ben Bowser. We hit it off right away. Every time they spoke about Meg, their eyes sparkled. The meeting went well. Now, all I could do was wait and hope.

At home the next evening, while I was cooking dinner, the phone rang. "Hi, Lauren, it's Meg Montgomery here. Have you got a moment to talk?"

"Sure," I answered, moving quickly with the cordless phone to a quiet room. My heart beat fast.

"I would like to offer you the job," she said.

I was overjoyed. After a few quick words and an assurance that I'd have the contract tomorrow, Meg said good-bye. I hung up and hugged Paul in celebration. This time, he opened a bottle of wine. Annie and Harry wanted to know what all the excitement was about. I explained, "Mommy has been given her dream job!"

"Does that mean you don't work for the dog in the manger anymore?" asked Annie.

"Not for very much longer!" I laughed.

On the way to work the morning I planned to resign, I grew nervous. I was anxious about Di's reaction, wondering how she would respond to my resignation. I also had mixed emotions about leaving a good company and close colleagues. Apart from the last eight months, the experience had been a good one. I wouldn't have considered leaving except for Deadly Di.

At the first opportunity, I drew deep breaths, marched into Di's office, and closed the door. I slid an envelope across the table.

"Di, I'm resigning."

With no expression on her face, she asked, "Where are you going?" She showed no regret whatsoever that I was leaving. Her reaction didn't surprise me, but it still struck me as lousy.

"I'm going to Harlow Kane as strategic marketing manager."

"No doubt, your role here helped you get that job," she said coldly.

I was determined not to let her take any credit for my success. "I think all my roles have helped me develop into the professional that I am."

She glared through me. "You'll leave today." She turned her back and started hitting her computer keys.

I sat for a moment, amazed. I had no option but to leave her office. I knew I would never have a doubt that I made the right decision to resign.

I started to do the rounds to let my colleagues know I was leaving. I had time to talk to only one friend before an email was circulated to the team:

> To all Marketing staff,
>
> Today, Lauren Johnson resigned from the company. She will leave immediately.
>
> Di

Insensitive, ungrateful pig! After eleven years with the company working in several divisions, I was dismissed by her with a single line! Evil woman.

What joy to be leaving!

Before I left that afternoon, the human resources manager asked if I would like to have an exit interview. I declined. I knew I would be too worried to answer certain questions. I didn't want to lie about my reasons for leaving, and I didn't want to risk the consequences of Di's rage if she found out what I said. I was disappointed in myself that I didn't have the courage to say how I really felt. But surely human resources and the executives already knew all about Deadly Di. If they were really concerned, they could have fixed things long before. Better for me to quietly move on.

Given that Deadly Di had terminated my employment immediately, I had a two-week holiday before starting with Meg. I enjoyed being a full-time mom: I dropped Annie off at school each day and picked her up. I gave Harry a break from preschool and we explored the city together. When Annie was home from school in the afternoons, we did something special. Baking cakes was a favorite. And I even managed to catch up with a few friends.

Before I knew it, it was the night before my first day at Harlow Kane. I went to bed early but lay awake, too excited to sleep.

4

First-Day Surprises

THE RUSH HOUR TRAFFIC CRAWLED as I wondered what lay ahead for me at Harlow Kane. I looked forward to working with Meg, but I was still nervous. After eleven years with the same company, I was now facing the unfamiliar.

A thought of Deadly Di flashed through my mind, and my first-day nerves dissolved. The last couple of weeks had given me the first Sunday nights I could remember—well, in the previous eight months—that I had not dreaded the thought of work the next day. I had faith that under Meg, I'd never have to experience that Sunday dread again.

I arrived at the reception area at eight-thirty and asked for Meg. Ben Bowser, whom I'd met at my second interview, came down to meet me. I was pleased to see a familiar face, and he greeted me warmly. He told me Meg couldn't meet me first thing—something had come up. Ben showed me around the building and around the Marketing department, which shared a floor with Information Technology and Human Resources.

Meanwhile, Ben told me about his twenty-four years with the company. He was friendly and chatted openly about Harlow Kane. I quickly got the feeling that he was beyond caring whether people agreed with his views. Beyond caring about how he looked, too. He wore a navy suit, shiny from being overworn, and a tie that was more fitting for a 1970s costume party than the professional workplace. But I liked his easygoing manner despite all that, or maybe because of it.

Ben introduced me to the team in Marketing—six others apart from Meg. I remembered Sandra Pearson from my previous interview. Everyone made me feel welcome. The team was relaxed and seemed comfortable with each other.

A good thing too, because the office layout had an open plan. I hadn't expected this. My two interviews at Harlow Kane had been in offices on other floors. Never mind. It was a relatively small thing, and no doubt I would get used to it.

Our workstations were arranged near the external windows, and in the center of the area there were meeting rooms with glass walls. Meg was in one of the meeting rooms and in the middle of what looked like an earnest telephone conversation. She didn't look happy. When she hung up the phone, she sat quietly for a few moments before coming out to the general work area. She apologized for not meeting me—something had come up. She asked Ben to look after me for the rest of the morning.

Around mid-morning, with Meg still not available, Ben offered to treat me to a coffee and walk me through the company's organization chart so I could start to understand the key players. He said we could walk to a coffee shop, Columbia's, which he preferred to the shop on the ground floor of the building.

As we walked across the foyer on our way out, we bumped into Nicholas Strange, the distracted exec I'd met the first time I visited.

"Nicholas," Ben said, "this is Lauren Johnson, who's just joined us."

"Hi. Pleased to meet you." He obviously didn't remember meeting me four weeks earlier, and his dominant handshake hadn't changed.

"What is your role here?" he asked. He *definitely* didn't remember me.

"Strategic marketing manager, under Meg Montgomery. I enjoyed meeting you and John Squires at my interview." If Nicholas now made the connection, he didn't show it. Perhaps he didn't hear me. Perhaps he wasn't listening.

"I've just finished a breakfast meeting where I presented to an industry forum," he said, glancing over my shoulder at someone else. "They like what we're doing here, and they're impressed with the prospects for our business. I've got a meeting with John now. Good meeting you, Lorraine. I hope you enjoy working with us."

Ben tried to correct him. "I'm sure *Lauren* looks forward to working here." Nicholas missed it. He went one way and we went the other.

We stepped out into the sunshine and walked through the park to the coffee shop. "Nicholas is quite a case," Ben said, happy to gossip. "He's very full of his own importance and doesn't suffer from a small ego. But he is a key personality around here." I absorbed the information, not ready to comment myself. It did seem odd for Nicholas to tell a new recruit about his breakfast meeting.

By now we were at Columbia's and ordering coffee—a cappuccino for Ben and a skim milk latte for me. It was a fine day, so we sat outside.

I asked Ben to fill me in on the senior people in the company. He was more than happy to do so, and he pulled out a lightly crumpled copy of the org chart from his coat pocket. "Apart from John Squires, the next most important person is Nicholas Strange. In fact, Nicholas has more impact than John. John brought him in about two years ago to push performance of the business. Driving performance isn't John's strength, which he knows. For Nicholas, being aggressive is natural. He excels at it." I could believe that.

"Soon after Nicholas arrived, he brought in Jeremy Hyde as the chief financial officer." There was a restrained tone to Ben's voice when he said the CFO's name. "Together, they've really shaken up the place. It's quite different now compared to two years ago." Better or worse, he didn't say. I sensed worse.

Our coffees arrived. Ben stirred three spoonfuls of sugar into his cup.

"As COO, Nicholas has the four sales and services directors reporting to him. They're all important. I guess the last key person is Hugh Worrell, the director of HR, more because of his influence with Nicholas and Jeremy than anything else." Ben leaned forward and dropped his voice, as though sharing a secret. "Hugh, Nicholas, and Jeremy are buddies—they own a vacation home together."

I nodded, sipping my coffee. I decided my first priority was to meet with each of the executives, form relationships with them, and gain their

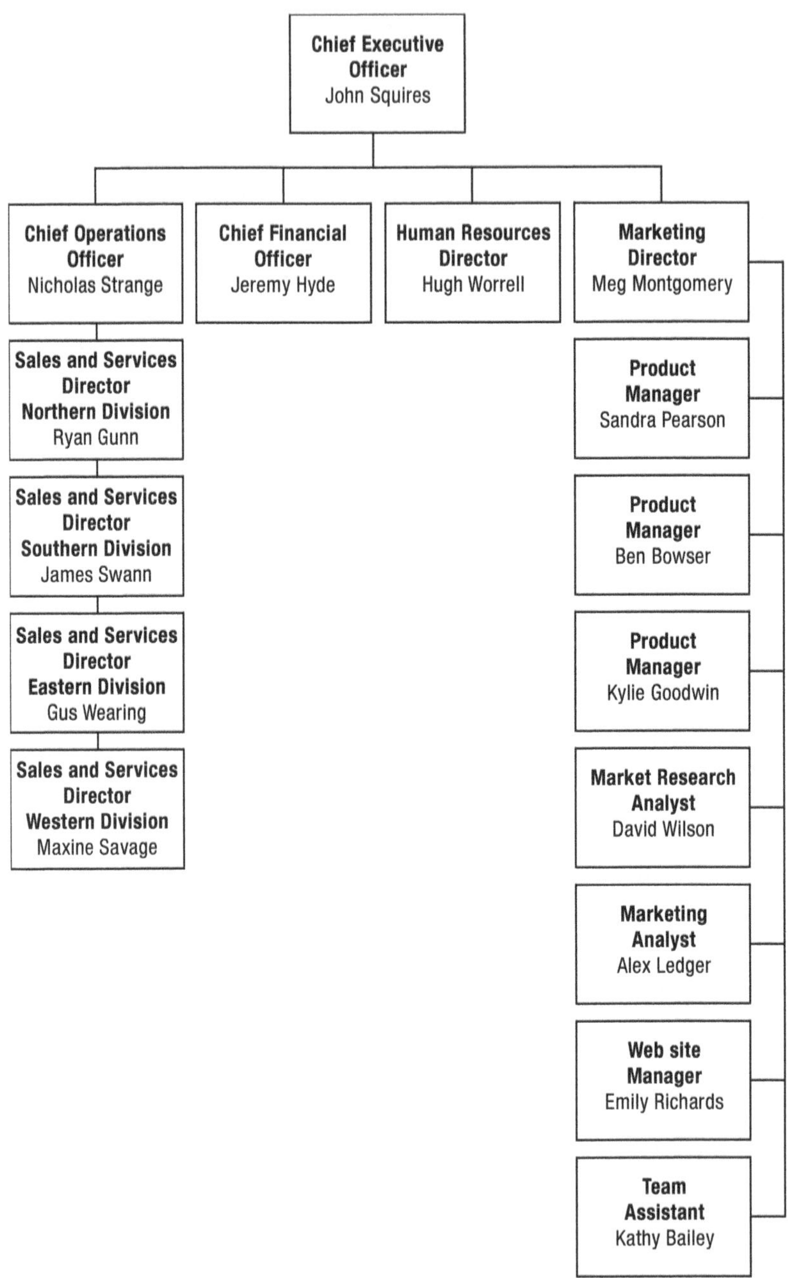
Chief Executive Officer
John Squires
Chief Operations Officer
Nicholas Strange
Chief Financial Officer
Jeremy Hyde
Human Resources Director
Hugh Worrell
Marketing Director
Meg Montgomery
Sales and Services Director Northern Division
Ryan Gunn
Sales and Services Director Southern Division
James Swann
Sales and Services Director Eastern Division
Gus Wearing
Sales and Services Director Western Division
Maxine Savage
Product Manager
Sandra Pearson
Product Manager
Ben Bowser
Product Manager
Kylie Goodwin
Market Research Analyst
David Wilson
Marketing Analyst
Alex Ledger
Web site Manager
Emily Richards
Team Assistant
Kathy Bailey

input into my review of the marketing strategy. Nicholas, Jeremy, and Hugh sounded like a key group.

"Do the executives support the Marketing department?"

Ben rubbed his chin. "John is a strong supporter. Nicholas tolerates us when it suits him. Jeremy is hostile, but he's like that with everyone—except Nicholas, of course. We don't see much of Hugh."

Ben sighed and said, "Just as important to our team are the Sales and Services directors, though—that's who we interact with most directly. Of the four, James Swann is the best. He's a good guy, believes in our work, and he's very inclusive. Two of them are okay—Ryan Gunn and Gus Wearing. The fourth—Maxine Savage—is aggressive and keeps us at a distance."

The relationships seemed more complex than I had hoped. My interview with John Squires had given me the impression that Harlow Kane had a much more positive team of executives. It was starting to sound like a very political place. When Ben had finished his explanation, I asked him about his own time with the company.

"I join the Quarter Century Club next year," he boasted.

"Twenty-five years of service—that's quite a stay. How have you found it?"

"It's been great. It's paid the bills, and I'll have a good pension in four years and three months." But who's counting, I thought.

"The thing to do," he confided, "is to avoid trouble."

I asked him what he meant.

"Senior people come and go. Sometimes you just need to hold on until a boss moves on—or is moved on. You never know who your next boss will be. Over the years, I've seen some bad managers. But in a few years the position changes, so the person who was the bad manager ends up being managed by the person they badly managed! Then it becomes interesting."

Ben's frank insights were helping me get a feel for the place. I encouraged him to chat as we headed back to the office.

When we returned to the fourth floor, it wasn't long before Meg appeared, apologized for being tied up, and invited me into the meeting room. As she closed the door, I sensed something was wrong. Meg's face was strained and pale. She was agitated, and she wasn't smiling.

"Lauren," she said, her voice husky, "I have some regrettable news."

My heart skipped a beat. I searched Meg's face for clues. What could possibly be so wrong?

Meg cleared her throat. "This morning, I resigned."

What? At first I didn't respond, her words didn't register. She waited. The word "resigned" hit me a second time—this time my brain connected. My smile evaporated. She waited.

"Oh, no!" My jaw dropped.

"I'm afraid so, yes."

"Why?" My mouth was dry.

"I'll tell you more when we have our team meeting. I just wanted to apologize to you first for resigning on your first day. I know it's a terrible thing to do, and it's not something I've done lightly. Something happened last week and it's left me with no other choice."

Tears welled and I fought to compose myself. "Was the thing that happened last week work related or personal?"

"Work related," she answered grimly.

What could it be, I wondered. It must have been horrible.

"I am so sorry for you, Meg, whatever it is that's forced you to resign."

"I'm really sorry to let you down," Meg continued, her eyes moist as well. "Believe me, I've agonized over this. I wasn't planning to leave when we were hiring you. I was very much looking forward to working with you, too. If I'd had any intention of leaving then, I wouldn't have recruited anyone."

I was thrown, my mind in chaos, a hundred thoughts competing with each other.

"Of course, I'm very disappointed," I said with a tremor in my voice. "The major reason I wanted this job so much was to work with you. You seem like a great boss. Your experience is so strong, and I could learn so much." I was distressed and suddenly uncertain about the future. Meg offered me a tissue.

"But whatever happened last week must have been terrible," I said.

"Yes, I'll talk about that in a minute. Kathy's organizing an urgent team meeting."

I felt shipwrecked. Within one minute, the world had spun out of control.

"When do you leave?"

"That still has to be worked out. I've given a month's notice. There's a meeting tomorrow morning to finalize the date."

I struggled to speak. "But . . . but you'll be here for the month, won't you? At least I'll have a few weeks working with you." I was drained, my excitement over my new job extinguished.

"Yes, that would be good," Meg sighed, "although Sales and Marketing staff who resign are usually asked to leave immediately. I'll let you know tomorrow."

Meg wiped her face with a tissue, perhaps trying to clear the strain. "The rest of the team will be here soon. Are you okay?"

For Meg's sake, I managed a weak smile. "I'll be okay. I'm just shaken."

Meg passed me another tissue.

"Sorry," I said. "I come from a long line of criers. You should see me at the movies, especially sad ones or romantic tearjerkers—I'm a mess!"

"That's okay," she replied. "There's just one piece of advice I can give on that—invest in Kleenex!"

We laughed and I felt a bit better. But this was not the first day I'd pictured.

5

Gems in the Dirt

THE REST OF THE TEAM SOON JOINED US, looking curious. Thankfully, I had managed to stop crying. Meg thanked everyone for coming, her face strained.

"I have some important news," she said quietly, looking from face to face. "I'm leaving the company."

She was unable to go on. She couldn't get any more words out for what seemed like ages. There were a few gasps, then everyone was silent—staring—waiting.

After a while, she continued, "This morning, I resigned." She paused again, steadying her breath. "Late last week, Jeremy Hyde verbally abused me, severely. It was unacceptable. And it has happened once too often. I decided over the weekend I wasn't going to take it any longer. I talked with my husband and decided I would resign."

The mood was tense. Everyone was shocked, disappointment written clearly on their faces. Some of the women were teary. Even the men had watery eyes. Someone went outside for more tissues. Meg must be a great boss, I thought, to have this reaction from her team.

Emily Richards, the Web site manager, started to cry, and then sobbed inconsolably. Sandra Pearson half joked that we should all leave with Meg and set up a consultancy. A few minutes later, she was tearful as well.

David Wilson, the market research analyst, shook his head. "I feel as though I've been kicked in the guts. Last week, I had a call from a recruitment agency offering me a job. I told them I wasn't interested, but I might call them back if you're not going to be here, Meg."

"Don't do anything hasty," counseled Meg. "Just take some time to let things settle and get back to normal."

"How can things get back to normal without you around?"

"You're a wonderful team," Meg said, wiping her eyes.

"You're a great boss," several responded.

Kathy Bailey, the team assistant, hadn't said anything—she just stared blankly into space, probably too upset to talk.

I wondered what on earth I had gotten myself into. The most appealing part of the job was the chance to work with Meg. I didn't doubt that Meg hadn't been planning to resign, but judging by the day's events, there was a lot going on beneath the surface at Harlow Kane. I'd thought it was a great company. It appeared not. Meg must have been going through a tough time to resign so suddenly, and with nowhere to go.

But then again, I couldn't have stayed where I was any longer either.

She looked at me. "I am very sorry for you, Lauren. This is a significant upheaval for your first day."

"It's okay, Meg. I feel for you, especially if you've been working in a negative environment." I knew exactly how that felt. "I know you must be making the right decision. I was going to be leaving my other company anyway, so don't be sorry for me."

Emily had stopped crying. "I feel so angry," she said. "I am so angry that someone like Jeremy can cause someone like you to resign, Meg. He should be the one that goes. It's all so political."

Ben cleared his throat. "When do you leave, Meg?"

"I don't know yet. I have a meeting tomorrow with John and Hugh to discuss that."

"And who will take over as our manager?" asked Kylie Goodwin. She didn't look too upset. Perhaps she wasn't sorry Meg was leaving.

"I don't know. John and Nicholas will decide what to do about that."

People seemed exhausted. We sat in silence. Everyone looked deep in thought about what the news meant for them. Kathy still stared without focusing, her eyes red.

Emily announced, "I think I'll have another baby!" She had things in perspective. We all laughed, sharing a welcome release of tension.

Ben leaned forward. "Meg, you are right to look after yourself. We all wish you well." He looked around the room. "I don't feel much like doing any work. It's nearly lunchtime. Let's head down to an early happy hour! How 'bout it, Meg?"

"Absolutely!" she laughed.

That was my first day at Harlow Kane. Not at all what I had expected. We went to a restaurant bar for the afternoon, and I learned a lot more about the senior bosses. Despite what John Squires had said, there appeared to be a lot of politics in the place. From what my new buddies were saying, a few on the executive team were motivated by power and ego, and others were yes-men and would never rock the boat. I was worried about what lay ahead.

I was talking with Meg and Ben at one point, standing around a tall table, when Ben asked Meg to share more details about what had happened. Meg looked uneasy.

"Last week, Jeremy Hyde threw a book at me," she said flatly. I was speechless.

"That was the end for me. I've endured tons of verbal abuse from Jeremy. Words are one thing; having a book thrown at you is another thing altogether."

"What were you arguing about?" Ben asked, with no hint of surprise about Jeremy throwing something.

"He'd been abusive to one of my team, so I went to talk with him about that—to defend my staff member and to insist on proper behavior. Well, let's just say that he didn't appreciate the discussion. He saw red, instantly turning angry."

"Who was the team member involved?" Ben asked.

"That doesn't matter, Ben," she said, waving her hand. "The important thing is that it was the end of the line for me with Jeremy and a couple of other key people. I wasn't prepared to put up with that sort of behavior any longer, especially with things flying at my head!"

Fair enough, I thought. I was already scared of Jeremy Hyde, and I hadn't even met him.

"Did you complain to someone?" I asked.

"Well, I talked with John. He's the only one I could talk to. Jeremy is very close to Nicholas, and they're both close to Hugh Worrell." Ben and I leaned forward to make sure we heard Meg over the noise in the bar.

"John was really concerned with what I said, but he wanted to know if there was a witness. I said no."

"Apart from the book."

Meg smiled at Ben's joke. "Look, John's a really nice guy, but he finds these issues hard to handle, and he doesn't want to get involved in politics or divide his team. If I made a big issue out of this, then the attack on me would get even worse. So I decided that I would leave. But I have told John he needs to know what's happening around him, that the culture of the place is changing and there's a whole host of issues that need his attention. He can ignore it all and hope it isn't happening, but it won't go away. It will only get worse. That was my advice to him."

I wanted to know more about the group of nasty-sounding executives I'd be left with. "Meg, how come you fell out with the others on the senior management team? I can't imagine why anyone would have a problem with you."

Meg paused. Ben jumped in. "I'll tell you what really happened," he said brightly. "Soon after Nicholas and his buddies started at Harlow Kane, Meg fell from favor—no offense, Meg." She smiled.

"I have this theory about management," said Ben. "Managers have a choice of being good at managing up or being good at managing down." Ben put his glass down so he could gesture freely. "To manage upward, you need to be political. But the behavior that impresses your bosses is a real turn-off to your staff. Things like not having definite opinions, not sticking up for what's important, not being consistent, favoring what your boss wants, and treating your boss as the top priority. If you become good at those things, you become less respected by your own troops. They see right through you and know they can't rely on you."

"What a disturbing theory," I said, lowering my glass and staring at him.

Meg looked toward the ceiling as if running through a list of the Harlow Kane executives. "Gee, Ben, you might be right. Most of them manage upward well and their people don't like them. Except for James Swann—he doesn't manage upward well and his people love him! And that's your point."

"It's tough to do both," Ben shrugged his shoulders. "I know hardly any managers who are good at both. My theory is that it's a trade-off."

I thought about managers I knew. Deadly Di sprung to mind, and I had to agree that her behavior supported Ben's theory. Somehow, Di Ashman always impressed her bosses—how, I didn't know.

Meg sipped her gin and tonic. "Well, I know I don't manage up so well to people like Nicholas and Jeremy. I struggle with playing their games, given what they value."

"And that's why we like you!" Ben picked up his empty glass and clinked Meg's.

I left the bar just after five and drove home in a distracted state.

Exhausted by all that had happened, I dropped my bags inside the front door and fell into the nearest comfy chair. Harry jumped on me and rapidly told me his news of the day. Paul yelled from the study that he was finishing on the computer. He soon joined me and asked me how my day had gone.

"Well," I said, holding Harry at bay, "for starters, Meg quit." And I filled him in.

Paul stood up in surprise. He laughed, pacing the room and shaking his head. "That is unbelievable! You could write a book, Lauren!"

I didn't share his laughter. I called out to Annie, "Annie, can you please bring me your fable book?"

Annie ran down the hallway, handed me the book, and sat next to me. I thumbed through the pages looking for the fable that captured my mood.

"Here it is."

> A cock, scratching the ground for something to eat, turned up a jewel that had by chance been dropped there. "Ho!" said he. "A fine thing you are, no doubt, and had your owner found you, great would his joy have been. But for me, give me a single grain of corn before all the jewels in the world!"

Annie looked at me in a curious way. "I don't understand that one," she said. "I'd take the jewel."

"We can talk about that later," I smiled. "Right now, we have dinner to cook."

6

Take Two

DRIVING TO WORK THE NEXT DAY, I realized that I had lost much of my enthusiasm. I wondered about the reality of Harlow Kane. With Meg leaving, my new role had lost its single most important attraction. And this was just day two.

Everyone else on the team seemed to be struggling as well. Emily said she had hardly slept, and Kathy had dark rings under her eyes. Meg spent a few moments with each of us at our desks before going upstairs for her meeting with John and Hugh. I commented to her that she appeared more relaxed than she had been the day before. She agreed. "It's a great relief to have made my decision and told the team."

By nine-thirty she was back and asked us into a meeting room.

"It's been decided that I leave immediately. I would like to stay and work out the month's notice so we could smoothly cover the outstanding projects and work through our good-byes. It's not to be. I've loved working with you all and will miss you dearly."

"They're being spiteful making you leave immediately," growled Emily, "and what sort of message does that send us?"

Meg paused. "John was happy for me to work the month, but Nicholas argued that my mind would not be on the job and that they would have to move forward without me. Hugh supported Nicholas, and John changed his mind and went along with them."

The only composed person from yesterday, Kylie Goodwin, asked again, "Who's going to take your place?"

My stomach knotted. My throat clamped tight. I prayed, *Not Di Ashman—please!* It was as though the world stood still until Meg answered.

"Marcus Pomfrey will take over."

Sheer relief! Logically, of course, with Meg resigning only the previous day, there had been no time to recruit externally. But that hadn't stopped me from being paranoid that Deadly Di might haunt me.

Gradually I realized that the room was silent. Out of the corner of my eye, I caught Emily grasping her throat with both hands to lift her head up. She smiled across the table at Sandra, who returned the gesture. (I would forget at the end of the meeting, however, to ask what that was about.)

"You're joking," someone said. It didn't sound like Marcus Pomfrey, whoever he was, was quite as popular as Meg.

"We really will miss you, Meg," was the general chorus. I looked around the room. It was clear how gloomy everyone felt, each person probably reflecting on what Meg's leaving meant to them personally. Meg was possibly the only one who felt mildly in control of her future. And Kylie looked okay.

The meeting ended and we wandered back to our desks. An email had just arrived from John Squires.

> To All Staff,
>
> With sincere regret, I have to inform you that yesterday Meg Montgomery resigned. Because of Meg's role as marketing director, her resignation takes effect immediately and she will leave today.
>
> We thank Meg for the positive impact she has made and wish her well. On a personal note, I have very much enjoyed working with Meg and I will miss her. Marcus Pomfrey will replace Meg as marketing director when

> he returns in two weeks from an international assignment in Hong Kong. Sandra Pearson will be the acting manager until Marcus's return.
>
> Regards,
> John Squires
> Chief Executive Officer

Ben came over to my desk for a chat. We returned to the meeting room.

"Tell me about Marcus Pomfrey," I asked.

"Marcus is a young guy going places. He used to work in this office before being transferred to our Hong Kong office twelve months ago. He's good at his marketing responsibilities. Pity about his people skills. Everybody was happy when he moved overseas. Marcus is about Marcus. That's his problem. He's a yes-man and likes looking good. He's good at managing upward, so John, Nicholas, Jeremy, and Hugh like him."

"Another manager who supports your theory," I smiled.

"Yep."

"Is he a bully?" I asked anxiously. I was worried that he might be cruel, like Deadly Di.

"No, I wouldn't say he's a bully. He's certainly self-absorbed, but he's more political and unpredictable than intimidating. He's more likely to frustrate you than scare you." I was pleased about this, in a weird sort of way.

"We call Marcus the ATC," Ben continued. "The Air Traffic Controller. People appear on his radar screen. He lands them and moves on to the next, forgetting about the one that just landed. Land them, move on. Off the radar, out of mind." Ben smiled. "I actually get on quite well with Marcus—only because I'm no threat!"

Better than a bully. Still, what had I gotten myself into? I reminded myself I couldn't have stayed any longer with Deadly Di and retained my sanity.

As we left the meeting room, Ben added, "We always knew that in a moment of madness, someone would promote him."

7
Badges of Rank

I DID MY BEST TO CLOSE THE LINES of useless thought and get into my new role.

Around mid-morning on the third day, I asked Ben to take me around the executive floor and introduce me to the senior team. I wanted to start meeting the executives, since my project would affect them most. I printed out the Harlow Kane organizational chart along with a few pages of my calendar to set up meetings.

On the top floor of the building, Ben swiped his security card and opened the doors to the executive suite. What I saw next made me stop dead in my tracks. It was like walking into a botanical garden. I knew the company was proud of its open offices, but this was something else! Unlike the tight spaces downstairs, on this floor the distance between desks was so enormous that the executives would never hear each other shout, let alone speak in normal voices to each other. Each workspace was separated by a maze of large exotic plants. If I got separated from Ben they might need to send out a search party to find me.

I turned to Ben. "This is amazing!"

"Yep—one of the benefits that come with the top job. Let's start at John Squires's side of the floor," he said, leading me to a corner section. John's area was clean and homey. Family photos decorated his desk, and copies of the day's newspapers sat neatly folded on his meeting table. John looked up from his desk and waved.

"Good morning, John," Ben greeted him. "I'm showing Lauren around Mission Control."

"Hi, Ben, how are you? How's your family? How's that big son of yours doing with his football?" smiled John, coming around his desk. "Hi, Lauren." John shook my hand firmly. I had forgotten how tall he was. "I'm really pleased you've decided to join us. Would you like to come back in a few minutes after you've finished your tour? We can talk then. I have about thirty minutes until my next meeting."

"Thanks, John. I'd like that. I'll see you shortly." Ben and I moved on.

"Next to John," Ben said, "is Nicholas Strange's office."

We made our way through the plants. Unlike the rest of the floor, Nicholas's office had walls. Neither Nicholas nor his secretary was there.

Ben whispered to me, "When Nicholas started at Harlow Kane he had walls built for his office. He apparently can't tolerate an open office for himself. But he says he can see the cost-saving benefit for everyone else. And if you look closely at the chairs at his conference table, you'll notice his chair at the head of the table is slightly higher than the rest." Ben looked around to make sure no one was listening and whispered, "He had the legs of all the other chairs cut down by about an inch."

"You're joking!" I examined his face, but there was no sign of a smile. "I believe everything else you've told me, Ben, but not that one!" I laughed.

Ben grinned. "He also measured his office space to make sure it was larger than everyone else's."

Again, I waited for a smile, but Ben only shrugged his shoulders.

Nicholas's secretary had now returned to her desk. Ben introduced me to her, and she agreed to set up a meeting for me to meet Nicholas. We moved on, accompanied by pleasant perfume wafting from the plants.

We walked past the stairway that led down to the meeting rooms on the nineteenth floor. The steps were about two yards wide, made of wood and varnished with a glossy veneer. I remembered seeing this staircase from the floor below when I was being interviewed. It was magnificent.

"The stairs that lead up to the top!" I laughed to Ben.

"Or that lead down," he quipped.

Most of the execs were out, and I had made only a few appointments as we neared the end of the tour. We had one office left before completing the circle back to John's.

"Over here we have Ryan Gunn, Sales and Services Director, Northern Division." Ryan was on the phone. As we approached, he hung up, complaining about being on hold.

"Ryan, this is Lauren Johnson," said Ben. "She joined us this week as strategic marketing manager."

"Hi, Lauren," Ryan smiled. He wore a coat and an expensive silk tie, probably Italian. His dark hair was spiked with gel, and he had pencil-thin sideburns that ended just below his ears. I figured him to be in his late thirties and obviously a high performer to achieve director at his age.

Ryan's use of space was different from everyone else's. While others had positioned their desks the fullest possible distance from each other, Ryan had his desk close to the main walkway. His secretary was stationed at the window.

After the usual greetings, I commented to Ryan, "I'm interested in the way you've organized your desk. You're by the hallway and your assistant is at the window."

"It's for Nicole's benefit," he said, pointing to his secretary who waved happily. "I'm often away from my desk at meetings, so this allows her to enjoy the light and the view. I think that's only fair. It's what a good manager does." I asked Ryan about setting up a time for us to meet. He apologized that he was so busy but thought he'd be able to make time for me the following Wednesday.

As we walked away, Ben sniggered, "With his desk so close to the walkway, he ambushes everyone as they pass by. You can't walk past him without being pumped for information. Did you notice he's also placed himself right next to John? Ryan always volunteers to be in charge of office moves so he can position his office to his best advantage." How interesting, I thought. Maybe Ryan's apparent friendliness and consideration for his secretary were fake.

"So, there you have it," Ben said, his arms open wide. "The executive suite—Mission Control."

"Is that all the execs?" I asked, trying to remember the organizational chart in my head. "Did we miss anyone in the maze?" We laughed.

"No," answered Ben. "James Swann, the fourth sales director, sits with his team on the tenth floor. He, and Meg before she left, were the only executives not on this floor. And I don't think it's because they're allergic to plants. They like to be with their teams."

I thought about Ben's theory—that managers are good at either managing up or managing down. I looked forward to meeting James Swann. I thanked Ben for the tour and he left me to my meeting with John Squires.

There was nowhere to knock to attract John's attention, and his assistant wasn't there. I solved my dilemma by calling out that I was back.

"Come and sit down, Lauren," he said, showing me to a chair at his round table. He moved the newspapers and a dirty coffee mug. "Welcome to Harlow Kane. I am pleased you joined us, although I am very sorry Meg resigned."

"So am I!" I said. "The opportunity to work with Meg was so attractive. But I'm pleased to be here. Thank you for giving me this opportunity."

"It's a pleasure. I'm sure you will do a great job. If ever I can be of assistance, please let me know."

"There is one thing that would help," I said, grabbing the chance. "How close do you want to be to my review of the marketing strategy? Do you want to be directly involved or just get reports on progress?"

John stroked his thick chin. "I'm happy to be as involved as you want me to be. My role has more to do with the external market and our board. Most of the operational activities are Nicholas's responsibility. In terms of your key project, Nicholas will be closer than I am and more critical to its success. But if you want to share anything with me, by all means let me know." He was pleasant but seemed more than happy to turn the future of his company's marketing over to someone else. It would appear that John Squires was a strictly hands-off CEO.

That night after dinner, I was eager to get Annie to bed to read her a fable as Paul tucked Harry into bed. I was still thinking about the splendor of the executive floor, the abundance of potted plants, and the extravagant use of space.

Yes, Aesop had found the same thing.

> There was war between the mice and the weasels, in which the mice got the worst of it, numbers of them being killed and eaten by the weasels. So they called a council of war, in which an old mouse got up and said, "It's no wonder we are always beaten, for we have no generals to plan our battles and direct our movements in the field." Acting on his advice, they chose the biggest mice to be their leaders, and these, in order to be distinguished from the rank and file, provided themselves with helmets bearing large plumes of straw. They then led the mice to battles, confident of victory; but they were defeated as usual, and were soon scampering as fast as they could to their holes. All made their way to safety without difficulty except the leaders, who were so hampered by the badges of their rank that they could not get into their holes, and they fell easy victims to their pursuers.

8

Ah, Sanity

I WANTED TO MEET JAMES SWANN. When I got to work the next day, I found his number and dialed.

"Hello, James Swann here," answered a cheery voice.

"Hi, James, this is Lauren Johnson." I was about to explain who I was, but it wasn't necessary.

"Hi, Lauren. It's great to hear from you. Meg mentioned you were coming on board. I'm looking forward to meeting you. Do you want to set up a time to get acquainted?"

"Yes. Actually, that's why I'm calling—to introduce myself and to see if we can meet at some point in the next week or so."

"Sure. But let's not wait that long! What are you doing this afternoon? I've got a pretty clear calendar today. I could meet you at around three. Would you like to have afternoon coffee?"

I liked his openness, his enthusiasm. "Certainly. Should I come to your office?"

"No, you're the new kid on the block. How about I come and find you?"

"I appreciate that, thanks, James. I'll see you at three."

Punctually at three o'clock, James Swann appeared. Ben showed him to my desk and introduced us.

"It's great to meet you, Lauren," James said. We shook hands firmly. He had smiling eyes.

"Let's go for coffee and get to know each other," he said, and we headed off to the elevators. James didn't like the coffee in the shop on the ground floor of the building either, so we made our way to Columbia's and chatted easily as we walked. On the way, he told me that he had worked for Harlow Kane for three years, all the time in the Sales and Services department as the director of the Southern Division. Before that, he was consulting for a year and before that he was with another firm for five years. All told, he had been in the industry for twenty-plus years.

He asked about my joining Harlow Kane and I mentioned the attraction of working with Meg.

"I'm very sorry she's left," he said, sounding truly regretful.

"I was so looking forward to working with her," I said. "You can imagine my shock when she resigned on my first day. Things must have been tough for her."

"It must have been a nasty surprise," he commented sympathetically. "Things were very tough on Meg for some time." He hesitated. "She was the victim of a concerted attack by Jeremy Hyde. For some reason, Jeremy didn't see eye to eye with Meg." He hesitated again and didn't go on.

We arrived at the coffee shop and ordered our coffee. "Anyway," I said, hoping to learn more about Meg's departure, "I can't fathom how anyone could not get along with Meg."

"Well," smiled James, "work's not all about logic. It's a lot about relationships and coalitions. You've probably worked with people you couldn't relate to, no matter how hard you tried."

I smiled that I understood. I was thinking of Deadly Di. And then my mind jumped to Marcus Pomfrey and my need to have a good working relationship with him.

"Well," said James, "let's just say that's what happened here with Meg. Certainly, through no fault of hers, she was in a situation of having to deal with some key people, some powerful people, who were very different from her. And no matter what she did, she couldn't win. I think she did the right thing in leaving. It will be much better for her."

I sipped my coffee and put my cup down. "But that's very disappointing. Workplaces should be more accommodating of different people."

"But that's life," James said evenly. "Look, what you have at work is a whole range of people coming together who didn't choose to work together. Of course there will be differences. Now, I hope I'm the type of boss who appreciates differences, but not everyone has the same attitude."

"Isn't that a pessimistic view of work?" I asked glumly.

"Not at all," he said, smiling. "Just realistic. You just need ways to cope with different situations."

"It sounds like you've had some testing times," I laughed.

"Well, yes. I have had some moments!"

I sensed a close bond forming between us. "What's been your worst work experience?"

James laughed. "That's easy!" He sipped his coffee and wiped his mouth. "At my previous workplace, before I went into consulting on my own for a year, I was a senior executive. All was well. Suddenly, my boss left and a new CEO arrived. This new guy was ruthless. For some reason, he thought I was against him. He sacked me in his first month. No questions, no discussion. Bang. 'See you later, James.' He concocted a restructure and paid me out. There I was, happily and loyally contributing to an organization when out of the blue everything changed, all because of one thing—The Boss."

"Wow! How did you cope?"

"Well, that's my point. How do you cope? My wife and I escaped to Fiji for a month and reflected on all the good things we had. I decided not to take the layoff personally. In the end, I felt sorrier for the good people who stayed in that shitty work environment. At least I got out."

He smiled and continued, "Later, I heard a joke that would've helped at the time." James finished his coffee. "It's about three envelopes. There was this senior boss who was being replaced, told to move on. During the handover, he told his replacement that when he'd arrived in the job three years before, his predecessor had given him three envelopes containing three very useful pieces of advice. 'I've done the same thing for you,' he said. 'The envelopes are sitting in the top desk drawer, numbered one, two, and three. When things get rough, open the envelopes in sequence.'

The new boss thanked the departing boss and went about settling into his new job."

James leaned forward, obviously enjoying his story. "After a few weeks, the new executive found the going tough, so he opened the first envelope. Inside was the first piece of advice: hold a planning meeting. Now, that seemed like good advice, so the new boss held a planning meeting, developed the division's strategy, and shared it with the board of directors and staff. Everyone was impressed with the new boss's directions and plans, and for a while things settled down.

"After a few months, the company was struggling again and the new boss began to worry. During a sleepless night, he remembered the envelopes, and when he arrived at work the next morning he reached into the drawer and opened the second envelope. Written there was a single word: restructure. So he reorganized his department and changed people's roles. There was a bit of fallout and a few people lost their jobs, but others commented that this new boss really meant business, and again the board congratulated him on his decisiveness. Of course, there was some discomfort in the company, but that was to be expected after a restructuring, and in time, things again settled down.

"But after another few months, the business was no better, and the boss was expected to do something to improve performance. This went on for a few more months until the pressure became relentless. The boss was at a complete loss, and with most of the fresh-ideas people gone in the restructuring, he was desperate. Then he remembered the envelopes. He reached into his drawer, dug around, and found the third envelope. He tore it open, eager to read more of the advice that had served him so well. He unfolded the paper and read the third piece of advice: prepare three envelopes."

Our laughing attracted the attention of people at nearby tables.

"So, that's one lesson learned from my experience. I guess the boss who sacked me thought he was doing the right thing. He was probably following the lead that he'd seen from others."

He moved his coffee cup to one side and gestured with his right palm. "But enough about me," he said. "How can I help you settle in? What are your plans?"

"Well, I have thought about that."

"Good!"

"I've started setting up meetings with each of the senior managers so I can get an understanding of their roles and their needs."

"Great! There's one technique I'd suggest. After you finish your first meeting with each person, write down five words that describe them."

"And put them in an envelope," I laughed.

"Almost! Those five words will give you plenty of information on the person's style and their motivations. People reveal a lot about themselves unintentionally—through the language they use, the topics they talk about, and the topics they don't talk about. Recording your first impressions will give you plenty of information on how best to work with them."

I reflected for a moment. "It seems judgmental to assess people so fast."

"Maybe," he nodded, "but think about it this way. By being aware of how people think and act, you'll be better able to interact with them and influence them."

I sat back, thinking and not saying anything.

"Just give it a try," he added. "You might find that your observations help you."

"Okay, James. I'll try it."

"Including this meeting with me," he teased.

"Oh, that's easy," I said. "Sharp, friendly, energetic, humane, helpful!"

We both laughed. "Thank you," he said. "That happens to be the way I'd like people to see me."

"I'll also decide on the five words I'd like the executives to say about me once they've met me," I said.

"Excellent," said James. "Now, a second piece of advice—you need to secure an early win. Something people will see as having a positive impact on the business. And it should happen in your first sixty days. In the next year or so, you need to have a major impact in your area of expertise, something seen as highly beneficial to the way we approach our marketing strategy. Don't forget, I'm happy to help you with anything."

"Thanks, James, I really appreciate it."

Soon after returning to my desk, I wrote down those first five words that described James. With bosses like James around, this would be a good place to work. I looked forward to working with him. I felt uplifted and more optimistic about working at Harlow Kane.

Later that night, I decided on the five words I wanted people to say about me: intelligent, enthusiastic, creative, committed, sincere. At least I hoped that's what they would say.

I thought about my own flaws—my avoidance of confrontation and my need to be compliant. I wondered what five words Deadly Di would choose for me.

9

The Jackdaw

HECTIC AS THE FIRST WEEK AT WORK WAS, I found when Sunday came I was still calm and enjoying Annie and Harry's antics at the zoo, not worrying about the following day. Joining Harlow Kane hadn't been such a bad idea, I thought.

On Monday morning, I met with Gus Wearing, Sales and Services Director of the Eastern Division, at his office. He welcomed me and shook my hand. His office was littered with paper, his shoes were scuffed and dirty, and he had a bad case of dandruff on his shoulders—they looked like they'd been dusted with a light covering of snow. I was slightly taken aback. I wondered if he approached his job with the same sloppy attitude, or did he simply suffer from a lack of self-awareness—or both?

He greeted me pleasantly enough, at least. "Welcome to the company, Lauren. How are you finding it?" he asked, offering me a seat.

"Fine, thanks, Gus. I'm still settling in, really. How long have you been here?"

"I've been here twelve years," he seemed delighted to tell me. "Came through the ranks. I started as a sales rep, then progressed to branch manager, and last year was appointed to be the sales and services director. I was a very successful sales rep. I had the record performance for five years in a row." He seemed to have a need to boast.

"That's impressive," I commented. "I look forward to working with you. The reason for this meeting is to introduce myself and also to understand the main challenges you face and find out where I can help."

"Before we get to that," he said, "tell me about yourself."

I thought that was nice of him. I told him about our family friend who got me interested in marketing when I was a kid. "When I graduated," I went on, "I worked for a multinational corporation and gained a lot of experience in a number of roles, and now I'm here."

"That's great."

"So what are the key challenges in your role?"

"Before we get to that, Lauren, what are your interests outside of work?"

I really wanted to get to the point of the meeting—why was he stalling? Or was he just being polite?

"Oh, well, I have a wonderful husband and two great kids—a seven-year-old daughter and a son who just turned four. We enjoy sports, mainly sailing and basketball. And I manage my daughter's basketball team." To be polite, I added, "How about you, Gus, what are your interests?"

"I'm very much into golf," he announced. "I play every weekend, and most of my holidays are organized around golf." He went to his bookshelf and picked up a photograph. "This is me on my last vacation at the Turnberry golf resort near Glasgow, Scotland." The photo showed Gus posing after he'd driven the ball off the tee. There was a lighthouse in the background.

"Good photo. It looks like a wonderful course. What was your score?" I asked, still being polite.

"Don't ask!" he said. And he didn't answer. "Okay, we'd better be quick," he said. "Otherwise we'll run out of time."

I was relieved to be getting to the point at last. "Okay, what would you say are the key sales challenges in the company? If I'm aware of them, I could try to support the sales teams."

"I think we're doing pretty well," he said with a blank look. "There's no one thing that stands out."

This surprised me. In his role, he should have been acutely aware of key areas needing improvement. I knew from the numbers I'd seen that Gus's division was the lowest performer. I tried a different tack.

"Have you ever lain awake at night, worrying about your work, wishing you had a magic wand you could wave to fix your problems? What would you most want to fix?"

"Well, yes, there is one thing," he conceded. "The quality of our sales reps. They're not nearly as good as I was when I first started. They don't have the right skills."

"Oh, why not?"

"About two years ago there was a cutback in sales training, and that's having an impact now. Some of our better reps have left and gone to other companies that have better career options, and our new reps aren't being trained as well as they used to be. Eventually, a lot of them get frustrated and leave. Our senior sales people lack the depth needed to fill more senior jobs, such as branch managers. The cutback in our sales training has been very costly."

"Thanks, Gus. That's helpful. I'll see what we can do about that."

"It's not really a Marketing issue, though," he said. "It's more a Human Resources issue."

"It shouldn't matter whose issue it is," I offered. "If, between Marketing and HR, we can support the Sales and Services divisions, that's the most important thing. I'll talk to Hugh Worrell about it."

Gus looked at his watch. I thanked him for his time and we finished our meeting.

As I walked away from his desk, a movement by Gus caught my peripheral vision. He had commenced flossing his teeth. Thank goodness no one else was around. I would have died of embarrassment.

As the elevator took me from the twentieth floor to the fourth, I reflected on my meeting with Gus. I wondered why he seemed so determined to prove himself to me, to look so important. Interesting that he tried to avoid the topic of the meeting and I had to push to cover the subject—did he not want to be exposed, or did he not want to risk expressing a view? Maybe he was a good sales manager but out of his depth as a director.

When I arrived back at my desk, I wrote down my first impressions of Gus, as James had urged me to do: evasive, conforming, purposeless, grubby, and shallow. I felt a little guilty that I was judging him so quickly, but I reasoned that I would change my assessment if Gus proved me wrong. When I spoke to the product managers, they *did* agree that the cutbacks in sales training were a problem.

Driving home that evening, I was thinking about Gus Wearing. I thought about his pride in his past achievements, but I wondered about his suitability for the role he was in now. I smiled as I remembered a fable that described a similar situation. When I arrived home, I dropped my bags and keys near the front door and went quickly to Annie's room to look at the fable book. Annie was there, playing with her dolls.

I picked up the book and found the fable I was thinking about.

> One day a jackdaw saw an eagle swoop down on a lamb and carry it off in its talons. "My word," said the jackdaw, "I'll do that myself." So it flew high up in the air and then came shooting down with a great whirring of wings onto the back of a big ram. It had no sooner alighted than its claws got caught fast in the wool, and nothing it could do was of any use. There it stuck, flapping away, and only making things worse instead of better.
>
> By and by up came the shepherd. "Oh-ho," he said. "So that's what you'd be doing, is it?" And he took the jackdaw, clipped its wings, and carried it home to his children. It looked so odd that they didn't know what to make of it.
>
> "What sort of bird is it, father?" they asked.
>
> "It's a jackdaw," he replied, "and nothing but a jackdaw. But it wants to be taken for an eagle."

I laughed aloud.

Annie looked up from her dolls. "Mom, can you read me something different tonight?" she pleaded. "I've had enough of fables for a while."

"But they're great," I exclaimed. "You can learn so much from them." Not wanting to turn her away from them, I conceded, "Maybe we can space them out a bit. I'll give you a rest tonight, and we can read them again another night."

She just screwed up her face and didn't say anything.

10

The Assassin

WEDNESDAY I HAD AN APPOINTMENT with Ryan Gunn, so I went back up to Mission Control. Ryan wasn't there, and his secretary, Nicole, had no idea where he was. I waited for fifteen minutes. He didn't show. Nicole apologized. I made another appointment for the following day. I was annoyed but didn't show it. For Nicole's sake, I made light of the situation and said I looked forward to the meeting.

The next day, I returned to Ryan's office. He was in a meeting with three other people. Nicole explained that an urgent meeting had come up and that Ryan would not be able to see me. Ryan was facing me, but he didn't acknowledge me. I was angry, but once again I didn't show it. I said I understood that things come up. Nicole took pity on me and changed Ryan's meeting with one of his team members that afternoon so we could meet. I returned at three, not expecting him to be available. Surprisingly, he was.

Without mentioning a word about standing me up at our two previous meetings, Ryan met me with a warm hello and a firm handshake. He suggested we go for coffee. His lack of apology for two postponed meetings left me cold, and the warm welcome struck me as false. He took me to the coffee shop downstairs, and without asking me what I wanted, he marched up to the counter and ordered two cappuccinos. How bizarre!

He took off his coat and sat down, leaning forward with his elbows on the table. He wore gold cuff links, and his sleeve cuffs were delicately embroidered with his initials.

"I need to leave my phone on," he said, spinning his BlackBerry in his fingers. "I'm expecting a response to a major bid we put in last week. If we get it, it will be the largest contract of its type that Harlow Kane has ever won."

"That's okay," I said as he glanced around the shop. "Customers come first. Tell me your background."

He looked back at me and pulled himself upright. "Well, I was working for one of Harlow Kane's competitors and performing extremely well," he said, pushing the palms of his hands down on the table, "when I got a call from a headhunter asking if I was interested in a real challenge. Turned out that when Nicholas arrived at Harlow Kane, he decided the then-director was not going to work out. Harlow Kane made me an offer too good to refuse—Nicholas really wanted me. When I started, I have to say performance of the division was at rock bottom. That was around eighteen months ago. The people reporting to me were generally dedicated and capable, just—let me see—poorly led. So I've turned things around by focusing on the basics."

"What are they?"

"Well, I spent my first thirty days getting to know the team," he said, glancing around to see if the coffees were coming, "and working out how the organization ticks and understanding current performance."

As he spoke, he slid the palms of both hands, face down on the table, toward me. His body language made me feel uncomfortable, and my chest and stomach pushed involuntarily back into my chair. "Within the next thirty days," he explained, "we held a planning session to agree on a vision and action plans. That session helped create a strong bond in the team. It also helped me get a sense of who was going to work out in the team and where the weak links were. I had to make a few tough decisions, but they were for the greater good."

I felt sorry for the members of his team who didn't make it based merely on Ryan's impressions of them. He continued.

"Then I monitored the scoreboard of performance closely each month for the remainder of the year. I worked out the strong areas that I could leave alone and the weaker areas where I had to pay most attention."

The coffees came. I thanked the waitress for mine. Ryan ignored her.

"And what are the current issues?" I asked.

"There are several," he said, playing with his teaspoon. "First of all, I'm concerned about the turnover of our sales reps across the firm. Our division has the lowest turnover, at around seventeen percent. Still too high, but lower than the firm's average of twenty-five." He leaned back in his chair and held up his hands as if surrendering. "The worst division has a sales staff turnover rate of thirty percent. This is a big problem for Harlow Kane." The way he said this made me think he wanted me to check out which division had the highest staff turnover. Later on, I did check it out—it was Gus Wearing's.

"Have you talked to Human Resources about it?" I asked. I tasted my coffee—yuck! I could see why others preferred Columbia's.

He leaned forward, both hands now pushing down on the table. I felt uneasy. "I did have a discussion at one point with Hugh Worrell," he said, "but he thought it was mainly an issue of management in the divisions, rather than a corporate problem." He continued to spin his BlackBerry and glanced around to see who else was in the coffee shop.

"What's your view?" I asked.

"My view about what?"

"Your view about whether the attrition problem is a divisional issue or a company-wide issue." Was he not even following what he himself was saying?

"I think it's a problem with some of our basic HR programs," he said. "Other divisions don't hire carefully enough—they tend to hire people who look good on paper. But our company doesn't train them properly, so they tend to be unproductive for the first few months. Our overall training and career path options for sales reps aren't good—HR really should improve some things. And they don't usually let people move from one division to another. So the good reps get locked into their current division, and it's almost impossible to get managers to free them up for a career move to another. Apart from that, we don't have any problems!"

His hands moved like mirrored puppets. One minute, both palms were being thrust at me, the next, they were pushing down on the table.

"What about other issues?" I asked, distracted by his hands. I was not enjoying my coffee and wondered if I should bother to finish it.

"I'm worried about our long-term competitiveness," he said. "We've been providing much the same products and services for a number of years, doing well, but I'm worried that unless we reinvent ourselves, we'll gradually lose our edge. When I did my MBA, I was fascinated with firms that could totally reinvent themselves. I did my MBA at Harvard, sponsored by my previous company. It was a good program. Have you done an MBA?"

He was boring me. "No, I haven't," I replied politely. "Would you recommend it?"

"Very much so. You learn so much, from the program and from other participants." He checked his BlackBerry for messages.

"I'm really interested in your views about how we need to reinvent ourselves," I said when I thought his attention was back with me. "I see that issue as the major challenge in my role as a marketing strategist—to identify the breakthrough products and services that will take us to another level and leave the competition behind."

"It is a great challenge. Whatever I can do to help, please let me know. I can tell you what we're doing in my division." He waved to someone at another table.

"Yes, please," I encouraged him. Perhaps I might learn something from our conversation after all.

"We've set up a major bids group. This group supports the branches with big proposals. I thought this would really help our revenue. And we're increasing our win rate. We have the best win rate in the company. We've been focusing on relationships with key clients. I've personally spent time with the senior executives of our top ten clients. This has paid off because we've seen more spending by those clients, which means more revenue and profit for us. We're leading the company in revenue per sales rep and in profit per sales rep." His hands were raised again, palms facing me and pushing toward me. I felt like I was being pushed away.

"That sounds impressive," I said, tired of hearing so much talk of his own importance. How could someone be so perfect?

"Thanks. It is, but I couldn't have done it without my team. They are well motivated and perform well. And I like to think I reward them well." By now, I was unable to work out whether anything he said was sincere.

He looked at his watch and hit his palms on the table. "I think we should leave it there. I have a team meeting shortly. I like to get the team together every week to look at performance and actions on key projects. It was good meeting you, Lauren. If I can give you any assistance in your job, please let me know."

I thanked Ryan for his time. I sat for a while in the coffee shop, recovering from the boring encounter—and the poor coffee.

When I got back to my desk, Ben Bowser asked me how the meeting went.

"Did Ryan keep his appointment?" Ben smiled. Part of Ben's job was to support Ryan on behalf of Marketing.

"Yes, he did." I didn't reveal that it was my third attempt.

"What do you make of him?" Ben asked. I knew what I would've liked to have said!

"The meeting went well," I said, avoiding the question.

"Be careful of Ryan," Ben warned. "He's known as the 'Smiling Assassin.' He smiles at your face while he stabs you in the back."

A cold shiver went through me, accompanied by memories of Deadly Di. Ben must have sensed my concern.

"I just want you to know, that's all," Ben said. "It's best to be warned. He's the sort of person who makes himself look good at other people's expense."

I felt nauseous. Ben couldn't know he'd triggered a "wicked boss" phobic reaction in me.

"Did he tell you about his major bids group?" Ben asked.

"Yes," I answered weakly.

"Well, the truth is, it was Meg's idea. She had to work really hard to persuade him to set it up. Reluctantly, he did. Now he claims it was his idea. I bet he didn't even mention Meg."

"No," I agreed, wanting to change the subject.

I thanked Ben for the warning, and as James had advised, wrote my first impressions of Ryan in my file: vain, cunning, unreliable, ruthless, and domineering. Ryan even earned a sixth word: boring.

As I sat at my desk, trying to concentrate, I thought about the positive culture that John Squires had described at my interview—"no game-playing." I was wondering about that now. While John and James were fine, I had strong misgivings about Gus and Ryan. I had already been warned about Jeremy Hyde, Hugh Worrell, and Maxine Savage. As yet, I was undecided about Nicholas Strange.

I had to admit that I'd been naive to accept a job based entirely on the quality of the manager I was to work for. I should have carried out more of an investigation of the company and the executive team. But now that I was here, I had to buckle down and deliver.

11

The ATC

"WATCH OUT, YOU IDIOT!" I yelled. Some mad driver in a black BMW cut me off in the parking lot. Typical male. Nothing was going to stop him from grabbing that space. I hadn't seen the driver or the car before. I reversed into a space opposite and watched him. He braked into his spot and turned off the engine, then checked his hair in the rearview mirror. Using three fingers, he fixed the front and sides of his receding hair. He poked his feet out of the car, black shoes shining. Then came the hand on the door handle, then his whole body. He adjusted his manhood as he stood and pulled up his slacks. Next he reached into the rear seat, picked up his coat, and put it on. With a glance at his reflection in the car window and a final lift of his slacks, he pranced to the front entrance of the office. Slightly repulsed, but intrigued, I followed at a distance. I was soon distracted by my early morning meeting and didn't think any more about him.

After the meeting, I headed back to my desk when Ben caught my attention.

"Lauren," he said, "Marcus has arrived. Come and I'll introduce you." I followed Ben to what used to be Meg's desk. Oh no—the idiot in the parking lot! My stomach dropped somewhere down around my knees.

"Marcus, this is Lauren Johnson," Ben said.

"H-ell-o, Lauren," Marcus beamed. "I am very pleased to meet you and looking forward to working with you." He looked me up and down. Sleaze. He made my skin crawl. Now, I thought, was a good time to lie.

"Same here," I smiled. His slacks were riding high on his waist, covering the slight protrusion of a belly. I made a mental note to check with Emily and Sandra about the throat signal they'd made when Meg announced Marcus as her replacement.

"I would like to meet with you as soon as possible," Marcus beamed again. "I am scheduling one-hour meetings with each member of my team. I would like a review of your projects and budgets. Please see Kathy to make a time." He turned his back to me and went back to his desk. That was it. That was meeting Marcus Pomfrey, the Air Traffic Controller. On the radar and quickly off again.

Later that afternoon, Marcus called a team meeting.

"Welcome, everyone," he said. "I'm delighted to be back from my overseas development assignment. I've had the pleasure of working with most of you before. For those of you I haven't worked with, I should point out that I'm a good people manager and I have an open-door policy. If you ever need my support, please don't hesitate to contact me for any advice or help. Are there any questions so far?"

The rest of us looked at each other. I caught Ben Bowser's eye. He smiled and shrugged. What a contradiction, I thought: If Marcus were a good people manager, he wouldn't need to point out that he was a good people manager.

"The next thing I want to announce," he continued, "is that I am planning to move offices. I'm not sure why Meg chose this floor when all the other directors are together on the top floor. My view is that I will not be able to represent you well enough from here. I need to be on the top floor with the other senior executives—close to John, Nicholas, Jeremy, and the others. Kathy and I will move as soon as possible to the twentieth floor."

Well, I thought, that established Marcus's priorities—closer to the executives than his own team. I looked at Ben who smiled and opened his palm toward the door, presumably signaling that Marcus was abandoning us.

"The next thing we need to be clear about is each other's roles and responsibilities. I want to develop a responsibilities matrix that will show each person's duties on a spreadsheet."

In my mind, everyone's roles and responsibilities were crystal clear to all of us—no confusion or duplication whatsoever.

"I've asked Kylie Goodwin to be project manager on this task," Marcus was saying. "Kylie will distribute a template by the end of tomorrow. Please complete the template and send it back to her by the end of the week. I will then review the final spreadsheet."

Kylie wore a smug look, like the one a teacher's pet would wear. Meg would have kept her in line, but Kylie would be in her element with Marcus. She'd no doubt pander to his ego and wrap him around her little finger.

"And finally," said Marcus, "please schedule a time with me, through Kathy, over the next few days so that you and I can meet individually to review your current projects. I look forward to working together and having a big impact on the success of the business."

That was that—meeting over!

As we left the room, I caught Emily's arm and asked if I could check something with her. We waited for the others to leave.

"Remember at that meeting with Meg a couple of weeks ago," I smiled, "you made a signal to Sandra with your hands around your throat? What was that all about?"

Emily laughed. "You mean like this?" She put her hands on her throat and pushed her chin up and back, simulating choking.

"That's it!"

"It's about Marcus," she grinned. "It's a code we have—he wears his pants so high they cut off his windpipe. We used to use it to warn each other that Marcus was around. It's a bit insensitive, but funny!"

I laughed along with her. "Yes, I noticed!"

I scheduled a meeting with Marcus for the next day. For some reason, he wanted to meet in one of the rooms on the nineteenth floor. As he closed the glass door, Marcus glanced at his reflection. Unfortunately, he checked only his face and hair, not the position of his slacks!

"Okay, Lauren, what are you working on?" He held a pen in his hand and leaned back in his chair.

Unbelievable, I thought. No questions about me or my background.

I explained to Marcus that I had been with the company for only two weeks and that I was still settling in. I told him of my plans to meet with the senior executives to understand their issues and how their ideas might fit with my role. As I spoke, he spun the pen around in his hand. He wasn't overly supportive of my plan, but he asked me to come back and see him when I had finished the meetings. I was surprised that he didn't like the idea. Surely, getting to know the executives was a good thing. Unless he wanted to keep that all for himself!

I outlined the six steps I was following to complete the whole strategy review. He drifted in and out of the conversation—one minute focused on me, the next minute blankly looking out the window. He said eighteen months to two years sounded like a long time to finish the project. But he didn't push it. Constantly, the pen moved through his fingers—one moment spinning, the next going from forefinger to little finger. It was hugely distracting.

I continued to explain the project. He listened without questioning, so I couldn't tell how much he was taking in. When I finished, he quickly closed the discussion. "Okay, fair enough, whatever," he said. "Let's leave it there." On the radar, off the radar. He checked his watch, put his pen in his pocket, and stood up to leave. I had no option but to go with him.

We walked together in silence to the elaborate staircase that led to the twentieth floor and Mission Control. Without saying good-bye, Marcus turned his back and slowly—deliberately—placed a foot on the first step. His shoulders seemed to become more erect as he paraded up the stairs. I thought I even detected a little wobble of his backside. I half hoped he would trip, but he made it safely to the landing by the time I had moved to the elevators.

I still didn't know anything about him or his story, and he knew nothing about me. It was as though he and I didn't exist up until that point, and then we just came into being and started working together without understanding what had gone before. I wondered what the future would hold with Marcus as my boss. I wondered whether I should have stayed in my old job—no, Marcus couldn't be as cruel as Di Ashman. He was more disinterested than aggressive, more preoccupied with himself than angry. I wondered about Ben's assessment of him as a yes-man.

Ben was in the elevator when I got on, heading back to the fourth floor. There was one other man in the elevator whom I didn't know. The man got out at the eleventh floor and as he left, I noticed he wore cuff links and embroidered cuffs. When the elevator doors closed and Ben and I were alone, I asked Ben about the cuffs.

He laughed, "That started just after Nicholas arrived. No one ever wore cuff links, let alone embroidered cuffs. But Nicholas wore them, and within a few days of him joining us, they suddenly appeared everywhere!"

As we walked from the elevator back to our desks, Ben said that he had just been speaking to Kathy. She was really upset.

"You know how Marcus is meeting with all of us?" Ben said. I nodded. "Well, Kathy asked Marcus when he would be meeting with her. He told her he was too busy and wouldn't be able to meet with her for at least two months. Can you believe that?"

I could not. I shook my head and stopped walking. "But Kathy is a key person. How could he not want to treat her as a priority? How could he not want to send her a message that she is really important to him?" I worried about what sort of boss—what sort of person—Marcus Pomfrey was.

We resumed walking, in silence.

12

With Friends Like These

THE NEXT DAY, I WAITED FOR AN ELEVATOR on the nineteenth floor after I'd finished a meeting. Marcus arrived at about the same time and pressed the elevator button. I smiled at him and tried to engage him in small talk, but he answered my questions with grunts and offered nothing to the conversation. He punched the elevator button several times. I didn't particularly want to be in an elevator with him alone.

I was relieved when two women, one much younger than the other, came out of the conference room area to catch an elevator as well. Both were well dressed, although the younger one, a visitor by the guest badge on her lapel, looked more professional and more at ease in her clothes and high heels. The older woman wore tight-fitting clothes and looked somewhat silly as she teetered on her heels.

I was surprised when they said good-bye to each other and the younger one disappeared into the stairwell. I wondered why she was taking the stairs, given we were on the nineteenth floor. The older woman greeted Marcus like they were friends. He called her "Maxine" so I assumed she was Maxine Savage. I didn't feel comfortable introducing myself, not wanting to intrude on their chummy conversation. Marcus ignored me, but maybe he assumed Maxine and I had already met. Maxine ignored me too.

The elevator bell rang and the three of us moved to the steel doors. Marcus held the door open, ushered Maxine into the elevator, and shuffled in behind her while continuing to ignore me. I went last. Marcus asked Maxine where she was going. She said the ground floor, and he pushed the appropriate button. I pushed the fourth floor for myself.

Marcus stood next to Maxine, his back to me. I felt about as big and as important as a flea. He asked Maxine why her visitor had left via the stairs.

Maxine grinned at him, "She suffers from claustrophobia and hates elevators." Her grin turned into a laugh.

Marcus laughed too. "Why didn't you meet her in a room on one of the lower floors, or even in the coffee shop?"

Maxine sniffed. "If she wants to do business with me, she has to meet me on my turf. It puts me in a better negotiating position." Marcus agreed that he would do the same.

As Maxine laughed, she wobbled on her heels. I half expected her to fall over, but like the Leaning Tower of Pisa, she defied gravity and stayed upright.

I couldn't extract myself from the elevator fast enough when it arrived at the fourth floor. Later, I realized the poor young lady must have walked up the nineteen flights of stairs as well as down them.

When I returned to my desk, I checked with Sandra to see if it had been Maxine Savage that I had just met. I described her to Sandra—the ill-fitting clothes and high wobbly heels. Sandra laughed and nodded. She also confirmed that Maxine and Marcus were friends.

It was my first interaction with Maxine. I didn't look forward to the next.

Ben was walking back to his desk and smiling to himself. He looked much happier than I felt. I asked him what he was smiling about. He said he had been visiting Gus Wearing.

"Gus's style hasn't improved," Ben laughed. "He's wearing a safety pin for a missing shirt button! Not even *I* would do that."

Normally, I try not to laugh at other people's expense, but I did this time. I could just picture Gus—scuffed shoes and snow-flaked shoulders, now complete with a safety pin shirt button. Ben always made me feel better!

Over the dishes that night, I told Paul about the incident with Marcus and Maxine in the elevator. Paul was disgusted and could hardly believe it. Annie was wiping the plates, and Harry was playing with his cars on the floor in the family room.

"Who are you talking about?" Annie asked.

"My boss," I answered.

"Has the dog gone with you?"

"No, this is a different one." Oh, no, I thought. What a horrid concept. "Hey, Annie, go and get your fable book, please."

"Do I have to?" she whined.

"Yes, darling. I want to check something." She lingered.

Harry must have overheard us; he raced off to Annie's room. "I'll get it," he shouted.

"You better not touch anything in my room," Annie yelled after him.

Harry was back in a flash, holding the book by its back cover, letting the pages dangle.

"Don't damage that book," said Paul.

Harry handed me the book. I checked the index and found the fable I was looking for.

"Do you remember this one, Annie? We read it the other night." But Annie had thrown down the tea towel and covered her ears as she ran from the room. Harry and Paul listened, but Harry lost interest halfway through.

> A man who wanted to buy an ass went to markets, and, coming across a likely looking beast, arranged with the owner that he should be allowed to take the ass home on trial to see what he was like. When the man reached home, he put the animal into his stable along with the other asses. The newcomer took a look around and immediately chose a place next to the laziest and greediest beast in the stable. When the master saw this, he put a halter on him at once, and led him off and handed him

> back to his owner again. The latter was a good deal surprised to see him back so soon and said, "Why, do you mean to say you have tested him already?"
>
> "I didn't want to put him through any tests," replied the other. "I could see what sort of beast he is from the companion he chose for himself."

"Paul, how am I going to get on with Marcus?" I asked soberly. "If you can tell a person by their friends, then I'm in big trouble!"

"Gee, I don't know," he said in a tired voice. "But I hope you work it out. Let's not go through another Deadly Di disaster. You'll have to try and get on with him. But make sure you stick up for yourself this time." He sounded grumpy.

We did the remaining dishes in silence. I wished Meg were still around.

13

Wicked Witch of the West

I HAD MANAGED TO GET MAXINE'S ASSISTANT to schedule a meeting for Maxine and me. The meeting was set for the day after the elevator incident. I arrived early and was gazing out the window when Maxine walked in. Yes, it definitely was the same woman who had cruelly expected her claustrophobic visitor to walk up and down nineteen flights of stairs. Maxine was a short person, slightly shorter than I. Her black-and-white checked suit was too tight, showing too many curves in the wrong places.

She walked in briskly, plunked her folder on the table, and let out a sigh as though she was far too busy for this meeting. I was immediately ill at ease.

"You must be Lauren. I'm Maxine." She didn't smile, avoided my eyes, and didn't shake my hand.

"Hi, Maxine, I'm pleased to meet you." I held out my hand, which she shook briefly. She gave no indication that she recognized me from the elevator.

She moved to the head of the table. I pulled out a chair at the side of the table and caught her looking me up and down as I sat. My back faced the outer glass wall.

"What's this all about?" She sat down and pushed her chair away from the table. She looked at her reflection in the glass behind me and patted her bottle blonde hair.

"Well, I've been with Harlow Kane for just three weeks. I wanted to introduce myself to you and discuss your ideas on what my priorities should be and how I can best add value to your division."

"That's novel," she said flippantly, and rolled her eyes.

"What do you mean, novel?"

"To have someone in your role offering to assist Sales and Services," she answered as she eyed herself in the glass.

Her comment threw me.

"Well, I'm eager to be of service to the sales groups," I said, struggling for the right thing to say.

"We'll see if it works out that way," she said, again glancing at herself in the glass. It felt like I was meeting with two Maxines—one in front and one behind.

I didn't know what to say. Eventually I offered, "One way to help me understand what I should focus on is to put yourself in my shoes for a moment. If you were doing my job, what would you do to support the directors in Sales and Services?"

"That's easy. I wouldn't do your job!" she said with a cynical laugh. She checked that her reflection enjoyed the joke as well.

Again, I was thrown. Why was she not helping me? It felt like she was deliberately obstructing my efforts to get to know her and understand how best to support her. She reminded me of Deadly Di. I started to get nervous, rapidly losing my confidence. If that was her intent, she was succeeding.

"I much prefer Sales to Marketing," she said, crossing her plump arms and legs. "Sales has much more impact. Marketing is a backroom support function, an overhead function. Sales is where it really happens."

"Have you not had good support from Marketing people in the past?" I asked, trying to hide my frustration.

"I've found Marketing people to be academic, sensitive, and too pure. In Sales, you have to be practical. You would be eaten alive in Sales if you were too analytical," she said with a sharp shake of her head, checking her reflection to make sure each strand of hair fell back into its right place.

I was becoming agitated but did my best to stay composed.

"Well," I said, "Harlow Kane has obviously decided that a Marketing function is important. Do you think there should not be a Marketing department?"

"I accept that a Marketing department is a necessary evil," she acknowledged begrudgingly.

"Well, the company has decided that the marketing strategist role is important, which is why I have been employed. Do you think Meg and John made a poor decision?"

"I don't know you," she said, "so I have no issue with John employing you." Her acknowledgment of John, and not Meg, interested me.

"Well," I pushed on, "now that I'm here, I want to be effective. Can you share with me your key sales challenges? How are we performing in the market? In what areas do we do well, and where do we do poorly compared to the competition? This might give me some ideas of what I should focus on."

"We are doing well at present, so I don't need a lot of help," she answered coldly.

"If there was just one thing that you would love to improve," I persisted, "what would it be?"

She paused for a few seconds. "The quality of our sales representatives," she said. At last, I was getting somewhere. "We lose quite a few sales reps, and we have trouble hiring quality replacements and getting them up to speed quickly. It would help if you could do something about that. Others have tried to fix it, but nothing's worked."

"Okay," I said, noting the point. "What else? With our products and services, are there any areas where we compare badly with our competitors?"

"No, we're doing quite well compared to the competition. Actually, we're killing them." She looked at her watch. I was about to lose her, which was partly a relief.

"Look, why are you asking me all these questions?" she asked in a cutting voice. "If you've got something specific to show me, then by all means, give me a call and we can discuss it. I haven't got time for this. And I'm not doing your job, so I can't tell you all the answers. Is there anything else, or have we finished?" She stood up, checked her reflection, and tried to iron out a few bumps.

"Y . . . yes," I said weakly, "I just wanted to introduce myself."

"Okay," she said, "you've done that. I need to go. Give me a call when you do have something for me."

Maxine marched from the room. I was exhausted from the encounter. Somehow, I struggled to my feet and dragged myself out of the room. I kept about ten paces behind her. She walked unsteadily, as if she suffered from a disability, but the problem was her shoes—the heels were too narrow for her round body. Watching her weave her way along the corridor, I was caught between giggling and feeling seasick. She managed to navigate her way to the stairs and wobbled back up to the twentieth floor and into her den.

After this, I went back to my desk and wrote the five words describing Maxine: oppositional, merciless, arrogant, intimidating, bitch . . . well, I crossed out the last one and replaced it with grumpy.

I was finishing my list when Sandra came back to her desk.

"I've just met with Maxine," I whispered.

"How did it go?" she smiled.

I looked around—we were on our own. "She's a bitch!"

"Yep, we call her the 'Wicked Witch of the West.'"

I grinned. "What I don't understand is why she gave me a hard time. I thought as a senior woman she would want to help other women."

Sandra let out a short burst of laughter. "You might think so, but do you know what she says about that? She says, 'I had to make it without anyone holding my hand. I'm not your mommy.' I've heard her say it!"

14
Meeting the Beta Alpha

I WAS STILL RECOVERING from the nasty episode with Maxine and becoming uncertain about my plan to meet each of the executives. Apart from James, the meetings had ranged from unsatisfactory to shocking. Next up was Nicholas Strange, Chief Operations Officer.

I left my decision of what to wear that morning until after I'd heard the weather report. It was to be a drizzly, cool day. I chose a dark dress suit with a blue top that suited the color of my eyes.

I was all set to leave but was momentarily delayed (and accepted that I'd thus be late for work) when Harry called out from the bathroom that he'd "done one." This was code for him wanting Paul or me to wipe his behind. I called out to Paul—no answer—darn. Harry yelled louder, insisting that someone help him "right now!" At the bathroom door, I was greeted by a four-year-old bottom pointing to the sky, Harry's hands and feet planted on the floor. Harry repeated his demand. I obliged.

I quickly washed my hands, kissed Paul and the kids good-bye, and set off to work, driving slowly in the crawling traffic. I turned the radio down and went over my thoughts about meeting with Nicholas. I decided that my plan was good—to be natural and to come across as an observant and analytical professional with an ability to make astute assessments of company strategies and competitive positioning. After all, that's what I was employed to do. So far, I'd made good progress. I'd reached an understanding of our current capability and could see how we compared with our competitors. I would share with Nicholas some of my early impressions.

The meeting was scheduled for ten-thirty. I arrived promptly at the arranged time but was kept waiting for at least ten minutes while Nicholas talked on the phone. The waiting annoyed me. I could've happily stayed at my desk, working productively, instead of wasting time like this. I knew it was all about power, keeping us "lesser" people waiting. Deadly Di had taught me that. I knew full well that if I'd been the CEO or a board member, Nicholas would have been punctual.

Helen, his assistant, invited me to wait in the chair outside Nicholas's office. While I sat and waited, I overheard some of Nicholas's conversation. He was complaining to someone about some tiling. Maybe he was renovating his bathroom or kitchen. He was criticizing someone about their lousy standard of work. He paused while the person on the other end of the phone was obviously speaking. He grunted a "thank you" and hung up. No doubt, he had won the argument.

"Hi, Lauren," he said, coming out of his office. He shook my hand in his dominant style. I was surprised that he seemed pleased to see me. "Come on in. Now, I have to apologize. I have a plane to catch, so we need to be brief." He pointed to his rectangular table and the chair I was to sit in. He sat at the head of the table.

My chair was slightly lower than normal, which made me feel awkward and disadvantaged. I recalled Ben Bowser's warning that Nicholas had had the legs of his subordinates' chairs shortened. Ben was right. I suppressed a giggle and looked forward to telling him later.

"As you know," I said, sitting as tall as possible, "I have just joined Harlow Kane. The reason I wanted to meet with you was to ask for your perspective on the company, which will help me in my role."

"Thanks for making the time," he said charmingly, looking me straight in the eye. "How about I start with an overall summary of the business?"

"That will be great," I said, feeling more relaxed. Good, he was going to cooperate. His voice was smooth and engaging.

He leaned back and placed his hands behind his head.

"First of all, we've been performing very well as a company these last eighteen months. Before I arrived, everyone was struggling. But I've made tough decisions and things have come together. The board likes our results."

He dropped his hands to the table and leaned forward. "The financials are in good order. We have improved our performance in major projects and major bids. When I first arrived, I did the financial analysis of where we made most of our profit. Until then, the analysis had not been done to the depth that we needed. What I found was that most of our profit comes from eighteen percent of our projects—the major projects for key clients. That's where our future lies." I wondered whose idea this was anyway. Ryan had claimed it as his. Ben had said it was Meg's idea, which was most likely correct.

"What parts of the business perform best?" I asked.

"The Western Division region under Maxine Savage is doing well. Southern and Northern divisions are doing okay. The Eastern Division is a basket case. You might try to get close to that group and see what you can do to support them."

He was being very frank, I thought.

"I am worried about Gus Wearing," he continued. "I don't know if he is going to make it. Have you met Gus?"

Suddenly, I was uncomfortable, and not so much because of the chair. I wanted to know his perspective of the business, but I didn't expect him to be so open—opinionated—about one of his direct reports. He waited for my answer.

"I have met with Gus," I answered carefully. "I have met with each of the sales and services directors."

"What do you think of them all?" he asked in a conversational tone.

"It's too early for me to say. I . . . I've only had brief meetings," I answered, trying to avoid the topic.

Nicholas continued in a casual fashion. "Gus is a worry. And have you noticed the way he dresses? Frankly, he's an embarrassment."

I squirmed in my seat and tried to change the subject. "When I was being interviewed for the role, people mentioned the challenges being faced by the company. What's—"

"Who said we were facing challenges?" he growled. His mood changed as rapidly as a switch being turned on.

"John and Meg," I answered hesitantly, mystified by his change of mood. "And Chester Osborne, the headhunter."

He slammed his fist down on the table. I jumped in fright. "Well, for starters," he scowled, pointing his finger at me, "Chester doesn't know a thing about us. And Meg doesn't work here anymore. And John is out of touch, lost!"

I swallowed hard, recoiling from his sudden aggression.

He went on angrily, his face bright red. "I don't know why they told you that. We are a well-run company that's doing great things. We're murdering the competition."

"I'm sure that's right, Nicholas," I said, my pulse quickening. "I think they were speaking more about the future." I regretted saying this as soon as the words escaped.

"What about the future?" he hissed.

I wanted to hide. "They were saying that there are early warning signs that we may slip behind our competition in a year or two."

Nicholas paused, stood, and walked to the other side of the table directly opposite me. He clamped his hands on the table and leaned toward me. I felt like running for the door.

"Listen to me, Ms. Johnson. It's all very well for you to come in here, sit on your judgment seat for a few days, and make negative remarks," he raved. "I'll have you know we've had an impressive track record over the last few years. I've turned this company around, made sure we can compete, and we certainly do compete—extremely well, in fact. Frankly, I am disappointed that you would say that we are in danger of losing that position."

I trembled, didn't know where to look, didn't know what to say.

"Sorry, Nicholas," I apologized in a small voice, "I didn't mean to be critical."

He looked at his watch. "We're going to have to leave it there," he said abruptly. "I have a plane to catch." I was relieved.

As fast as he had turned aggressive, he switched back to being sugary sweet. He was calm now, a totally different person. "You know, I'm a big supporter of Marketing." He flashed me his best smile. "If there is anything I can do to help you, please come and see me. I want to help you be successful."

This worried me. I sensed he was thinking the exact opposite!

He quickly packed his bag and glanced again at his watch. As I left his office, he yelled a command to his assistant, "Helen, I'm running late for my plane. Call the airline and have them hold the flight for me."

Surely I didn't hear that correctly—hold the flight for him? I could tell from his agitated look that he was not being funny. And from Helen's expression, I knew it wasn't the first time he had demanded such a thing.

"And tell my driver I'm on the way down," he shouted.

I returned to my desk and collapsed into my chair, still shaken by the ordeal. All I could think about was Deadly Di and the abuse I used to take from her. And now, the same thing had just happened with Nicholas Strange. I went to the kitchen, poured a glass of water, and tried to think about something else. I flicked a single tear from my eye. I had to be stronger. I breathed deeply and went back to my desk.

Despite my trembling hand, I managed to write my first observations about Nicholas: autocratic, arrogant, detached, unpredictable, tyrant.

* * *

That night, I told Paul about my meeting with Nicholas. He laughed when I described the shortened chairs. He joked that I must have made it up. But he believed the chair story after I told him about the plane. He knew I wouldn't have invented that one! He howled. I, however, was in no laughing mood. Harry wondered if I was telling a fable.

"But what about the abuse?" I exclaimed. "What do I do about that?"

"I don't know." Paul shook his head. "Maybe you'll run into this everywhere, especially in the senior roles you're now getting into. I'm out of my depth here. I don't understand workplaces like yours. I can give you a massage though, if it'll help."

"I'd love one, but I don't have time." There was a basketball meeting that night, and as manager of Annie's team, I had to attend. I was so exhausted from the Nicholas episode. But if I didn't go to the meeting, the team would lose points, and we didn't have many to lose.

I left Paul and the kids at home and drove to the meeting. It was a waste of time, just a lot of boring things to cover, which seemed to be major deals to some of the people there.

Driving home, I reflected on my meetings with the executives. I now had met with almost all the senior managers, all except Jeremy Hyde, the CFO, and Hugh Worrell, the HR director. Nicholas Strange ruled the roost. For some reason, John Squires had apparently conceded his power to Nicholas; or perhaps Nicholas had snatched it. And Nicholas's behavior was being mirrored by those closest to him. The Wicked Witch of the West, Maxine Savage, and Ryan Gunn, the Smiling Assassin, were similarly self-absorbed, and the jackdaw among eagles Gus Wearing seemed to lack confidence. Gus was probably well aware of Nicholas's opinion of him and was running scared. Marcus Pomfrey lacked sincerity, but managed upward well, so he fit in. James Swann was the exception. He was genuine and enjoyed leading, and his self-identity did not seem dependent on his position.

With a less-than-positive view of the executive team, I worried about what the future held for me.

Paul was still up when I arrived home, and we sat in our comfy chairs and chatted about the kids. He said we needed a family vacation.

"Paul, I've just started at Harlow Kane. I can't take vacation yet."

"But it's been ages since we had a break together. It would be good for us. School holidays are coming up."

"Look, I've had a terrible day and I'm tired. Can we talk about this some other time?"

"Okay," he said, "but I don't want to see you getting down again like you did with Deadly Di. Don't take it all so seriously."

"But it *is serious*! I want to do well, and that's important to me," I argued.

"Just keep it in balance. And I do think you need a vacation."

"Let's talk about this another night. I'm on such a short fuse after today."

"That's exactly my point!" he blurted, standing up. He waited for me to respond, but I was too tired.

He said resignedly, "I'm going to bed."

I turned on the TV and vegetated in front of some mindless late-night trash. About twenty minutes later, I woke up on the couch and crawled into bed.

15

Trying to Add Value

IN THE TWO WEEKS Sandra had been acting manager, she'd approved a trip to an external marketing conference for me—and a good thing too, because Marcus tried to cancel it as soon as he found out.

He couldn't see why I needed to attend a conference when I had been with the company only a few weeks. Irritated, I had to explain to him that the subject matter related closely to my responsibility for developing marketing strategy.

"Anyway," I said, "the money's already been paid." Begrudgingly, he let me go.

At the conference, impressive speakers covered a range of amazing subjects. I came away with plenty of stimulating ideas that I couldn't wait to share at Harlow Kane. It didn't take great deductive powers to realize that the company needed to find ways to reduce the staff turnover of sales representatives, most likely through induction and training. Achieving this would have a high impact on the retention and morale of the salespeople, and consequently improve sales and profit. From what I had learned at the conference, I had a good idea of how the problem could be fixed.

I tried for several days to meet with Marcus to tell him some of the ideas that I felt were worth exploring. It took me two weeks to finally get him to see me. I met him in his office, which by now was on the top floor at Mission Control, positioned nicely in the botanical garden.

"Marcus," I said, "the conference was very good."

"Fine," he responded unenthusiastically, spinning his pen. "Did you learn anything?"

Grateful for the opening, I began, "Sure did! I picked up a stack of useful ideas that could work well for us. One of them is excellent for training sales reps. Another is an anthropological approach to market research."

"What was that?" he exclaimed, his eyebrows raised.

"Anthropological studies. You might call them archetype studies."

He looked at me blankly.

"We are a service company," I began, pleased for the chance to explain, but concerned about the raised eyebrows. "But what does service mean in the various countries in which we operate? Concepts and words mean different things in different countries; for example, the concept of time. In Switzerland, it means 'exact.' In Latin countries it can mean something quite different." I paused. He looked at me as though I was speaking a foreign language.

"What's that got to do with us?" he asked impatiently, moving his pen through his fingers.

"Well, in business it's important. There have been studies done on the meaning of quality. In Japan, quality means 'perfection.' In Germany it means 'technical precision.' In France, it's 'luxury and style.'"

I paused, trying to gauge Marcus's reaction. From his vacant look, I knew I had lost him. Most people were interested in this stuff. Maybe he didn't follow me. I had to hit the punch line soon. I raised my voice a fraction to try to regain his attention.

"It's all about understanding how our customers decide whether we're a good company to deal with." I'd definitely lost him and I had to finish.

"As a service company, we need to know what 'service' means in different countries. If we understand this better than our competitors, then we'll be in a better position to compete."

"Okay, fair enough, whatever," he said, closing the discussion. This one never even got on the radar. He put his pen in his pocket.

I realized too late that I wasn't going to be able to explain my idea about training sales reps. But I had to give it a shot anyway.

"Marcus, the more urgent issue I want to talk to you about has to do with training sales reps. I picked up an idea at the conference that will really help. It's a straightforward idea that I would like to implement."

"No, I don't think that's a top priority here," he said, flattening my enthusiasm. "Our main focus in Marketing should be the development of products and services and launches. Now, I'm running late for my meeting with Nicholas. I'll see you later." With that, he was gone.

I stayed glued to the spot, shocked that he showed not the slightest interest in what I had said. I wondered if I should have pushed the point. What did I do wrong? I felt dazed as my enthusiasm quickly disappeared. He was a champion at killing energy and motivation.

But I knew deep inside that I could not drop this issue. What I had learned at the conference would definitely help with the major issue of sales rep training. It would also provide me with the quick win I needed to demonstrate my value, the quick win James had urged me to achieve. I realized that I had confused Marcus by talking about anthropology and had completely lost him by the time I'd talked about sales rep training. I needed to approach him again.

I arranged another meeting with Marcus. I had to believe that if I could hold his attention long enough to share the idea with him, I would be on my way to success. This time, however, I would have to explain it to him very simply—get it on his radar!

A few days later, we again met in his office at Mission Control.

"Marcus, you know I have been meeting with the sales directors to introduce myself and to understand their challenges and areas for improvement. Well, one thing that immediately stood out to me is the turnover of our sales reps. I think we can help."

"I don't think so," said Marcus.

"Why not?" I said, frustrated by this short, negative response.

"It's not the main game. I want the team focused on issues that are clearly within the Marketing department's goals. We don't own staff turnover. That's an HR issue."

I couldn't believe that he was not interested in even hearing the idea. But I was determined. I had to keep pushing, uncomfortable as that was for me.

"But I have an idea that might work," I said, annoyed with myself that I found confrontation so difficult. "Staff turnover is everyone's problem. Losing a high proportion of sales reps has to be important to Marketing."

"Forget it," he said forcefully. "I told you to forget it last time we talked. I'm not going to do Hugh Worrell's job for him. I want you to focus on the things that will make the biggest difference to our department. There is no end of real challenges, Lauren. I don't want you getting distracted. Have I made myself clear? Now, is there anything else?"

"No." End of discussion.

Driving home that night, I was angry at myself for not being confident enough to push an argument, and I was angry with Marcus that I had to argue in the first place. Why should I have to be good at handling conflict, anyway? It was supposed to be a workplace, not a battleground.

I had to keep going with the idea of solving the sales rep issue. I had to make an impact. If I didn't win executive support and get this early achievement, it would be even harder to accomplish my main task, a comprehensive review of marketing strategy.

16

Dr. Jekyll and Jeremy Hyde

"WHO'S THAT SHOUTING?" I asked Ben. We were on the thirteenth floor, the floor occupied by the Finance department. Ben had agreed to help me gather financial information for my sales rep training proposal.

I couldn't believe what was being spewed out from the other side of the floor. The language belonged in the gutter, not the office. Sailors wouldn't have tolerated it. Ben sighed, "That'll be Jeremy."

"No way!" Ben was about to meet with one of the financial analysts, and I was to meet with Jeremy Hyde, the CFO, whom I had not yet spent any time with.

"Afraid so. Jeremy is legendary for his short temper and hurling truckloads of abuse. And he has absolutely no remorse."

"But the swearing and personal attack someone is getting, surely that isn't accepted."

"Well, that's Jeremy. He's given a lot of latitude."

"But no one should have to put up with that—the poor person on the receiving end!" My stomach churned. I knew I could never take abuse like that. I felt awful for whoever was receiving the verbal assault.

At that moment, accounting staff started to leave the floor.

"What's happening now?" I asked.

"Let's ask Marcia," Ben replied, pointing to a lady hurrying toward us.

"Marcia," said Ben, "where's everyone going?"

Marcia looked at us but didn't pause. We fell in step with her. She looked over her shoulder before she answered. "We always escape for a while when Jeremy is in an abusive mood. We're going for coffee until things settle down."

It was inconceivable to me that she, and the staff, were so used to doing this.

Ben asked her quietly, "Who's getting it this time?"

Marcia shook her head and looked down. "George Banks, the accounting manager."

Marcia kept moving, and we followed her into a crowded elevator. At the ground floor, she set an urgent pace and we rushed to keep up.

"Do you know why?" Ben continued.

"The accounts receivable news wasn't good." She was puffing now. "And our collections of money haven't been up to budget, plus, cash is a bit lower than expected. Jeremy threw a tantrum and he's taking it out on George."

"Why were collections bad?" Ben asked.

"Well, they're not disastrous," answered Marcia. "But they are a bit below budget because we're training a new revenue clerk." Under her breath she added, "The last one left because of a similar abusive session. I don't think the new clerk will be with us for long, either. George is defending her. He must have known it was coming because he sent her on an errand about an hour ago, so at least she's missing this."

"Can we forget the reason?" I interrupted. "Collections aren't the issue! The abuse is the issue! How long has this been going on?"

We were now outside in the fresh air and sunshine and Marcia relaxed, slightly.

"As long as he's been with us."

"I just can't understand how this behavior can be tolerated. Why doesn't his boss do something?" I asked. "Or if his boss won't, how about HR?"

Marcia shrugged her shoulders and answered, "Jeremy used to work with Nicholas Strange at another company, so Nicholas must have known all about Jeremy's short fuse before he hired him."

Ben added, "The problem is that Nicholas, Jeremy, and Hugh are all very close. Hugh is godfather to one of Jeremy's children. They all socialize together. I told you about the beach house they own together."

Marcia said she felt better, now that she was outside. "Most of us are getting sick of it. Too many of us have been on the receiving end of his tongue-lashing."

"Has anyone gone to John Squires?" I asked, wondering why the CEO would not intervene.

"One time, soon after Jeremy had joined us, one of the managers went to see John," Marcia said angrily, gritting her teeth. "That manager said John didn't want to know about it. He said Jeremy must have been misunderstood. And John must have told Jeremy because the manager who complained got fired soon after. No one has gone back to John since."

We let Marcia catch up with her colleagues—strength in numbers. Ben and I went back inside, heading to the fourth floor. I was glad we had the elevator to ourselves.

"What else do I need to know about Jeremy Hyde?" I asked.

Ben shook his head. "He's one mixed-up, disturbed individual, that's for sure. He doesn't trust anyone, and he's always on guard. Once, there was a young finance graduate who joined us, and he and a few others had to make presentations in front of Jeremy. The three people before him got absolutely scorched by Jeremy. It was his turn next and he was petrified. Lucky for him, time ran out and he didn't have to make his presentation. But he'd got himself into such a state, he nearly soiled his pants. He quit the next day."

My hand flew to my mouth. What on earth was I doing here? My hands started to shake.

"Ben, how absolutely horrible!" This was a nightmare. "Is there anything else?"

"Oh, the list is endless. And Jeremy can't take criticism, even in the nicest form. He gets so angry."

"So, tell me again, why does John tolerate him?"

"He's good at his job," said Ben. I studied Ben's face, looking for humor. He saw the irony in what he'd said. "I mean, he's good at the technical side of finance. He runs a tight ship and is a good manager of money.

John turns a blind eye to his behavior because John doesn't want to worry about financial matters. And remember, Jeremy is supported by Nicholas and Hugh."

"But it's such a dispiriting environment for his staff," I said. "How can people be expected to work properly in such tension? Imagine the effect on their health and the psychological damage. I can't believe this is tolerated in this day and age." I thought of Paul's reaction to the story I would tell him that night.

"No wonder Meg resigned," I said.

"Yeah. Meg never mentioned everything that happened with Jeremy. I guess chucking the book at her was the straw that broke the camel's back, and she decided she wasn't prepared to tolerate it anymore."

"Good for her. No one should have to take that."

I avoided a "get-to-know-you" meeting with Jeremy.

17

A Good Idea

ALTHOUGH MARCUS HAD GIVEN ME no encouragement whatsoever with my sales rep training idea, I decided to persist. My colleagues helped me with the proposal, and I was ready to take the idea forward.

I was now into my sixth week at Harlow Kane, and the importance of developing the capability of sales reps was a clear priority across the Sales and Services divisions. I arranged to meet Hugh Worrell, the HR director, who was happy to meet me when I called.

When I arrived at Hugh's office at the appointed time, he kept me waiting for just a moment. I could see him talking with Nicholas. When they'd finished, Hugh came to the lounge area where I was waiting and introduced himself.

"Good morning, Lauren. I'm pleased to meet you." He shook my hand with a strong grip and invited me to sit down at his round table.

He was smartly dressed in a colorful shirt with cuff links and, of course, embroidered initials on his cuffs. His silk tie exactly matched his shirt. His shoes shone. His pants were carefully creased and he moved confidently. He definitely had style—the exact opposite of Gus Wearing. Hugh also showed early signs of an emerging stomach.

"I'm pleased to meet you too, Hugh."

"Now, what's this about sales training?"

"Well, I've been meeting with the sales directors and talking with them about their key challenges. Just about all of them said the same thing, that there's a need for better sales rep training. Now, I have an idea that I—"

"Why were you talking to them about sales training?" he interrupted.

His tone surprised me. I started to worry that he might attack me, like Nicholas had. Maybe he thought I was invading his turf. I had to be careful.

"I hadn't gone to talk to them specifically about training. I'd gone to them because I wanted to understand the big picture and help them where I could. I asked them their one challenge they would most like to overcome. Almost all of them agreed it was sales reps and that better training would make the biggest difference."

"Fair enough. Why didn't they come to me?" he leaned back in his chair.

"I guess it came up because I asked them. Anyway, I wanted to share this finding with you and to share an idea I have. I believe it could put us at the top of the industry."

"I'm listening," he said, leaning forward. Good, I had his attention.

"The idea is that we implement online sales training with a program from Garrison Business School. The program is already available, and we don't even need additional computer capacity."

"I don't believe in online learning," he objected, waving both hands in dismissal. I waited for him to explain. He waited for me to go on.

"Why don't you believe in online training?" I asked. I hadn't anticipated that the HR director would have a problem with this method of training; maybe other executives would, but not HR!

"I think people learn best in a classroom. They need to be taught by and interact with an experienced person."

I already had an answer for that.

"I have thought about that," I responded. "We would train local facilitators from within Harlow Kane who would coach and mentor the younger sales reps. Each office would have its own mentor who would coach the reps and reinforce their online learning."

He put his fingers to his lips and slowly tilted his head from side to side. Perhaps he was warming to the concept.

I went on. "The benefit of online training is that we can deliver training to people wherever they are, and at a time that suits them. We won't have logistical problems of coordinating classroom education."

"And," he joined in, his eyes bright, "our salespeople could do the program after hours."

"Well . . . they could," I hesitantly agreed. It did worry me that the sales reps would be expected to work their full week and fit the training into their personal time. They definitely would not thank me for that.

I changed the subject. "And all the material is written by Garrison, based on research they have conducted on effective selling. It's right up there with Harvard's research."

"How much will this cost?" I knew I was winning him over if he was asking about price. I was confident he would support the idea.

"With the help of a colleague, I've crunched some numbers," I said and handed him a pack of information. "Sales reps are currently leaving us at the rate of twenty-five percent a year. This is a high labor turnover, and given that it takes around three months to recruit a sales rep and another three months to have them operate at an effective level, this is a multimillion dollar problem for us yearly. We know from the sales directors that the number one issue of concern is an absence of good training. The financials supporting this training are strong."

"Yes . . . and what does it cost?" he repeated, leafing through the folder.

"Around ten thousand dollars for a license and three hundred dollars per student per course. It's much cheaper than the classroom alternative."

"It sounds like a good proposition," Hugh acknowledged, nodding thoughtfully. "Thanks for raising this, Lauren. Have you shared this idea with any of the other executives?"

"No, I haven't had a chance. Because it relates very much to HR, I wanted to share it with you first."

"Okay, leave it with me. Best not to tell anyone else about it at this point until I consider the proposal, and then you and I can discuss it some more. Thanks, Lauren. Good work."

As I left his office, I began to feel confident that I was finally getting somewhere and that this would be the early win James had talked about. I was excited and couldn't wait to tell Paul.

18
Change of Plans

"LAUREN, COULD YOU COME UP AND SEE ME?" When Marcus rang to summon one of us to the top floor, he generally overlooked normal pleasantries. I cheekily signaled to Emily—with a quick hand choke of my neck—that I was going to see Marcus. We laughed.

The enormous number of plants in Mission Control still surprised me. On my way to Marcus's office, I passed the gardener. She was busily pruning and watering.

"Come on in," said Marcus when I arrived at his office. He stood up and came from behind his desk and sat down at his round table. He gestured for me to sit.

"I've just come from a meeting with the executives. Hugh Worrell presented a terrific idea. He thinks we should train our sales reps online and supplement the training with local Harlow Kane facilitators who will act as coaches and mentors for our sales reps in their actual locations."

"Yes," I said, pleased, and waiting for more.

"Not only that, but he says we can get immediate access to the latest and best program from Garrison Business School."

"Yes, I know, didn't Hugh—" Marcus was still talking.

"The executive team loved it. Hugh is putting together a task force to implement the idea. What I would like is for you to be our representative on the task force. Could you do that? I know you have an interest in this issue with sales reps."

"Well, I'd love to. But, um—did Hugh say where the idea came from?" I waited anxiously for the right answer.

Marcus frowned, trying to recall. "No, not really. I got the impression that he'd talked to the sales directors about their biggest challenges and then came up with this solution. It was very well received—immediate unanimous support. It really hit the mark."

I felt sick. My brain yelled, "Tell him the idea was yours! Stick up for yourself, for goodness sake!" But I remained silent. I was confused; my head was doing cartwheels. I couldn't work out fast enough how to explain the truth without calling the HR director a liar and a thief.

Marcus had some calls to make, so I left quietly. Demoralized. Stunned. I struggled back to my desk.

Fifteen minutes later, I was still gazing blankly at my computer screen when Marcus called again, asking me back up to Mission Control. I wasn't in the mood to signal to Emily. What did Marcus want this time?

"Please sit down," he said when I returned to his office. This time, he remained seated at his desk and pointed for me to sit opposite him. "I called Hugh Worrell to tell him you would be our representative on the sales training task force. For some reason, Hugh doesn't want you on the committee. What have you done to him?" Marcus leaned forward with his elbows on his desk and rubbed his temples.

What have *I* done to *him*! This idea was to be my quick win, a demonstration of my value to the business. He had snatched it, like a wolf.

"I haven't done anything to him," I snarled. "I've only met him once."

"Well, anyway, he's asked Kylie Goodwin to represent Marketing. You're off the project."

* * *

I couldn't get the children into bed quickly enough that night. It seemed to take ages to settle them. I fought my impatience. Finally, Paul and I had some time to ourselves.

"I know what's coming," he smiled. "Another work story." He handed me a mug of hot chocolate.

"Thanks, darling. I could use this. You're so thoughtful."

We sipped our drinks, ate cookies, and laughed at each other's frothy moustaches. I was less angry now.

I started to explain how Hugh had ripped off my idea.

Paul was amazed. "I'm so glad having my own practice keeps me out of these sorts of games," he said. "What are you going to do about it?"

"I don't know. I'm still recovering from the shock."

"Maybe he did acknowledge your contribution. Or maybe he plans to," said Paul, always thinking the best of people. I shook my head.

"Maybe. But I think it was a straight steal."

"Well, you can't just leave it and fume," he said.

"But I don't want to make a fuss. I don't want to argue with people, especially a member of the executive team. I get so nervous just at the thought of an argument."

Paul placed his mug on the table and scolded me. "There you go again, Lauren. Why won't you stick up for yourself? If you don't, this will just keep happening."

I was drained, exhausted by the struggle. "I just want to do a good job and make a difference. Why do I have to play these games?"

"What do you think you should do?" he asked, reaching again for his mug.

I thought about facing Hugh and trying to demand an explanation. Tears welled in my eyes. "He's the head of HR," I said weakly. "I can't call him a thief. Who would I even tell?" Paul handed me a tissue. "I'll just have to get on with my job."

"Lauren, for God's sake, you must stick up for yourself. You can't keep letting people walk all over you."

"But how could I ever win, confronting the HR director? I'm new, and no one knows me. I don't want to get on Hugh's bad side, and I don't want to be looking for a job again. Maybe it serves me right. I should have taken the idea to someone I knew I could trust."

"Lauren, this is definitely not your fault. I love you for the fact that you do trust people. But you shouldn't have to worry that a director will steal your idea at work. Don't blame yourself."

We sat in silence for a while.

"Can you talk to James Swann about this?" Paul asked.

I shook my head. "I really don't want to involve him in my issues."

We finished our hot chocolate and most of the cookies. Paul reached out his hand to mine. I held it and he pulled me up. "Let's go to bed. I love you, Lauren. Don't let them get you down." He put his arm around my shoulders and squeezed me. He gently nudged me ahead and rubbed my shoulders as we walked.

I lay awake in bed for a long time. I must have dozed off eventually because I jolted awake at around four o'clock. I didn't sleep for the rest of the night.

When I drove into the parking lot later that morning, Hugh was there, sitting in his Mercedes convertible. I parked my car only six spaces away from his, but he leaped out and rushed off to the foyer without acknowledging or waiting for me. Maybe he hadn't noticed I was there.

I dragged myself out of my car and arrived, exhausted, at my desk on the fourth floor. I made a note of my assessment of Hugh: unscrupulous, pretentious, calculating, destructive, and cowardly.

19

Mind Games

SOON AFTER MARCUS POMFREY became our manager, he took a dislike to Alex Ledger. Alex was our marketing analyst and a whiz at analysis and spreadsheets. While the rest of us dealt with sales and business, Alex performed miracles with analysis. He was a perfectionist. Sure, he had his quirks, but he was easily the best at what he did. But it was obvious to everyone that Alex's style had become painfully annoying to Marcus.

The rest of us gave Alex a lot of latitude and we tolerated his eccentric ways. Not Marcus. The rest of us understood that Alex had a different makeup than the rest of the team. Not Marcus. The rest of us knew that the way to get the best out of Alex was to encourage his expertise and present him with detailed analysis problems. Not Marcus. We learned to plan projects so that Alex could comfortably work the numbers without delaying the rest of us. Not Marcus.

Marcus got tired of Alex and deliberately tried to embarrass him in front of us. Alex told us that Marcus was putting pressure on him about his performance. None of us could understand this; we could see no problem with Alex's performance. It didn't make sense. Marcus said the company didn't need or want the detail that Alex took so much time over. He said that Alex was making work for himself and was trying to look important. He demanded that Alex work faster and satisfy himself with less detail and finesse.

Concerned, we asked Alex if things were getting bad enough that he might resign.

"No way," he said. He wasn't going to let Marcus push him out. He intended to keep battling on. We were relieved to hear this.

After three months of putting solid pressure on Alex, Marcus finally took action. One morning, he summoned Alex up to Mission Control. Minutes later, Alex was back, looking shell-shocked.

"He's eliminated my position. I've been laid off!"

We quickly gathered in the meeting room to hear his news.

"What do you mean?" asked Sandra. "We *need* you—he can't do this!"

"Well, he has!" Alex slumped into a chair. His face was pale.

"Why don't you protest?" I asked, hurting for him.

"Who to?" He held his hands up in surrender.

"Well, HR for starters," I said before I'd properly thought that through—I'd forgotten that Hugh Worrell couldn't be trusted. "What about John Squires?"

Ben responded, "John won't get involved with something like this. Marcus would have had Nicholas's and Jeremy's support before he acted. So there's no one to protest to."

"That's it then," conceded Alex. "I'm to pack my things and leave this afternoon."

"Are they giving you outplacement help to get another job?" Emily asked.

"If I want."

"Is Marcus going to come down and make an announcement?" asked Sandra.

"I don't think so," said Alex. "Just the standard one-line email, no doubt."

We offered him our sympathy and support and slowly returned to our desks. None of us could concentrate on our work, so we left early.

In the days that followed Alex's departure, Marcus seemed perfectly content. The rest of us were a mess. We not only had lost a colleague but also knew full well that our output would suffer without Alex's wizardry.

About a week after Alex left, Marcus asked us how we were doing without him. Unanimously, we answered that we were struggling without him. Marcus murmured that perhaps we still needed the analyst role. His master plan became apparent two weeks later when he called a team meeting. He said he'd originally thought we didn't need the analyst role, which was the reason he'd eliminated Alex's position. He said that from the feedback he'd received from us, it was clear we *did* in fact need an analyst after all. He said that he was big enough to acknowledge his error and would fix the problem for the sake of the team.

"I have a colleague," he announced, "whom I worked with at another company some years ago. Fortunately, he is available to join us. His name is Kurt Wolfe, and he will start with us next week. Kurt is a high performer and will fit in wonderfully. Please make him welcome when he starts."

How convenient! What a sham! Marcus had obviously squeezed out Alex to make room for his buddy.

Sandra must have felt the same. "Why didn't you ask Alex back?" she demanded, giving Marcus a fiery look. He glanced away. I admired Sandra for her courage.

"No, once someone leaves, that's it for me," answered Marcus smugly.

"But that's not fair," Sandra protested.

Marcus rubbed his neck and smiled. "Well, that's the way it is. Kurt will be a strong team member, and I expect you to treat him like a professional."

After the meeting, I grabbed Ben. "I thought you said Marcus was okay!" I exclaimed. "When we first talked about him, you said he wasn't a bully. You said he was preoccupied with himself but not hurtful."

Ben shrugged. "This is the first time I've seen him pull a stunt like this. He must have learned a few tricks in Hong Kong."

On the surface, Kurt Wolfe looked the part. His dress style was sharp: cuff links—not yet with embroidered cuffs, those came later—classy Italian ties, immaculate shirts, gleaming shoes, and a smile that matched his Rolex. I never once saw him with a hair out of place. He looked like success in a suit.

About a week after he joined us, Kurt invited me to coffee at Columbia's so we could "get to know each other." I thought that sounded interesting, so I agreed.

Columbia's was busy, and most of the tables were full. We finally found one at the back and ordered coffee. I was cautious about Kurt, given that he was a plant of Marcus's. He asked about me and my role. I gave him short, carefully worded answers—nothing that Marcus could take offense at. Kurt was open and enthusiastic. He quickly finished his coffee and ordered another. I was still finishing my first and declined his offer of a second cup.

Suddenly, Kurt's tone changed. "I hope that you and I can have a close relationship, Lauren."

"I hope so too, Kurt," wondering why he needed to say so.

"We should commit to each other," he said. This was strange.

"What I mean is," he continued, "if we hear something significant about the other person, we should pass it on. Like, I know that Marcus says that for him and the other executives, the jury is still out on you. I'm not sure what he means by that, but I thought you'd want to know. Do you want me to find out more?"

I was stunned. Without thinking, I said, "Yes," then wished I hadn't.

"I'm sure it's nothing," he said nonchalantly, smoothing his hair with his right hand. "Forget I said it." I was devastated, but he had more. "There's something else I wanted to ask," he said. A lump caught in my throat.

I hadn't recovered from the last piece of news and he was piling on more. "I detect," he continued, "tension between you and Kylie. I heard she applied for your job. Do you think she's resentful?"

It was true, I didn't have much time for Kylie and didn't trust her, but I tried not to let that show. What I didn't know was that she'd applied for my job—if that was true. Kurt had been on the scene only a week. How did he pick up any so-called tension so quickly? What had he heard? What had she said? *What had Marcus said*?

"I don't think so," I said, unable to come up with anything better.

"You don't think she resents someone coming in from outside, doing a job she thinks she could easily do? You don't think she resents the higher salary you have?"

"I really don't think so," I said, although I wasn't feeling so sure this time. He was trapping me with his clever questions.

"Well, that's great then," he said breezily. "Forget I said anything." He smiled, as if there'd been an innocent misunderstanding. I stared glumly into my empty coffee cup, not knowing what to say. Kurt wasn't finished.

"Just one other piece of advice," he said, leaning over the table toward me. I wanted to escape. "From what I've seen this last week, you shouldn't believe that people who are friendly to you are necessarily your friends, or that people who are unfriendly to you are necessarily your enemies." And with that, he downed the last of his coffee and jumped out of his chair before I could speak.

What a malicious and clever thing to say, if you want to make someone paranoid.

I drifted through the rest of the day, my mind a long way from my work. I began to doubt people who smiled at me and wonder about those who didn't.

This is ridiculous, I thought. I had to see Sandra and Ben and clear this up—find out what they knew about Kylie and about Kurt's wicked comments. But neither Sandra nor Ben was around at the time, so I didn't get a chance.

I struggled home. Knowing Paul would give me another lecture on sticking up for myself, I couldn't bring myself to share with him what Kurt had said. I couldn't bear the tension.

I read Harry a story that night. Afterward, I got Harry to go to my room and fetch the fable book. Best if Paul didn't see me reading Aesop—he might ask me about work.

After Harry fell asleep, I squeezed in beside him and swapped his book for Aesop. I read a dozen fables. Aesop knew plenty about the Kurt Wolfes of this world.

> A young hound started after a hare, and when he caught up to her, he would at one moment snap at her with his teeth as though he were about to kill her, while at another he would let go his hold and frolic with her, as if he were playing with another dog. At last the hare said,

"I wish you would show yourself in your true colors! If you are my friend, why do you bite me? If you are my enemy, why do you play with me?"

20

Torture Chamber

OVER THE NEXT FEW WEEKS, I worked hard on my analysis and research, and I started to build a view about directions in marketing strategy and the company's brand. I worked with Sandra on some product ideas I was considering, and Emily Richards helped me with research on our competitors. I missed Alex Ledger's help on analysis and kept well clear of Kurt Wolfe and Kylie Goodwin. Those two were as thick as thieves. On her own, Kylie had been manageable. Kylie and Kurt together poisoned the team. And with Kurt such good buddies with Marcus, we constantly felt spied on.

I talked to Sandra and Ben about Kurt. They said Kurt had had similar chats with each of them about sharing confidences. Both of them had told him to go jump into a lake. They recommended I tell him the same. But I wasn't sure I could.

I had been working for the company for about four months when I received an email from Marcus sent to the Marketing team. It was time for our performance appraisals, and he asked each of us to make a time to see him.

Finally, something I could look forward to. I wanted to clarify my job goals with Marcus—something that had never been done—and get feedback from him on how I was doing. I scheduled my review for Friday afternoon at two o'clock.

I was about to head up to Mission Control for my meeting with Marcus when my phone rang. It was Paul. He told me he couldn't pick up the kids that afternoon because he had a patient who needed urgent treatment. He asked me to collect them.

"It's going to be tight," I said. "I have my review with Marcus now. I don't know how long that will take."

"I really need you to do this, Lauren," he pleaded. "There's no alternative."

I was anxious, torn between my work and my parental duties. I agreed to do it, but wasn't sure how.

Now I was in a rush to get to Marcus's office. I dashed to the elevators and raced to his office, arriving five minutes late.

Julie apologized that Marcus had been called to see Nicholas and that he might be a little late. I sat in his office, catching my breath and waiting for Marcus to arrive. There was no need for anxiety about being late, but now I was getting worried about picking up the kids on time. I pushed that worry to the back of my mind and focused on the discussion with Marcus that was likely to unfold. At the very least, I hoped to get clarity on my role and be given the opportunity to discuss in detail my project goals.

Marcus's arrival interrupted my thoughts. "Another drama this afternoon, but nothing we couldn't resolve," he muttered, whirling into his office. He looked at his calendar, probably checking the reason for my sitting there.

"Okay, this meeting is to discuss your performance appraisal," he said, as if he was reminding me.

He picked up a file and sat in the swivel chair behind his desk. He scooted the chair to the round table where I was sitting.

"How do you feel you have performed this last year?" he invited, leaning back in his chair, putting his hands behind his head and giving me a good view of his underarm sweat.

I glanced away from his slightly discolored white shirt and was annoyed that he couldn't even remember that I'd started at Harlow Kane just before he'd returned from Hong Kong.

"I've been here only four months," I corrected.

"Yes, of course," he recovered. "It feels longer. Anyway, how do you think you've done with your job goals?"

"Well," I said, "we've never talked about my job goals, except that when we first met, you might remember I outlined the project steps I planned to follow."

He brought his hands down with a rush and sat forward in his chair. "We can do the goals now," he said, "but we can also talk about your performance without worrying about job goals."

"If you like," I answered. "But I was hoping to talk about job goals so that you and I are clear and agree that I am focusing on the right things." If I didn't get him to agree on my objectives, then Marcus and I might argue eternally about my work.

"Okay," he said. "Let's get to job objectives later. First of all, let's talk about your contribution so far. How do you think you've done these past four months?"

"I think I've done well," I answered cautiously, wondering where he was going with the conversation and whether he would want to discuss job goals at all. "I have contributed a number of significant outcomes to a number of the Sales and Services divisions, and I have helped the product marketing managers a lot with ideas and strategies. I have also started to make good progress on the Strategic Marketing Review—I have completed the analysis of the internal capability and finished the analysis of competitors—even though I've not yet had a chance to talk with you about it. And I believe I have contributed to a positive team spirit. So, I think it's been a good four months."

I wanted to talk about my idea for training sales reps, but Hugh Worrell had stolen that from me without giving me any credit. It was too late to use that in evidence.

He paused for a moment, spinning his pen in his fingers. "I have some reservations," he declared, clenching his teeth.

I cleared my throat nervously. "What are they?"

"Well, you haven't made any significant impact on revenue and profitability. And we've not made any progress at all in improving client satisfaction. I don't believe you have much to show at all for your first four months."

I was thrown. There was a storm brewing. I had to recover my bearings, quickly.

"Umm . . . in my role as a marketing strategist," I said, "you wouldn't expect me to have an impact on revenue, profit, and customer satisfaction in four months. The time frame of my job is much longer than that." I was recalling what Meg had said about the impact of the project, and the time it would take to do it properly. I wished it was Meg doing my appraisal.

"I disagree," he said. "The whole team is responsible for these outcomes, and we should all share in them. Frankly, Lauren, I'm disappointed."

Disappointed! *He's* disappointed. Dumbstruck, I struggled to respond. Too often in these situations, I get trapped in a quiet zone. I should fight, but I'm too scared to be confrontational. True to form, I remained silent.

Marcus continued, "In terms of overall performance, I rate you a three."

"What's a three?" I asked, bewildered.

"A three is an overall satisfactory rating," he answered. I'd never been assessed as just satisfactory. My shoulders slumped. I managed to say, "What's the scale?"

He showed me the back page of the appraisal form. "A one is exceptional. A two is above expectations. A three is meeting expectations. A four is below expectations, and a five is unsatisfactory."

A three sounded a bit tough to me. I didn't consider myself merely "satisfactory" or "meeting expectations."

Deflated, and struggling to defend myself, I murmured, "I believe I'm more than 'meeting expectations.'"

"Three is a good rating," he said. Why, then, did I not feel good about it?

"In my view," he continued, "if a person is new to a role, it is very difficult for them to be rated higher than a three in their first year."

Was that supposed to make me feel better? I was still trying to work out the system. I needed to talk to James so that he could educate me on how all of this worked.

"Anyway, that's your rating," said Marcus, tapping his pen on the table.

I didn't know enough to argue. But I wondered why it had to be like this—like a judge's sentence.

"Can we discuss my job goals so we can avoid this uncertainty next year?" I asked hesitantly.

"We can," he said flatly, "although I do believe in a fair degree of flexibility in job goals and plans, to allow for changes throughout the year."

"Yes," I said, unsure of the implications of his point. "Can we discuss job goals now?"

"Why not?" he answered, as if he were indulging me.

I breathed deeply, trying to control my heartbeat and regain my confidence.

"The key point," I started, "is that with my responsibilities, you can't expect an immediate impact. My role is different from a product manager's role. That role shows an impact in three to six months, whereas the impact of my job is around eighteen months or more. In about two years, we'll be able to properly assess my impact."

Marcus squirmed in his seat. He picked up his pen and twirled it through the fingers of his right hand. His face turned red and he looked annoyed.

"I don't accept that for one moment!" He glared straight into my eyes. I looked away. "A two-year time frame for assessment is ridiculous!" His voice was getting higher. "Any job needs to be assessed at least monthly. I want to see progress each month and each year!"

That was not my point, but I didn't have the stomach to fight back. I knew I was going to be in deep water if I couldn't persuade him to accept this time horizon for my job. Couldn't he understand my role was different from others? If we couldn't agree on this point, the future was sure to be stormy.

"Well," he said, in a calmer voice, controlling his anger, "we might need to agree to disagree on that. Let's leave it there. How about you draft your job goals as you see them and we can talk about them later. Meanwhile, I have completed this form. If you can sign the back page, I'll submit it to Human Resources."

He had already written a three rating on the form. I was uncomfortable signing it but felt compelled to do so.

"How is the form used?" I asked. "What are the implications of a three rating?"

"Not much. The forms are filed away in HR, and no one really looks at them."

I looked at the job goals section on the front of the form. He had written a few generic goals relating to revenue, profit, and customer satisfaction.

"We have now clarified that," he said, sitting back in his chair. He looked at his watch and sighed. "Just sign it and let's move on."

The kids would be waiting. Reluctantly, I signed the form and handed it back to him. At least the confrontation was over. I was out of the building in ten minutes.

* * *

The deflated feeling was hard to get rid of, though. It was still there on Sunday morning as Paul and I lay in bed. He suggested we take the kids to a carnival later in the morning. I wasn't in the mood, still flat from Marcus's judgment of me and his nasty way of saying things. I said they could go without me. Paul wasn't happy.

"Are you still feeling shitty about your appraisal?"

"Yeah, I guess."

He pushed himself up on his elbow. "For God's sake, Lauren, get over it! Do you think Marcus is spending one second worrying about this?"

"But it's not his career getting trashed!"

"We should spend time as a family," he said. "The kids love the carnival."

"You go without me." I buried myself into the pillow.

"We might just have to."

He got up. I lay there feeling miserable while Paul dressed quickly and silently left the bedroom.

I struggled out of bed ten minutes later, showered, and got dressed in old sweats. I didn't want to leave the house, and I looked like it.

Paul got the kids ready while I read the Sunday papers. He said they would be leaving in fifteen minutes. Annie picked up the clues that I didn't want to go.

"Come on, Mom, please come!"

"I don't feel like it," I said, sounding like a spoiled ten-year-old.

"Please, Mom," Annie pleaded.

"Pleeeeease," Harry added, grabbing my knees.

They had me. "Okay. Just give me a few minutes to change."

Paul hurried the kids into the car and secured Harry's seatbelt. I was in my seat by the time he got into the driver's seat. He leaned over and kissed me on the cheek. "Thanks," he whispered.

I was glad I'd changed my mind. The kids ran around trying rides and finding new junk food to beg for, pulling Paul and me after them. After a full day's hard playing, we drove home a happy family. The kids were exhausted, and after an early bath and dinner, went to bed without debate. I thanked Paul for a good day. He was pleased and thanked me for brightening up.

Now, I just had to get myself ready to face work the next day. So much for not dreading Mondays.

21

Oaks and Reeds

OVER THE NEXT WEEK, the rest of the team trekked to and from Marcus's office for their appraisals. There were very few happy campers.

At the end of the appraisal week, a few of us were having lunch together at a nearby café. After we ordered, Ben opened the discussion.

"How did everyone survive this year's torture?" he asked, smiling.

There weren't many returned smiles. Embarrassed by my three rating, I didn't want to comment.

"He's a pretty tough judge," David offered.

"Executioner!" Ben corrected, laughing.

Emily said, "It's tough that your salary review is directly linked to your rating." That got my attention.

"I didn't realize that," I said.

"Sure," said Emily. "There's a link to both your salary and your bonus. Only people rated one and two get a bonus. And base pay increases differ quite significantly from the high to the low ratings."

"Funny thing is," said Ben, "we're told that a three rating is good. If a three rating is a good rating, we wouldn't have to be told it's a good rating!" I identified with that.

"And," he continued, "if it's a good rating, then there would be a bonus payment attached to it." Everyone murmured agreement. "And don't forget," smiled Ben, raising an index finger, "the system is designed so that most people are rated average." I snorted involuntarily at Ben's insight. "For me," Ben concluded, "I'm not too worried. I know the system. A manager can give out only a few ones and twos. I'm a safe target for a three. I expect it every year, so I just take it, and I don't attach any importance to it. I've been around too long to worry about the rating. It's just a once-a-year thing, so I let it pass." I admired Ben for his philosophy. If I could detach from the appraisal like him, at least Marcus wouldn't be able to ruin my weekends.

"Well," said Emily, "my discussion with Marcus was interesting. I'm still trying to follow the logic. He assessed me as meeting expectations. He also said that I performed extremely well. I asked him how that fits—I'm doing an excellent job, but I get the meeting expectations rating. He told me I was employed because I'm a high performer and high performance is what's expected. Therefore, I am performing to expectations!"

I had trouble believing that Emily would be rated only a three. She was so effective in her role, and her clients loved her. I couldn't decide if that made me feel better or worse about my own rating.

As always, Kylie had a self-righteous look on her face. "I think the system is fair. It encourages people to deliver, and I think Marcus is a good judge," she said. Kylie may as well have branded a one or two on her forehead.

I felt awkward about this "post-torture" discussion and didn't want to talk about my own rating. I changed the subject and asked people what they thought of the continuing war in Iraq. That did the trick. Everyone had an opinion, and it was fairly divided. We didn't return to the subject of our annual reviews.

When we left the café and returned to the office, I happened to be walking next to Ben. It was a windy day and my hair was blowing across my face. I held it back as best I could with my hand.

"Ben," I said, "have you ever read Aesop's fables?"

He stopped walking and smiled at me. "Where did that come from?" he laughed.

We resumed walking. "I've been reading fables on and off for the last few months. Quite a lot really accurately describe the things that go on at work."

"I read some years ago as a kid, but I forget them now," he said, scratching the back of his head.

When we reached the front doors of the building, he held the door open for me to go in first.

"What made you think about fables right now?" he asked.

"Just something you said over lunch. I'll bring the book in and show you."

"What was it I said?" He hit the button for the elevator.

"That you don't take appraisals too seriously."

"Yeah, bring it in and show me." The elevator bell rang. "I assume you had a tough appraisal," he said gently. I nodded. We entered the elevator along with some others, and we didn't continue the discussion.

The next day, I brought in the book of Aesop's fables. I chose a moment when most of the others were away from their desks. I went over to Ben's workstation and whispered for him to come into the meeting room. I had the book in a plastic bag.

"Here's the fables book," I said as we sat down. I took the book out of the bag and opened it to the spot I had marked. "Here's the one that describes your approach to appraisals." I slipped the book across the table to him.

He read aloud.

> An oak that grew on the bank of a river was uprooted by a severe gale of wind and thrown across the stream. It fell among some reeds growing by the water and said to them, "How is it that you, who are so frail and slender, have managed to weather the storm, whereas I, with all my strength, have been torn up by the roots and hurled into the river?"
>
> "You were stubborn," came the reply, "and fought against the storm, which proved stronger than you. But

> we bow and yield to every breeze, and thus the gale passed harmlessly over our heads."

"That pretty well describes it!" he laughed. Ben took the book and paged through it. "I could tell you a fable of my own!"

I laughed again and sat back in my chair. "Do tell."

"There was this guy on a horse. The horse was madly galloping along a road. There was another person standing on the side of the road. As the horse dashed by, the person standing by the road asked the horseman why he was going in that direction. The man on the horse answered, 'You might as well go in the direction the horse is galloping.'" He laughed, enjoying his own joke.

"Thanks, Ben."

"Thanks for what?"

"Thanks for making me feel better."

"Try not to take it too seriously, Lauren. Like Aesop says, bend with the breeze."

We agreed that we should get back to work. Ben asked if he could borrow the book. "Of course," I said. I thought I would probably buy myself another copy. I looked forward to sharing more Aesop with Ben.

22

Oh, to Feel Valued

MY FIRST SALARY REVIEW happened soon after the appraisals were finalized. Marcus summoned me up to his office one Friday afternoon. Oh no, I thought, not another Friday disaster. I gave Emily and Sandra the throat signal that I was going upstairs to meet the ATC.

Marcus was his most suave self. He wore a yellow tie I'd not seen before. It complemented his blue checked shirt beautifully. His slacks, however, were riding as high as ever.

"Lauren," he said, inviting me to sit at his round table and playing with the neck of his tie. At least he wasn't playing with his pen. He slid an envelope toward me. "I have reviewed your salary. I've taken into account your performance rating and your salary compared to other members of the team, and I have decided to give you an increase of one-and-a-half percent."

"Thank you, Marcus . . . any raise is welcome," I commented, even though the raise was miniscule. There would surely be further explanation.

"I have taken into account the fact that you have been with us for only four months. So, I have calculated the average increase for a third of the year."

"Okay," I said, "thank you." But I wasn't appreciative; the increase was too low for me to accept as encouragement. I didn't know what else to say, so I took the envelope and left.

Yet again, I went home feeling dejected, my confidence shaken. Yet again, I bashed Paul's ears after dinner.

"My enthusiasm has taken a dive the last few weeks," I said glumly. "First, there was my average appraisal, now there is this average raise."

"But it's only your first four months," Paul consoled. "Best not to read too much into it. And it doesn't mean you're not regarded highly," he said, trying to be helpful. "There's no reason to think you're not doing a good job."

"But for people like me who take pride in their achievements," I continued, "the only time we get to see our scores on the board is when we have appraisals and salary reviews. That's when we get our feedback and know we're performing well. To look at the scoreboard and see an average score is demoralizing."

I'd planned to spend a few hours on work projects over the weekend, but after my meeting with Marcus, I decided I couldn't be bothered. He didn't appreciate my work anyway. I silently vowed never again to have discussions about salary and work performance on a Friday.

That night in bed, Paul asked me what had happened to the fable book I had been reading to Annie.

"I took it to work to show Ben," I said, turning out the light. "He loved it, so he's borrowed it for a bit. Why?"

"I was going to read a few fables," he said. It was dark, so I couldn't see the expression on Paul's face, but I thought he sounded serious.

"Are you kidding me?" I asked.

"No!" he laughed. "I enjoyed reading them as a kid, but I've forgotten a lot of them. I thought I'd read them with you. There may even be a few in there to help you."

I rolled over and cuddled him. "That would be fun. I did mean to buy another copy."

"We'll buy one tomorrow," Paul said, rubbing my back and giving me a kiss.

On Sunday evening, with the worry of work on my shoulders, a wave of nerves suddenly hit. I was chopping onions for spaghetti sauce when my chest felt tight and my heart beat faster. It was a horrible, trapped sort of feeling. Despite the challenge of my project, the support of my immediate team, and the feeling that I was really making a difference, the old feeling of dread I thought I'd left behind after escaping from Deadly Di had returned. I *did not* want to go to work the next day.

23

Feeding the Horses

AS SOON AS I ARRIVED AT WORK the next day, Ben grabbed my attention. He wanted to talk in one of the meeting rooms. I dropped my bags under my desk, turned my computer on, and dashed into the room.

"How was your weekend?" I smiled. He had the Aesop book with him.

"It was good. Full of the kids and their sports activities. But it always goes too quickly. How 'bout yours?"

"Fine, thanks." I didn't want to bore him with my anxiety. I looked across the table at the book.

"I've really enjoyed reading this," he chuckled. "What a classic. I wanted to share one with you that beautifully describes the way Marcus treats us."

Quite a few of the pages were marked with sticky notes. He opened the book and took a moment to find the fable he had in mind. He read it to me like an actor delivering his lines.

> A soldier gave his horse a plentiful supply of oats in time of war and tended him with the utmost care, for he wished him to be strong to endure the hardships of the field and swift to bear his master, when need arose, out of the reach of danger. But when war was over he employed him on all sorts of drudgery, bestowing but

> little attention upon him, and giving him, moreover, nothing but chaff to eat. The time came when war broke out again, and the soldier saddled and bridled his horse, and having put on his heavy coat of mail, mounted to ride off and take the field. But the poor half-starved beast sank down under his weight and said to his rider, "You will have to go into battle on foot this time. Thanks to hard work and bad food, you have turned me from a horse into an ass, and you cannot in a moment turn me back into a horse."

"What do ya think?" he asked. "Doesn't that describe him to a *tee*? He should be keeping us motivated and conditioned, and instead he leaves us alone and unfed. Yet the good work he gets from us only 'meets expectations.'"

"Yeah, tell me about it," I said resignedly. I enjoyed Ben's humor, but the fable was sadly true. "Keep reading, Ben." I left the room to log on and get started for the day.

When I walked out, Sandra was just arriving. She saw me, waved, and made a beeline toward me. She noticed Ben sitting in the room.

"Come into the room for a sec," she said with a wry smile. I was curious. She shut the door after us and Ben closed the book.

"What's up?" he said as we sat down.

Sandra shook her head. "You know how I've been invited to speak at that conference?" We nodded. It was a great compliment to Sandra. "Well, I completely forgot to tell Marcus about it."

She pushed her seat back and crossed her legs. Ben pushed his chair back and rested his elbows on his thighs, ready to hear the story.

"About a month or so ago, I received the invitation and didn't give it any more thought. Well, on Friday the conference brochure arrived. He must have gotten a copy as well. Anyway, I got summoned to Mission Control." She paused, shaking her head again.

"What happened?" I asked, wondering what was coming.

"Marcus was angry that I'm speaking at the conference!"

"Why?" we asked, puzzled. What could possibly be wrong with Sandra speaking at a conference?

She gave a broad grin. "He told me *he* should be the one doing the presentation! If the conference brochure wasn't already printed, I'm sure he would have taken the gig."

"That's disgusting," I said a little too loudly. Suddenly, I was worried that someone outside the room might hear.

Ben roared.

There was a knock on the glass, and Kurt put his head through the door. "Sorry I can't join you," he smiled cynically. "Ben, we have a meeting that's about to start. Our visitor is waiting downstairs."

"Oh, shit. Sorry, Kurt, I'll be right with you." Ben stood up, and when he got to the door, turned and whispered so Kurt couldn't hear, "You do your presentation, Sandra, and you do it well." As he left the room, he put a hand behind his back and gave a thumbs-up sign.

"Oh, Sandra," I said flatly, "what are we going to do about Marcus?"

"Nothing," she answered happily. "There's nothing that can be done. He's here. He's a fact of life. Don't get so worried."

"But he's so draining," I sighed.

"Only if you let him be."

"I don't know how you can be so easygoing. I admire you for it."

We agreed that we should be getting back to work. As we left the room, I caught Kylie watching us. She quickly looked away.

As I sat at my computer, I decided that all I wanted was to get on with my project and to keep the momentum going without any distractions like the appraisals and salary reviews Marcus conducted.

But Marcus had one more trick up his sleeve—career planning. I managed to postpone my meeting with him several times, but finally he nailed me for a ten o'clock meeting on a Tuesday. At least this time it wasn't a Friday.

I was slightly delayed by a phone call from a client, and the elevators were busy, no doubt due to morning break traffic. I rushed into Marcus's office at Mission Control five minutes late. He was drumming his fingers loudly on his desk.

"I would appreciate it if you could attend these meetings on time," he spat. "The topic of career planning is an important one, Lauren."

The hypocrite. He had no right to criticize me about punctuality, given his own bad example. But I took the criticism silently.

"So," he said, moving to the round table, "I've scheduled this meeting so we can discuss your career plan. I'd like to assist you in completing this HR template." He waved a piece of paper in front of me.

I had given the topic some thought, since I knew this meeting was coming. The form hadn't been part of my plans.

"What you need to work out," continued Marcus, "is whether you want to progress as a technical specialist or a business leader."

What a tiresome start. I was hoping the subject would be about my learning and development. But he narrowed it immediately down to advancement. Why bother, I thought. I'll let this storm bend me instead of fighting, just like the reeds. Marcus droned on, and I waited glumly for him to finish planning my career.

Finally he said something that jolted me back to attention. "Of course, I think you are better suited to a technical specialist role."

"Why is that, Marcus?" I asked irritably, not that I wanted his opinion.

"You're regarded as a good technical person. You are not considered a leader."

Suddenly, I was no longer a reed but an oak being battered.

"Why do you say that?" I said, fumbling for composure.

He leaned forward, elbows on the table. "Some people have the ability to be noticed. You are not one of them. I don't know what it is about those who impress. People have commented that you're good technically, but that you lack influence."

"That's very surprising, Marcus," I fired, struggling to control my anger. "This has not been a problem elsewhere."

"That's probably because our people are such high performers."

Did I hear right? Did he mean that I might have been noticed in other companies because I was working with "lower" people? And now, here I was, working with a constellation of stars and finding it difficult to shine?

Marcus continued, "Kylie Goodwin has the ability to be noticed. People want Kylie on their teams."

Oh, good for Kylie. The teacher's pet. If he wanted me to behave like Kylie in order to be noticed, he could go pound salt.

I slowed my breathing. "You say people comment that I am stronger technically. Who made these comments?"

"A few people that I talk with about these things," he said and waved his hand to the side.

"But who are they, what are their roles, and how much interaction do they have with me?" I asked, feeling more controlled and slightly stronger.

"I can't share that information," he shrugged, "but I believe they are entitled to their views."

"But surely it depends on whether those views are based on evidence."

He repeated, "People are entitled to their views." He looked away.

I gave up and stayed silent for the rest of my so-called career planning review. He made notes on the form and I left promptly without signing it, leaving him to explain that to Human Resources.

Driving home that evening, still angry, I pulled into a quiet side street and stopped the car. I turned up the volume on the radio, held the steering wheel tightly, and yelled at the top of my voice, "I JUST WANT TO DO MY JOB . . . I JUST WANT TO DO MY JOB . . . I JUST WANT TO DO MY JOB!"

I felt better. I turned down the radio and resumed my journey home.

When I walked in the front door, the place was a mess. The kids were yelling and Harry was running amok. I hit the roof.

"Harry!" I bellowed, "will you stop running around? I've had a hell of a day and I need some quiet!"

Harry stopped dead in his tracks and started to cry. He ran to his room. I did the same, to my room. Paul came in. He said that I should not be bringing my work worries home. I knew that. I got up from my bed and went to Harry. I apologized and hugged him. He seemed okay, but I was exhausted.

24

Secret Information

THE NEXT DAY, I STRUGGLED INTO WORK, a little later than normal. I had just turned on my computer when Kurt Wolfe bounded up to me like a playful puppy. "Lauren," he yapped, "I have some news that I thought you would like to know."

Unable to match his mood, I answered flatly, "Sure, Kurt, what is it?"

"Well, I was in the elevator just now with two senior execs," he began, confiding in me as if we were bosom buddies. "I heard one of them ask the other, 'So, what do you think of Lauren Johnson? Is she performing up to par?' I don't know what it means, of course, but I thought you'd like to know. After all, what are friends for?"

I was thrown. Why did Kurt feel a need to share this with me? Perhaps he genuinely thought this was useful information, although I didn't know what I was going to do with it.

"Who were the two executives?" I asked.

"I can't say," he said, acting shocked. "That would be unprofessional."

"Unprofessional!" I said angrily. "You dump this on me, but then you won't give me the full picture so I can do anything about it. Thanks very much, Kurt."

He shrugged. "I just thought you'd like to know, that's all. If you want to talk about what you can do, just let me know. Should we make a time to talk more about it?"

Did he honestly think he was being helpful? Maybe he was making it up, trying to rattle my cage.

"No thanks, Kurt, I think you've done quite enough."

My head was spinning with the seed of fear Kurt had planted in my head. Why were these two executives talking about me? What else was being said?

That night, I told Paul about the Kurt incident and how it was worrying me.

"You know," he said, "I reckon there's a fable that describes him."

"What one's that?"

"I forget. It's one I can only vaguely recall from my childhood. I'll look out for it when I read the book. So how about we get the babysitter in tomorrow night and go out for dinner?" Paul asked.

"Great!" I smiled. I leaned over and kissed him.

"Where would you like to go?"

"I'm not sure."

"Well, choose your favorite restaurant. You've earned a good night out."

"Mmm . . . let me see." I scratched my head and thought about restaurants people had raved about lately. Nothing stood out. "Well, you know what I would really like to do?" I smiled, hoping he'd agree.

"No . . ."

"I'd love to go to a movie and have dinner afterward." It had been ages since we'd gone to the movies.

"Great idea. Do you know what's playing?"

"No idea."

"We'll have a look in the paper tomorrow. Maybe ask people at work too."

"Sounds great—thanks, darling."

I spent the next day at work looking forward to my evening out with Paul. I got through some good work on my project. I called Sally Morton, the consultant, and talked with her about the anthropology study and the meaning of service. I could almost cover her fees from the original budget; thankfully, it had been set before Marcus took over the reins. Talking with Sally made me very excited. The study, if successful, would be a breakthrough, the first of its kind. My level of energy over the project accelerated. I was like a Formula One racing car roaring around the track; nothing could stop me when I was in this mood.

Paul and I chose to see *Amélie*. We'd missed it the first time around, and it was replaying at a retro cinema. It was the perfect choice—a love story, charming, funny.

Afterward, over dinner and an expensive bottle of wine at an intimate Italian restaurant, we talked about the kids and our dreams for them. We talked about how fast they were growing up and whether we were raising them the right way. We thought, all in all, we were doing a good job, the best we could.

"As long as I don't take any anger over work out on them."

"No work-talk tonight," Paul chastised. "And I won't talk about the vacation we should be planning."

"Okay," I smiled. "What about dessert?"

"I'm going for the tiramisu!" Paul licked his lips.

"I might just have a taste of yours."

"As long as it's just a taste."

After dinner, we took the long way back to the car. We walked slowly, holding hands, past some shop windows. The late crowd was coming out of the last showing at the movie theater. Couples were laughing, arm in arm.

When we got back to the car, Paul opened my door, and as I stooped to get in, he held my face and kissed me just as we'd seen in the movie—gently kissing my right eye, then my left eye, and then my lips.

25

In a Hurry

MY HORRIBLE MOOD, which had been an aftereffect of annual reviews, had subsided, but there were still a few negative changes to deal with. One was that Marcus had made it clear that he held me accountable for making a time with him and taking him through the findings on my project, no matter how hard it was to schedule a meeting with him. I organized a time, and giving an uppercut signal to the chin, let my buddies know I was heading to Mission Control.

When I arrived, Marcus was in deep discussion with Grace Reece from HR. I sat outside his office and waited among the flora. He signaled me to join them. I smiled at Grace as I entered and took a seat at the round table. She threw me an uncomfortable look in return. Was I in trouble?

"Lauren," Marcus said pleasantly, "just bear with us for a moment, would you? Grace is reviewing my succession planning. I'm on the list as a high potential leader and we were just working through my development plan."

Grace squirmed in her chair. "Marcus, we shouldn't be discussing this in front of Lauren." She looked at me. "Lauren, it's nothing personal. It's just that this topic should be discussed only with the individual concerned."

"I agree completely," I said, getting up to leave. "I'll go back to the waiting area."

"It's okay," Marcus insisted. "We're almost finished. Stay there, Lauren; we'll be done in a second."

I stayed. Marcus continued the discussion with Grace. I pushed my chair away from the table, feeling awkward. I gazed down at my shoes, trying to appear disinterested in the conversation.

"In summary," Marcus announced to Grace and me, his captive audience, "I'm ready for sequential appointments to the key roles of sales and services director, chief operations officer, and chief executive officer." I felt his eyes on me. I was still studying my shoes.

"Well," observed Grace, "you feel you're ready. So far, Nicholas and John haven't given their reviews. They may or may not agree."

"Whatever," said Marcus. "I'm sure they'll agree with me. The international assignment has prepared me well."

"The objective of this meeting," Grace pointed out, "is to prepare your development plan. We need to complete this and send it to John."

"Yes," Marcus responded, "that's where we were before Lauren arrived. I don't need a lot of development. I have all the skills I need." He reflected for a moment, looking at the ceiling. "I'll tell you what development program I would most appreciate." I thought he was going to admit to having some sort of weakness. Maybe he was going to give us a rare insight into a gaping hole in his career. Grace must have thought the same as she raised her pen, poised to write. The moment of hope didn't last long. "Anything that helps me become CEO," he declared, straight-faced. "That's all I need. Just let me know what that is, Grace."

This self-inflated ladder climber was the man who assessed *my* performance, reviewed *my* salary, and advised me on *my* professional development! I glimpsed a look of disbelief on Grace's face, but she quickly recovered and stopped short of a smile. It was clear the meeting wasn't going to reveal any big insights after that, though. Grace gathered her papers and said she would return another time to finish the exercise.

As she left, Marcus looked at his watch. "I'm sorry that meeting ate into your time, Lauren. We'll have to catch up later. Sorry, but that was important."

Yes, I thought, as I too got up to leave—important to Marcus because it was all about Marcus. Well, at least this time I got an apology.

"Actually, there is one other thing I would like to cover." Marcus pointed for me to sit down again. What now?

"We need to organize the annual Sales Managers Meeting. I would like you to lead that project, please." His use of the word "please" indicated that this was a favor for him. Still, it sounded interesting.

"What's the Sales Managers Meeting?" I asked. "We haven't had one of those since I've been here."

"Marketing holds it once a year to brief the managers on directions for the year and to give updates on the sales incentive plan, new products, that sort of thing. I'd like you to organize it."

Although I'd be doing him a favor, I was very pleased to be given the challenge. And he must have thought I'd do a good job; otherwise he wouldn't have entrusted such an event to me.

"Sounds great, Marcus, thanks!"

"All the others on the team are very busy," he said. I wished he hadn't added that. "Kylie organized the event last year, so you can ask her how you should go about it. Even from Hong Kong, I heard she did a fabulous job. You have big shoes to fill, but I know you can do it."

This comment did nothing for my self-esteem or motivation. But this project was a chance to show what I could do, so I welcomed the challenge.

"I'm also thinking," he added, "that this is a high profile event, and it will give you an opportunity to be noticed. That should help you with the things we talked about in your appraisal and career discussion—to be seen as a leader."

I didn't know whether to be grateful or insulted.

He asked me to draft a project plan and come back to him to review it. I agreed to do so and got up to leave.

"Oh," Marcus said, sticking his index finger up in the air, "when you go downstairs, could you ask Sandra to come up immediately?"

"Sure," I said. "I'll let her know."

When I got back to the fourth floor, Sandra was at her computer. I told her Marcus wanted to see her urgently. Sandra grumbled something about everything being urgent, dropped what she was doing, and went up to Mission Control. About ten minutes later, she was back.

"Come into the room," she said. I saved the file I was working on and joined her.

"I need to share this with someone," she said, red-faced. "That man never ceases to amaze me." She crossed her arms. Obviously, she was referring to Marcus. "He wanted to see me urgently because he apparently has to prepare something on succession planning. He said he has to nominate someone on his team to be a high potential. He said that *someone* was me. And then he said, 'I need to prepare something for a presentation tomorrow to a review committee. Could we spend ten minutes now to throw something together—we can make it up if we have to'!"

"Oh, no," I gasped, "he just wants to do it so he can check the box?"

"Exactly!" she bellowed, unfolding her arms and gripping the arms of her chair. "That's the level of importance he places on my development and progression. And, by the way," she mimicked Marcus with an impassive face, "in case there's no real reason for me to be 'developed,' we can make it up!"

Ben knocked and came into the room. "Can I disturb you two?" he asked. He had the Aesop book with him.

"What have you got there?" Sandra asked.

"Lauren's book of fables," he beamed. Sandra nodded and said she'd love to have a look at the book later.

"I've been reading them, and I'm blown away at how relevant they are to this place," I said.

Ben opened the book and looked at me. "You know how I told you about my galloping horse fable?"

"Yeah."

"Well, wouldn't you know it, I must have recalled that story from a fable I heard as a boy, 'cause I found one just like it last night." He smiled and read:

> A young man, who fancied himself something of a horseman, mounted a horse which had not been properly broken in and was exceedingly difficult to control. No sooner did the horse feel the man's weight in the saddle than he bolted, and nothing would stop him. A

> friend of the rider's met him in the road in his headlong career, and called out, "Where are you off to in such a hurry?" To which he replied, pointing to the horse, "I've no idea. Ask him."

We laughed and I said, "That's just like Marcus with his own succession planning." I told them how I was forced to witness Marcus's meeting with Grace and how he'd concerned himself only with any development that would improve his chances of promotion to CEO.

"Not only that," said Ben closing the book, "but he shamelessly admitted it to you and Grace."

"Exactly!"

Two days later, Sandra signaled for Ben and me to join her in the meeting room. Ben was finishing a phone call. I joined Sandra, and Ben came in soon after.

"I've just had a meeting with Marcus on this high potential thing," she hissed. "I am so angry." She was pacing the floor. Ben and I sat, looking up at her.

"What happened?" we asked together.

"He said he made the presentation and talked about my abilities. The presentation was to most of the executives. He said it was going along fine and then Ryan Gunn made a comment about me."

"What did he say?" I asked.

"It's not going to be pretty," Ben predicted.

"Why not?" I asked.

"The Smiling Assassin never says anything good about anyone." Ben opened his arms and raised an eyebrow. "Am I right, Sandra?"

"Dead right!" she snarled through clenched teeth. "Ryan apparently commented that I'm not a team player."

"You're joking!" I exclaimed. "You're one of the best team players I know."

"Well, that's not what he said." Her tone was flat.

"It's a pretty easy shot at someone," Ben said. "It probably means that you disagreed with him once, so you became branded as a non–team player."

"But he and I have hardly done any work together," Sandra complained.

Ben laughed. "That wouldn't stop him from judging you!"

"Did anyone ask him for evidence?" I asked.

"I asked Marcus that—apparently not. Well, James Swann asked, but Nicholas bit into James about not letting people have their say. Nicholas said that Ryan may have a point, and they would have to keep their eye on me."

I shared Sandra's hurt. "Being nominated as a high potential is supposed to be a good thing," I said, my elbows on the table and fingers over my eyes. "But it sure hasn't turned out that way."

"I'm so annoyed," she spat. "I wish Marcus hadn't told me. And now I've been put in a box labeled 'non–team player.'"

26

The Smiling Assassin Strikes Again

WHEN I TOLD SANDRA THAT MARCUS had asked me to organize the Sales Managers Meeting, she looked puzzled.

"But he asked me to do that," she said. It wasn't possible for us both to be in charge. Sandra said she would clear it up right away and called Marcus.

"Marcus, regarding the Sales Managers Meeting, who are you asking to organize it?" She rolled her eyes in annoyance while listening to Marcus's response.

"Yes, I know you asked for my ideas. But you've also asked Lauren to be in charge." Pause.

"I know Kylie organized it last year. Who do you want to organize it this year?" Pause.

"Of course more than one person can be involved," Sandra exclaimed, with a shake of her head, "but we should have only one person in charge. Who do you want to be the project manager?" Pause.

"Okay, thanks." She slammed the phone down. "You're the project manager, Lauren—congratulations!"

We laughed about Marcus's ATC behavior causing confusion, and she offered to help brainstorm ideas and to fill me in on past events.

A few days later, Sandra, Kylie, Ben, and I met together to come up with the initial plan for the Sales Managers Meeting. Some great ideas emerged, and we also decided that a project team was important. Kylie volunteered to be on the team and said that from past experience, Ryan Gunn's assistant, Nicole Webb, was a wizard at organizing events. I agreed to ask Ryan if Nicole could assist. I would have preferred Ben or Sandra to be on the project team instead of Kylie, whom I could barely tolerate, but they were busy with other commitments, and, I conceded, it would be good to have the benefit of Kylie's experience from the previous year's meeting. I also thought it would give me a chance to work closely with her and hopefully form a better relationship.

After the meeting, I called Ryan. Nicole answered and said Ryan was in a meeting. I called his cell. He didn't answer, so I left a message asking if he was prepared to make Nicole available to help organize the Sales Meeting. He called back within a minute! I was impressed, and a little surprised. A quick response from him was out of character. He said he wanted Nicole to assist and he would talk with her immediately. Nicole called me a few minutes later, confirmed that Ryan had talked to her, and said she was happy to help out.

We had only five weeks to organize the event, which wasn't enough time, thanks to Marcus's delay in delegating. I put off most of my work on the major strategy project while I prepared for the annual sales meeting. Not that I minded too much. The sales event was high profile and urgent, and the strategy project could wait.

Tasks were delegated mainly between Nicole and me. Kylie's main input was to ensure continuity from the year before. Nicole looked after the critical details—the venue, the travel, and the food. Luckily, all the attendees had been notified of the date. The only gap had been Marcus informing me!

Because I was responsible for setting the agenda I met briefly with all the key players—John Squires, Nicholas Strange, and Hugh Worrell (Jeremy Hyde was never available)—as well as the four sales directors—Maxine Savage, Ryan Gunn, Gus Wearing, and James Swann—to ascertain their needs. I also called several sales managers from other locations to take into account their needs. I was pleased with the way it was all progressing.

I had weekly progress meetings with Marcus about the upcoming sales meeting. The day before one of these, about two weeks before the event, Ryan came to one of our project team meetings. I was surprised to see him there, as I hadn't invited him, but I still appreciated his interest. He listened and asked a few questions. He seemed impressed and left us to it.

The next day, I met with Marcus and brought him up-to-date on the status of the program. When I finished, he leaned forward with a very earnest look on his face.

"Ryan said he reviewed this plan with you yesterday. He's concerned that things aren't progressing as well as they should."

Excuse me! What on earth had Ryan said to Marcus? On the contrary, I knew we were extremely well prepared. As usual, though, I was at a loss for words.

Marcus sat back in his chair. "Ryan also mentioned to Nicholas that the event was at risk." Marcus couldn't have dug the knife in any deeper. "Ryan's offered to get involved, to make sure it runs smoothly. It's too big an occasion for me to risk a poor event, Lauren, so I accepted his offer. Nicholas thought Ryan's involvement was a good move." Marcus had an impassive look on his face.

I'd been hit by a shock wave. I tried to make sense of Ryan's strategy. It took me a moment, but I did manage to work out that I was in a catch-22. If Ryan became involved and anything went wrong, it would fulfill Ryan's prediction and I would get the blame. But if he became involved and everything worked out well, then he would claim the credit as the savior! I knew we didn't need his help; the event was well organized. There was, frankly, nothing for Ryan to do, and I didn't want him to take the credit. But if I declined, then Marcus would force Ryan's involvement anyway.

"I don't think we need his help," I protested.

"I think you should take it," he responded, lips tight. He picked up his pen to spin.

"But everything is really in order."

"I am not prepared to take that risk. I trust Ryan," he said. "Quite honestly, Lauren, I'm disappointed you don't want someone's help, someone who knows what he's doing." And then he really turned the knife. "I also checked with Kylie. She agrees Ryan's involvement would be a good idea." I'll bet she did!

Argument over, I left Marcus's office infuriated. I had to concede that Ryan was a clever bastard, having masterfully manipulated the situation so that he would be the hero no matter what.

Ryan joined us at one more progress meeting before the event, and he contributed very little.

The Sales Managers Meeting was an outstanding success. The program was received enthusiastically. "The best ever," people said. Everything went beautifully, the content was greatly appreciated, and no criticism at all was voiced. In his closing address, Nicholas Strange thanked the organizers.

"Ryan has advised me that there are a number of people to thank for organizing the event. Thanks to Kylie Goodwin for again being involved; thanks to Nicole Webb for her exceptional skills in organizing everything; and thanks to Lauren Johnson. Also, my thanks to Ryan Gunn for overseeing the project." Everyone clapped.

I saw red! This was unbelievable! The nerve of Ryan, the Smiling Assassin. No one but Kylie, Nicole, or me would be any the wiser about what had really happened. I was still fuming twenty minutes later when James Swann came over and thanked me.

"Well done, Lauren. That was a fantastic event—congratulations!" He must have noticed I was upset.

"What's up?" he asked, concerned.

I looked around to make sure that no one was within earshot and filled him in on what Ryan had orchestrated.

"Yep," he conceded, "that sounds like Ryan. Listening in at your meeting two weeks ago, he must have concluded that the project was going very well. Otherwise, he would have stayed well clear. This way, he gets the praise without any risk. All he had to do was drop a word of concern to Nicholas and Marcus, and they would have asked him to get close and keep control. He knew he was on to a sure thing!"

I drove home with mixed emotions. Yes, I was satisfied with the event and with the impact I had made. But I was livid at Ryan's shameless act of getting himself in the spotlight. I could clearly see why he so richly deserved his nickname.

I was just as frustrated at myself, however—at my naivety, my weakness, my fear. How could I ever stand up to people like the Smiling Assassin? I felt like I was in a corner, with no way out.

27
Hare or Tortoise

FOR SEVERAL MONTHS AFTER the Sales Managers Meeting, I had a good solid run at my project. But I regretted not having Alex Ledger around. I missed his analytical ability and responsiveness. Apart from having to be wary around Kurt Wolfe, he just wasn't in the same league as Alex when it came to analysis. As a result, I had to do more of that myself.

Sally Morton and I were enthusiastic about the opportunity to do a major review of the company's positioning and to understand the buying motivators of our customers. Sally would also assist me with the anthropological study on what the concept of service actually meant to our customers. Studies had been done on the meaning of *quality* in various countries, but not on *service.*

I had also asked Sandra to be involved in the project so I could gain her input from a product perspective. Sandra had very much wanted to help, but she explained that she was also spending a lot of time with Maxine Savage. Maxine was demanding more time from Sandra, expecting her to help with product initiatives Maxine wanted for her division. But Sandra said she would still make time to help me.

Sally and I, and Sandra when she could squeeze in the time, made a close and energetic team. We worked patiently and thoroughly, despite some hassling from Marcus for outputs. Whenever I tried to catch up with Marcus to update him, he was always too busy. Consistently, Sally would come to the office specifically for us to review the project with Marcus, only to have him cancel the meeting at the last minute. This was a complete waste of time and hugely frustrating. In the end, we just assumed that Marcus would not appear at any meeting we scheduled with him. Sally and I would always have our files with us and use the time as a working session.

One day, Marcus canceled yet another review meeting with Sally and me because apparently Nicholas Strange had called him at short notice. We were leaving Marcus's office at Mission Control, annoyed we had again been put off, when we happened to pass John Squires, our friendly CEO. John politely asked how things were going. I introduced him to Sally and mentioned that we were making progress on the marketing strategy review. He asked if we had time for coffee, which of course we did, and we went to his office to talk. We filled him in briefly on our thinking on the project and he seemed impressed.

"There is one thing I would like your advice on," I said.

He nodded.

"We struggle with the dilemma of speed versus quality. On the one hand, we need to deliver an outcome of our review promptly, but I don't want to sacrifice thoroughness. Can you help me with that, John?"

He paused, glanced at the ceiling in thought, and said, "I obviously don't know the details of your project and what time line is reasonable, but I think the main consideration is whether the review is time critical. Are we desperate for the outputs? What's your reading of that?"

"I don't believe the review is time critical. Our current strategy and products are fine. Our current competitive position is sound. So, no, it's not time critical."

"Well," he said, "that may give you the answer. If we are not hurting right now, or don't expect to be in a critical state in the next few months, then the most important thing appears to be quality. Another way of answering is that if we worked in haste and came up with the wrong answer, then we might suffer permanently. Imagine if you gave us the wrong answer, Lauren, and we went down the wrong path. We might never be able to go back. The time impact on what you are doing is at least five to ten years. So, please, take your time."

"It's a bit like the fable of the hare and the tortoise, where slow and steady ends up with a better result."

"I agree with that," he grinned. "If you need my support, please let me know."

As we left John's office, Marcus was walking out of Nicholas's office. He didn't notice us at first, his head down as he marched impatiently in our direction. When he did look up, he seemed pleased to see us.

"Ha!" he said. "Fancy running into you two. Come into my office, would you?"

We went in and sat down at his round table.

"Now, how is the review of marketing strategy coming along?" He leaned forward.

"We're making good progress," I answered. "We're undertaking the external research of customers through Sally, and I have concluded our internal analysis and the comparison with competitors."

"Why haven't I been briefed?" he asked, aggressively.

"We've tried," I said calmly. "We've made appointments with you several times, but the meetings keep getting put off."

"Well, I'm becoming impatient with the lack of progress." He spun his pen in his fingers. "This is an important project. It's been several months now, Lauren, since your performance appraisal and, frankly, I would have thought I'd be seeing outputs by now." He glared at me.

Sally cleared her throat and tried to help. "What's happened, Marcus, to make this so urgent all of a sudden?"

"I've just had a meeting with Nicholas on a range of issues, and he asked me about this project. I was embarrassed not to know the project's status. You should both keep me in the loop. You should not put me in such a position, and I don't want to be put in that position again. Please set up a review meeting with me as soon as possible."

I was annoyed beyond belief! Sally kept her composure.

"What we can also do," she said, "is send you an email with a summary of where we are and the next steps we are taking. We'll also send you an outline of the time line."

"Okay, that will be good. Thanks. Let's leave it there," Marcus said.

I followed Sally's lead. "We could give you an update right now, if you'd like."

"No, I don't have time right now."

We left his office, carrying his criticism silently with us. I walked with Sally to her car. I knew I could trust her, so I shared my frustrations about Marcus. I shook my head, infuriated that he'd blocked our efforts to keep him informed, that he'd canceled so many meetings. And now that Nicholas had embarrassed him, he'd pointed the finger of blame squarely at me, and suddenly the project had become incredibly important. Sally counseled that for whatever reason, we now had his attention. I, on the other hand, did not know whether that attention would be a good thing.

Sally also suggested we might need more support on the project, given that Sandra was working with Maxine Savage and couldn't spend much time with us. But everyone on the team whom I would want help from—Sandra, Emily, or Ben—was fully occupied, and we definitely didn't want help from Kylie or Kurt.

28

The Last Word

SANDRA PEARSON STORMED BACK TO HER DESK, FUMING.

"What's up?" I asked. "Have you been with Marcus?"

"Worse—I've just had a meeting with the Witch!" We went into a meeting room for some privacy.

"What happened?"

"I want to take two weeks off. Tom and I need a break, but Maxine won't approve the time off. She's known about this for weeks—since October! And it's Christmas! Maxine's too stingy to let me go. Three weeks ago, she said that I could have the time off. Then a week later, she said I could have the time off, but that I might need to come back early. Just now, she said she doubted I could take the time off at all. And she said she was disappointed that my career didn't come first!"

"Is the project at a stage that you can't afford to take time off?" I asked.

"No, nothing like it. The two weeks fit right in with her product project. Nothing will happen while I'm away. She's just pulling power plays with me."

"What does Marcus say?" I asked. "He's your actual boss. He's the one who ultimately approves your vacation."

"He didn't want to buy into the argument. He said I need to work it out with Maxine."

I felt inadequate to give advice. I knew if I were in Sandra's shoes, I would meekly accept that Maxine had power over me. I wouldn't argue the point nor insist on my rights—not that I would be happy with the situation. My lack of assertiveness worried me. I didn't stick up for myself. I let people like Maxine and the dreaded Di Ashman walk all over me.

Instead of giving advice, I asked Sandra what she planned to do.

"I'm going to tell Maxine I'm taking the two weeks. I'm not going to sacrifice my vacation time with Tom." I admired her courage.

Sandra went straight back to Mission Control. Within five minutes, she'd returned. By now, Emily was also at her desk; the three of us went back into the meeting room. We asked Sandra how it went.

With fists on her hips, Sandra replied, "Well, I went into her office and said, 'Maxine, I've thought about our discussion about my time off. I have considered what you said, but after weighing it all, I've decided that I will take the two weeks off. Tom and I have been planning this vacation for several months, and I want to spend time with him. I have planned it so that the project will not be compromised. I'll send you an email with the dates.'"

"What did she say?" Emily and I chimed in together.

"As I was turning to leave, she said, 'I might need to contact you while you're away.' I looked back at her and said, 'I'll be out of contact, with no fixed address. See you when I get back.'"

I smiled at Sandra and shook her hand. We laughed.

"Way to go!" I said. "I don't think I could've done that. I would have been so intimidated and so nervous. I would've sacrificed my vacation and not made a fuss. Not that I'm proud of that."

"She's just a bully trying to exercise power over me. And what's she going to do to me anyway? She might not talk to me for a while, but that's no great loss!"

Luckily, I didn't have the same issue about taking vacation. I'd finally agreed with Paul to take time off over Christmas and had cleared the vacation time with Marcus.

Annie and Harry excitedly helped pack the car, and we left for our family holiday. We drove first to my mom's and had a great time. My brother and sister and their families were there as well. Then we drove for two days to see Paul's mom and dad. They, too, were excited to see us, especially their grandchildren.

When I told Paul how much I'd enjoyed our vacation, he took the opportunity to remind me that we still should take a long break and go somewhere exciting. I answered that I'd think about it, but I really had to finalize my project first.

When I got back to work I caught up with Sandra about her time off. She'd had a great time, going downhill and cross-country skiing with Tom in the Rockies for most of the two weeks.

I waited expectantly for her first interaction with Maxine, which happened the first afternoon she was back. After her meeting, Sandra came back to the fourth floor with a wry grin on her face.

"What happened?" I asked, waving her into a meeting room. Emily joined us.

Still smiling, Sandra said, "Well, I went up to Maxine's office for our catch-up meeting. I walked in and said, 'Hi, I'm back.' I expected her to ask me about my holiday. But no, of course, she didn't. I expected her to ask about the ski resorts. But of course, she didn't. All she said was, 'There's one thing I need to fill you in on that happened while you were away,' and she was immediately on to work stuff. Not one polite question about my vacation! Anyway," Sandra added, "Tom and I still had a great vacation, regardless of Maxine's meanness."

Soon after, Maxine arranged for a change of product manager for her division. Sandra was taken from the Western Division and Kylie Goodwin, Miss Goody Two-shoes, was assigned. Kylie made a great show of the change. Sandra took it in stride and generously briefed Kylie on the work in progress. Sandra took over Kylie's responsibility supporting James, which was a welcome change for her, James being so efficient in the way he worked.

For me, Sandra's "sacking" was a big bonus. It meant she now had more time to spend with me on my project, a change Sandra was happy about as well.

29
First Looks

AWARE THAT MARCUS—and therefore I, too—was under pressure from Nicholas to show progress on my marketing strategy project, I decided to arrange a meeting for Nicholas, Marcus, and me. I hoped to gain Nicholas's support for the ideas that were emerging from my investigations.

Before setting up that meeting with Nicholas, I met with Marcus alone to bring him up to speed. I wanted to gain his support for several key conclusions I'd arrived at based on my assessment and gap analysis. Unfortunately, he seemed more preoccupied with the timetable than the substance of the ideas, and he was critical that I had not shown more progress on final outputs. I pointed out that the final outputs would come from the staged work along the way, some of which I was now taking him through. And I reminded him that I had also worked on the Sales Managers Meeting. He begrudgingly seemed to accept that.

Because Marcus insisted that Nicholas be brought up to date on progress, I wanted to make sure that I had Marcus's support for the stages I had completed, so I summarized them quickly once I'd gone through the details.

"Do you agree with what I've done so far, Marcus?"

"Yes, it looks fine."

Fine was not strong enough for me. "When you say 'fine,' what do you mean?"

"It's good." Still not strong enough for me to know where he stood.

"From your point of view, is there anything missing?"

"No."

I searched his face for anything hidden, but he was impassive. "Do you agree with my assessment of our internal capability? Do you agree with the competitor analysis? Do you agree with my conclusions about the way the market is changing and the expectations of our customers?"

"Yes, that all looks fine," he said impatiently.

"And how about the way Sally and I are setting up the anthropological study?"

He dropped his pen. "Just leave that out when we talk to Nicholas."

"Why?"

"I think it's crap."

What could I say to that? I was pleased with his support to that point, so I didn't push it. But I also didn't want to leave that hanging.

"I'll leave it out of this review, but you and I can talk about the anthropology study again another time—it will be valuable." I wanted to get his input on the study, but it was so hard to nail him to a time and hold his attention. He was missing out big-time if he didn't understand the uniqueness of that approach.

"Okay, Marcus," I said, closing my pad, "if you are supportive of what I've done so far, I will go ahead and make a time for us to meet with Nicholas."

He nodded. "Is that it?" he said, getting up.

"Yes, that's it."

It had been some time since I had seen Nicholas. He was hardly ever around. On such rare occasions as when we'd been in the same elevator together, the interaction between us had been awkward, and he'd had little to say.

Since my last meeting with Nicholas, though, even casual encounters were terrifying. I wondered if he remembered how angry he had gotten in our first private meeting together.

I spoke to Sandra and Ben about my fears. Like the good friends they were, they offered to give me a trial run. We made a time and booked a room on the nineteenth floor. When we were settled, Ben asked about the words I had first written down to describe Nicholas.

"Yeah," I said, "I checked my notes on that this morning. The words I wrote back then were autocratic, arrogant, detached, unpredictable, tyrant."

"That pretty much has him pegged," Ben laughed. "You could add competitive, manipulative, and untrustworthy, if you want to be generous and give him eight words!"

"I'll second that," said Sandra, putting her hand up.

"So, how do we want to do this?" I asked.

"How about we both play Nicholas?" said Sandra, opening her file, ready to take notes. We agreed that they would both imitate Nicholas and listen from his perspective. I went through my presentation, being careful not to be critical in a way that might anger the COO, as I had inadvertently done last time. When I finished, they clapped.

"Thanks," I beamed, "but still play Nicholas, please. What will he be thinking?"

"He'll be impressed," Ben enthused. "You covered everything really well."

"How about you, Sandra?"

"I've seen this project of yours develop over the last few months, Lauren, and it's very, very thorough. Advanced, really. Just one thing I would do differently with Nicholas. I'd start out with a statement that causes a 'yes' response." I asked her what she meant. "Something that makes him think, 'Yeah, this is interesting.' Something that grabs his attention, something that he will nod his head at."

"Okay, good idea. I'll work on that."

"Otherwise, it was great."

"Thanks, guys. I really appreciate it. Now all I need to do is relax!"

A short while later, I was sitting at my desk, ready for my meeting with Nicholas and Marcus, which would begin in just under ten minutes. I had just grabbed my materials to head up to the twentieth floor when my phone rang. Maybe the meeting was postponed—if only.

"Hello, Lauren Johnson," I answered hesitantly.

"Hello, Ms. Johnson," said a formal voice I didn't recognize. "This is Barbara McKinley from Harry's school." Harry had recently turned five and had started kindergarten.

I immediately thought the worst. *Oh no, what's happened?*

"Harry's had an accident."

"Is he okay?" I shouted into the phone.

"Yes, he's okay, really he is." I relaxed, slightly. Ms. McKinley went on, "But you should come pick him up right away. He's cut his leg quite deeply and should be taken to the doctor. We've bandaged his leg, but he may need stitches. Can you come right now?"

"Y . . . yes, my husband or . . . or I . . . one of us will come now." I thanked her for calling and hung up the phone. Poor Harry. But what dreadful timing! I knew Paul had back-to-back patients this morning. He couldn't pick up Harry. I looked at the clock on my computer—10:58. Just two minutes until my meeting. I'd never be on time now. I called upstairs.

"Marcus—"

"Where *are* you?" he hissed. "You *cannot* be late for this meeting."

My stomach twisted. "I'm sorry, Marcus. I've just had a call from my son's school. Harry's cut his leg and needs stitches. I have to take Harry to the doctor right now. I'm sorry, but there's nothing I can do. We'll have to reschedule." Silence from the other end.

"It's an emergency," I pleaded.

"Fine." He hung up.

Most of my teammates looked on sympathetically. Kurt was grinning and seemed to be enjoying the drama. Emily offered to walk with me to my car. I thanked her but declined, picked up my handbag, and hurried off to be with my son.

When I got to the school, Harry was in good spirits, proud of his bandaged leg. We drove to the doctor and waited for an hour. Harry's wound eventually earned him nine stitches, but he was a brave boy. I treated him to lunch at McDonald's and then dropped him at Paul's clinic.

I was back in the office just before three. I went straight to Marcus's office, wondering what mood he would be in and what trouble was in store for me.

"Sorry, again, Marcus, about the family emergency," I said, expecting a barrage of rebuke.

"That's fine, really," he responded pleasantly. I was surprised but pleased with his reaction. I didn't know what had caused him to settle down, but it was a good thing he had. Marcus ran his fingers through his hair.

"Nicholas still wants to meet today. I'm to call him the moment you're back."

Damn, I thought. I had hoped for a reprieve.

"Hold on, I'll go check with him," Marcus said as he jumped up from his chair and dashed to Nicholas's office. He returned quickly.

"We can see him in fifteen minutes. He's changed his afternoon around for us."

"Okay," I managed with a smile, my stomach twisting with nerves. "I'll go and get my files and come straight back."

"Okay, see you shortly."

I raced downstairs, quickly reported to everyone that Harry was fine, and dashed back up to Mission Control. I indulged in a slow walk from the elevators to Marcus's office, trying to control my breathing. I mentally practiced my opening and the key sections of my presentation.

Marcus was waiting outside Nicholas's office and beckoned me over. Nicholas came out as soon as I arrived.

"Come in," he said.

"Sorry about this morning, Nicholas," I said. "My son cut himself and I had to take him to the doctor to get stitches."

"That's okay, Lauren. These things happen." I was relieved to hear that.

He gestured for us to sit at his round table. Sitting in the stunted chair again disoriented me, and I was momentarily thrown off balance. Fortunately, I didn't need to start talking immediately. Nicholas was relaying a story about how his own daughter years ago had been rushed to the hospital when she was about eighteen months old. It had been a false alarm. Marcus laughed at Nicholas's story. Thank goodness for the banter—I now had my nerves under control.

"Okay, Lauren, what have you got?" Nicholas leaned forward, his hands folded on the table.

I sat as upright as I could. "What we've got is a status report on the review of our marketing strategy," I said in a strong voice. "And a prediction that the final outcome will substantially increase market share and profit, and the market will assess it as a breakthrough."

"Good," he nodded. Excellent. Feeling more confident, I continued.

About five minutes into my presentation, while I was covering my analysis of current capability and competitive positioning, Nicholas became distracted. His eyes wandered around the room, and he seemed to look right through me at people passing outside. He tapped his pen loudly on the table and glanced at his watch. Obviously, I was losing him.

I knew from past experience that Nicholas wasn't fond of negative news, but I didn't know how to cover the facts any other way, and I couldn't conceal them. At this point, however, I couldn't even tell if he was paying attention. I spoke quickly for another few minutes, trying to draw his attention to the slides, and then I cut the rest of my presentation short so I could answer his questions.

When I had finished, he raised his eyebrows and said, "Is that it?"

"Yes," I said, and waited. My heart was racing.

He looked at me impassively. I waited.

"I am completely underwhelmed," he said, slapping his hand on the table.

He could not have thrust the knife more deeply. Frozen in my chair, I felt the room closing in on me. I had nowhere to hide. I gulped and waited helplessly for an explanation of his verdict.

"I just don't see any value in this proposition. It's contrary to the direction we are following. It does not fit with our strategy. The basic assumptions are just plain wrong."

Slowly shaking his head, he turned to Marcus. "Have you looked at this, Marcus? Do you agree with her proposal?"

"Not really, Nicholas," Marcus lied. "I had a brief look at the skeleton of the idea and have not had a chance to consider it in detail. I agree with your reservations, Nicholas, and of course, I expressed these concerns to Lauren earlier."

The coward! The liar! I looked from one to the other, stunned.

"Lauren," Nicholas said, getting up to check his cell phone, "I expected better than this. Frankly, I'm disappointed. And there is no real insight or breakthrough."

Hadn't he listened to anything? Maybe I should tell him about the anthropology study. No, Marcus would hit the roof.

"Let me know when you've reworked it," said Nicholas from behind his desk, cell phone to his ear. End of meeting.

Quickly, I gathered up my anger and my papers and stumbled out of Nicholas's office. Marcus had his cell phone to his ear too, although I hadn't heard it ring. He told me we would talk later. Just as well—I was furious enough to kill him.

I took the elevator to the ground floor, dropped my files with the receptionist, and escaped outside for some fresh air. The wind was howling, but the day was dry, so I went for a walk to try to clear my mind. I was totally deflated and angry as hell—angry at Nicholas's rudeness, at Marcus's two-faced performance, at his cowardice. Angry at Nicholas's arrogance in passing judgment on my proposal without taking the time to properly consider it and showing me some respect. It wasn't like I hadn't thought about it. I hadn't just woken up that morning with my ideas. I had worked on this for months. This was my profession! I was angry that my ideas were considered wrong just because they were different from Nicholas's. I was angry with myself for not defending my proposal, angry that I went quietly and took criticism so meekly.

I wondered about Nicholas's daughter, the one who years before as a toddler had had a false-alarm visit to the hospital. She would probably be old enough now to be working. What sort of boss did Nicholas hope she worked for? Someone who treated people better than he did, I bet. The bastard.

I lost track of time. I wiped the tears from my face as I walked and eventually composed myself enough to return to the office. Luckily, there were only a few people around when I got back to my desk. I knew there was little chance of running into Marcus again that day. He would stay well away from our floor and hide in his office up at Mission Control. I left work early.

As soon as I walked into the house, Paul knew something was wrong. My grumpy mood gave it away. He suggested we take a break from cooking and go out for dinner. I agreed, and the kids needed no persuasion. Harry was limping, but he insisted he was fine.

Being close to my family restored some balance, marginally. By the time we got home, I had settled down a little.

When the kids were tucked in bed, Paul asked me what was wrong. When I told him, he tut-tutted and shook his head.

"What a lousy bunch of assholes. I just don't get them."

I shrugged. What else was there to say?

"They're true-to-life walking fables!" He'd been reading the Aesop book we'd bought that Saturday.

I felt too weary to speak.

"Do you know the one about the coward who raced off and left his friend at the first sign of danger? And then when the danger was over, he returned, brandishing his sword?"

I nodded.

"Well, that's stupid Marcus, the coward. And there's any number that apply to that ass Nicholas Strange!"

I smiled.

"And I still need to find a few to help you. I'll keep a notepad and a pen beside me when I'm reading."

"Thanks, sweetheart," I managed.

After having slept little that night, I dragged myself to work the next day. Fortunately, James Swann made a thirty-minute time slot for me—I wanted his advice.

Tears welled in my eyes as I described the horrible meeting. He reached for a tissue.

"I'll be okay," I sniffed. Damn, I promised myself I wasn't going to cry.

"Do you think Nicholas and Marcus are thinking about that meeting right now?" he asked.

"No," I answered, "they probably forgot about it right away."

"To Nicholas," he said, "it was just another conversation, like most everyday conversations he has. Trust me, I know."

"The problem is, though," I said resignedly, "it makes me less confident about coming up with new ideas and less energized to keep going with this one. It's knocked the enthusiasm out of me."

"Do you believe it's the right idea?" James challenged.

"I do."

"Do you believe it will help Harlow Kane?"

"I do."

"Do you believe you made the right analysis and defined the problem correctly?"

"I do."

"Do you believe you have given the matter deep thought?"

"I do," I said, feeling slightly more confident with each affirmation.

"Then you must back your own judgment and your professional ability. You know you're good at your job. You know in the past that your judgment has been spot-on. You must keep going with the idea and come at it from a different angle. Maybe, when you present it next time, the idea will be enthusiastically accepted."

"Thank you, James."

James had a wonderful ability to make me feel better. I wished he were my boss. I could do anything if he were.

* * *

I kept going with my project, and taking James's advice, went back to the basics to think of another way to explain and present it. Perhaps my weakness was a lack of ability to communicate the idea.

I found myself being much more cautious, though. Injuries don't always mend quickly. I took more time than I should have to finalize the idea and prepare myself for another round of possible rejection.

30

The Trumpeter

KURT RUSHED TO MY DESK. He had something to tell me.

"Not here. Let's get a meeting room."

I didn't like this. What was such a big secret that he couldn't tell it to me right at my desk? I knew I should've told him to get lost, but I followed him anyway. We found a spare room and he shut the door after us.

"There's something I think you'll want to know," he said. He looked flustered.

"What's up?"

"How do you think you're doing in your job?" he asked. Oh, no. Not another one of those conversations.

"I'm doing well," I said, weakly. My mind raced back to my recent meeting with Nicholas. "What sort of question is that?"

Kurt leaned forward with a friendly frown on his face. "If I heard something about you from upstairs, you'd want to know, right?"

I should have said no. Instead, I said, "Yes."

"I just overheard Nicholas Strange and Maxine Savage talking. They mentioned you."

I should have followed Ben's and Sandra's advice and told him to go jump . . . "And?"

"It didn't sound good," he teased.

My stomach sank.

"What exactly did they say?"

"Well, I couldn't hear every word," he said. Then he stopped again. This really couldn't be good if he was trying to spare my feelings. Or was it for effect, the nasty game player.

"So . . . tell me . . . what did you hear?" I pressed.

"Not much, really," he replied. "But I don't think they were praising your work."

My stomach, finding that it couldn't descend any further, shrank into a tight ball.

I put a brave face on. "Kurt, forget it," I said. "If you didn't hear clearly, then you don't really know what they were talking about, do you? Maybe they weren't talking about me at all."

"Oh, they definitely mentioned your name. And they were definitely saying that they haven't seen much output from the strategic marketing review. Nicholas used the word *underwhelmed*."

My other internal organs decided that my stomach had the right idea. Why would Nicholas share his assessment with Maxine? It was none of her business! This was all I needed.

"It's probably nothing, but I thought you'd like to know," he added, smiling broadly. I didn't want to hear any more of this.

"Let's leave it, Kurt," I said.

We got up to leave, but instead of opening the door, he waited. I realized he expected me to thank him for sharing his priceless information with me. No way.

I glumly plodded back to my desk, dragging my entrails after me. Kurt skipped back to his desk.

Trying to concentrate for the rest of the day was a hopeless task. I left early to get home to Paul. Annie and Harry were playing when I arrived. I begged Paul to come into the den and I updated him on Kurt's malicious game.

We sat brooding for a while. Harry came in, whining that Annie had pushed him. Paul ushered him out and distracted him with something else. I didn't know what. When Paul came back, he was carrying the fable book and his notepad.

"Listen to this!" he cried. "You will not believe this one."

> A trumpeter marched into battle in the vanguard of the army and put courage into his comrades by his warlike tunes. Being captured by the enemy, he begged for his life, and said, "Do not put me to death. I have killed no one. Indeed, I have no weapons, but carry with me only my trumpet here." But his captors replied, "That is only the more reason why we should take your life; for, though you do not fight yourself, you stir up others to do so."

He closed the book and dropped it loudly on the coffee table. "Does that explain this character, Kurt?"

"It does," I smiled tiredly. "But does it help me?"

"Well, you have to call him for what he is. You have to stand up for yourself."

I knew he was right, but I kept wishing the problem would just fade away. I wished I wasn't so scared of conflict. I wished I wasn't still suffering the irrational fear of loss developed in my childhood principally because my parents had divorced.

By now, the kids were hungry and squabbling with each other in the hallway, which wasn't doing my mood much good either.

Paul laughed. "Ah, and here's one of my favorite Nicholas Strange fables. I couldn't find it last time." He read as we walked into the kitchen.

> Some mischievous boys were playing on the edge of a pond. Catching sight of some frogs swimming about in the shallow water, they began to amuse themselves by pelting them with stones, and they killed several of them. At last one of the frogs put his head out of the water and said, "Oh, stop! I beg of you. What is sport to you is death to us."

I managed a smile.

Harry came screeching down the hall, his leg still bandaged. The stitches would be out in two days, and then he'd have tape on it for a while to prevent a scar. I picked him up and cuddled him.

"You beautiful thing." I kissed his ear and rocked him gently to and fro. Annie sat on her favorite stool at the breakfast bar and opened her coloring book. I put Harry down and kissed Annie on the head.

"Were you and Dad talking about your bosses again?" she asked with her head down, a purple pencil in her hand.

"Yes, darling. They're quite a handful."

She looked up from her book and said, deadpan, "I don't think I want to play with bosses when I grow up. Boys are bad enough."

Paul and I laughed, and I started peeling the carrots.

31
The Meeting from Hell

SOON AFTER THE DUST HAD SETTLED from my presentation to Nicholas, I found myself back on the nineteenth floor, facing Nicholas and his band. Marcus was on vacation, and because Sandra was also away, I'd been delegated to attend the monthly senior executive meeting in his place. All the senior executives were expected to attend, except John Squires. John had delegated all operations reviews to Nicholas.

The meeting was due to start at ten o'clock. I arrived five minutes early. When no one had joined me at a few minutes after ten, I had a horrible feeling I was in the wrong room. I was about to check the venue when James Swann arrived.

I asked him if we were in the right room. "Yes," he said, "these meetings never start on time." He sat in the chair next to me.

At about ten past ten, Jeremy Hyde, Maxine Savage, and Ryan Gunn ambled in. Ryan dropped his file and BlackBerry on the opposite side of the table and came around to shake my hand.

"Welcome, Lauren," he said encouragingly. I thanked him politely.

Jeremy and Maxine treated me as though I were invisible.

Soon, Hugh Worrell and Gus Wearing arrived. Hugh looked at me and glanced away. Maybe he had a guilty conscience about stealing my training idea. Gus sat on the other side of me, smiled, and said hello. His blue tie was stained and his shoes were still a mess. Dandruff sprinkled his shoulders. Better, though, to be sitting next to Gus than Hugh or Maxine.

At twenty minutes past, Nicholas Strange finally arrived, sweeping into the room with great gusto. No one apologized for keeping others waiting.

Nicholas perched himself at the head of the table and looked around the room.

"I can see everyone's here, so let's get started. First, we need to review the business results for last month." I was disappointed he didn't welcome me to the meeting, but at least he didn't challenge my right to be there.

He continued, "There is nothing to be pleased about, and we have serious work to do. I am particularly concerned about costs and would like to spend a fair amount of this meeting deciding on ways to cut them." Wow, that was direct. He stood up. "I have to leave for a short time. Jeremy will cover the details of this month's results."

One minute into the meeting and Nicholas had left the room! What could possibly be more important than attending this meeting?

Jeremy Hyde covered the financial results, focusing on areas where sales were low and where costs were high. He never congratulated anyone on areas where sales were above budget. At the end of his presentation, he moved to the topic of cost-cutting. He said that the company had to save three percent of costs in the remainder of the year. He asked us to write on a piece of paper the areas where costs could be saved. With our heads down, we were busily writing when Nicholas walked back in.

"What the hell's going on?" he demanded.

"We're writing down areas where we can save money," answered Jeremy.

"Don't waste your time!" Nicholas exclaimed. Jeremy shrank back. "I can tell you where costs need to be saved. Every department will save fifteen percent on travel costs. There will be no training for the rest of the year. We will save on stationery and publications. We will put a hold on IT investment and do an early review of charges from IT suppliers. We will have a salary freeze this year, except for exceptional performers. What do you think of that?" He glared around the table.

Hugh fiddled with his pen. "I think that's a good idea, Nicholas. Training programs can be easily deferred. In fact, we may be able to eliminate a few training staff positions and engage consultants next year. And in terms of a salary freeze, the outside market is slowing down, so we'll tell staff that it all has to do with the external market. We'll call it a market-related salary pause."

Nicholas nodded his appreciation. This was the first time I'd seen the executives interact with each other. It was intriguing.

"The IT department is a champion at spending money, so a bit of pain there won't hurt," agreed Jeremy. I was surprised he spoke so negatively about one of the groups that reported to him.

I could see the yes-men joining in—followed quickly by the yes-woman on the team.

"Travel is a good item to focus on," said Maxine, pursing her lips. "We spend a lot of money across the company on travel, and some of it is wasted. I have an international convention to attend next month, but I would be happy to defer that until next year." She beamed in her self-satisfied way and looked around the room. She lingered at her reflection in the window and touched her hair. Her head had moved another thirty degrees before she dragged her eyes away from herself.

"Thanks, Maxine," grunted Nicholas. "Let me know if your convention needs to be an exception. Any other comments?"

"Yes." James raised his hand slightly. "I don't like it. I think if we go out with a salary freeze and stop all training then—"

"That's what I've come to expect from you, James," Nicholas shot. "You are an obstruction. You are an obstacle to progress. I am sick of you arguing and bickering and contesting and debating every time we want to make improvements. You have to get on board, James."

I shrank into my chair, scared of what might follow. James maintained his even manner and his face showed no effect from the assault.

"That's fine, Nicholas, but if you don't want my opinion, then don't ask for it."

Nicholas rolled his eyes and let out a loud sigh. "Okay, give me your opinion."

"I was just giving it. If we freeze salaries and stop training, then that will send a dramatic message to staff and frighten them no end. And giving salary increases only to outstanding performers will cause incredible division across the company."

"Oh, so now you're not wanting to look after the high achievers," fumed Nicholas, his face red. "You are going for the lowest common denominator and pulling everyone else down. You are so narrow in your thinking. We must look after our stars."

"That's fine, Nicholas, then don't ask for my opinion. I just think there is a better way to achieve the outcome."

"Why didn't you say so?" said Nicholas, throwing up his hands.

Unruffled, James asked, "Do you want to hear it?"

"Okay, but make it snappy," Nicholas hissed.

James looked at everyone around the table. Most heads were down, perhaps avoiding the hostility of the number one ape. Ryan was playing with his BlackBerry, no doubt sending an email. Gus was doodling on his pad.

James opened the palm of his hand. "I am assuming from the financial results that we expect the final year results to be okay if we can save three percent overall in costs."

While James was talking, Nicholas got up from his seat, moved to a side table, and poured himself a glass of water. The instant he sat down, Gus stood up and did exactly the same thing—went to the side table and poured himself a glass of water. What's with the copycat behavior? I wondered.

James was continuing his argument. "If we defer hiring in areas outside of sales, then at current attrition rates we will save a fair part of that cost. If we review and limit travel and conferences, we will save about one percent. In regard to training, each of us should do a review of training plans over the next week and come back with plans to prioritize and save on training without having to stop it entirely. In relation to salaries, we could let staff know that we are reviewing costs and that if we save the three percent, then there will be the normal salary review at the end of the year."

"Look, James," said Nicholas coldly, "we don't have time for this. Your method is all very nice, but it's too time-consuming and it won't work. Doing it your way, we'll spin our wheels for a few weeks and still be stuck where we are. No, I have decided. Jeremy will give you all a memo with the costs to be cut. I expect you to give this your enthusiastic support," he scowled. "If anyone has a problem with that, let me tell you, it won't be me who won't be here next meeting."

I couldn't believe his disgusting behavior, his resorting to bullying as his only means of getting what he wanted. Next to me, Gus was nodding stupidly in agreement at everything Nicholas was saying. Jeremy got up and wrote notes on the whiteboard.

"Now," continued Nicholas, spreading his arms with his palms face down on the table, "there is something else I want to implement. I want to increase the number of sales reps by transferring people from non-sales departments."

James started to object, but Nicholas held up a hand and glared. "We are going to do this redeployment and we don't need to debate it," he commanded.

There was a knock at the door. "Come in," barked Nicholas. Janice Waters from IT poked her head in.

"Why are you here, Janice?" asked Nicholas impatiently, looking at his watch.

She eased into the room. "I was asked to update you all on the new sales tracking system."

"That's now on hold," snapped Nicholas.

Janice misunderstood. "Do you want me to come back later?"

"No, the whole project is on hold. We're about to stop it. Jeremy will talk to you later."

Janice left the room looking very embarrassed. I felt sorry for her. I was ashamed of the carrying-on, of the little Hitler running the show, of the sickening toadying behavior of most of his generals. John Squires, as CEO, should be aware of this. Does no one tell him? Does he not care?

"Let's continue the meeting," said Nicholas in a calmer voice. "I want to talk next about an executive coaching program I want all my directors in Sales and Services to be part of. Hugh will take you through it. I have to leave for a moment."

Hugh looked disappointed that his boss had apparently little interest in the subject as he started to explain the coaching program that was soon to commence. The first stage was a one-to-one review with the coach, followed by a review with Nicholas and then ongoing coaching.

"It's pretty simple," said Nicholas, striding back into the room and taking over. "John and I want to make sure that we are a high-performing executive team. We want insights into your strengths and weaknesses."

"Development areas," interrupted Hugh.

"What?" asked Nicholas, looking confused. "What are you talking about?"

"Weaknesses are termed development areas."

"Whatever," said Nicholas, with a wave of his hand. "The coach's name is Bill Whatman. I know Bill from years ago. Hugh will give you his contact details; Bill is waiting to hear from you. Have your first meetings with him within sixty days. Are there any comments?"

"Yes, I have a question," said James, undeterred. "How much is this going to cost? Given the pressure on costs, couldn't we defer this to the new financial year?"

"There you go again with your narrow, limited outlook," shouted Nicholas angrily. "I am absolutely sick of you getting in the way. I know exactly what your assessment report from Bill will say—obstructionist, pigheaded, not a team player. This is a strategic initiative to enhance the impact this executive team has on the business and no, it cannot be deferred."

"That's fine, Nicholas. If you don't want my opinion, don't ask for it," said James calmly. My heart was racing for him. I wondered if James needed to be saying anything at all—was it worth all the abuse he was getting? I admired his courage, but it bordered on martyrdom.

"Okay," said Nicholas. "If there are no other comments about the coach, let me repeat that you make sure you've completed your visits to him within the next sixty days."

Gus went to the side table for another glass of water. This time, he returned with two glasses—one for himself and one for Nicholas at the head of the table. Nicholas hadn't appeared to signal that he wanted a drink!

Nicholas moved to the next item on the agenda—a proposal for an employee opinion survey. Hugh invited Grace Reece into the room.

Hugh then introduced the topic. "Grace is proposing that we survey staff to assess their opinions on a range of subjects. I asked her to join us today so we can consider the idea."

Ryan put his BlackBerry aside and Gus took up his pen. Maxine seemed to be staring out the window—or perhaps at her reflection.

Grace looked around the room and started her presentation confidently. "I am recommending we undertake a survey of our staff to gain an understanding of their views and to provide us with possible actions to enhance employee commitment to our business. We—"

"What makes you think our employees aren't committed?" Nicholas interrupted.

"I'm not saying they aren't," she responded politely. "Rather, I am saying that we don't know what matters most to staff. I am proposing that we need to know. We need to know what staff members feel positive about so we can continue those things, and we need to know areas where staff are not so happy so we can take the appropriate action."

"Grace," said Nicholas curtly, "I would rather you got on with more important things." He turned to Hugh. "Hugh, this is rubbish. Why doesn't your department just get on with actions we have agreed to?"

"Well," said Hugh, "I am feeling much the same as you, Nicholas." Stupid coward, I thought. A good buddy for Marcus. "It's just that Grace has been badgering me to do this survey. I told her to bring it up with this group." Hugh turned to Grace. "Looks like the answer is no, Grace."

No one said anything. With her head down, Grace packed up her papers and left. She had been in the room for less than a minute. I imagined it would be some time before she put forward another idea, and even longer for her to brave visiting this meeting again. Poor Grace.

"Okay," commanded Nicholas, "we're out of time. I have an important call to make. Hold all other topics over to our next meeting. Inform anyone else waiting outside that we will see them next time."

Nicholas left the room and the rest of us followed.

I caught up with James and went with him to his floor. We found a meeting room to talk.

"James," I said, not hiding my contempt, "please explain to me Nicholas's behavior. He's so rude, and why is he in and out of the meeting like that?"

"Pretty simple, really," James said, shaking his head glumly. "He thinks he's much more important and intelligent than everyone else. He doesn't see a need for anyone else's input on things. He runs these meetings because John wants him to, but he puts no value in them. He's always got something better to do."

"Why did you keep speaking up and expressing your opinions? You must have known he was going to attack like that."

He rubbed his forehead. "I just need to do my job as best I can. To do that, I need to share my opinion. That's what I'm paid for. And I'm not going to let a bully stand over me."

"I admire your courage, but I'm not sure it's worth it."

"I need to be able to look at myself in the mirror, that's all."

"But doesn't he frighten you?"

"No," he shrugged.

"What if he gets so angry that he sacks you?"

James squinted. "Yeah, that would be his ultimate threat. He might own my paycheck, but I'm not selling him my soul. Anyway, I can't see him sacking me while John's around. Now, if John left, then I reckon I'd be on the next bus out of here, with Nicholas's boot print on my rear end!"

32
Duck Season

STILL STUNG THAT THE COO WAS UNDERWHELMED by my review project update, I revisited a number of assumptions and invested more time with Sally Morton on the external research. The research still supported my original assessment of the market and overall direction of the strategy. And the anthropological aspect of the research had revealed surprising information on what customers in our country meant by the word *service.* It was breakthrough stuff.

Our attempts to have Marcus review the findings were fruitless. I managed to snatch about thirty minutes to meet with him, but he wasn't interested in the detail and didn't seem to listen. He spun his pen and asked irrelevant questions. He insisted I present the preliminary findings of the external research to the Senior Executive Operations Meeting. Oh, no, I thought, not that crucifying audience. But Marcus wanted to test the research findings before embarking on the solutions themselves. And he wanted me to explain the anthropological study because he was unconvinced about this step.

I prepared my presentation carefully, knowing that the credibility of the idea, and my own reputation, depended on a convincing delivery. And I knew I had to turn Nicholas around. With the bitter taste of the last executive meeting still lingering in my mouth, I knew I would be in for a tough time.

I sat outside the meeting room for what seemed like an hour, reviewing my presentation and trying to ignore the chaos within. Finally, I was admitted and Marcus introduced the topic. "Lauren has been conducting research associated with her plans to review our marketing strategy, our brand, and our products and services. Over to you, Lauren." I was disappointed he didn't give any personal commitment in support of my research—the coward.

"Thank you, Marcus. And thank you," I said, looking around the room at everyone, "for the opportunity to update you this morning. I plan to take fifteen minutes to tell you about the research we have been conducting on our products and services and to share with you the early findings of the research." As I looked around, I noticed, gladly, that Maxine was absent.

Marcus leaned toward Nicholas and whispered something to him, which immediately distracted me.

"Excuse me, Marcus," said James, "I'm finding it hard to concentrate on what Lauren is saying."

"Sorry," replied Marcus, unabashed.

"As I was saying," I resumed, "this is an update on our marketing strategy research. We engaged a consultant to investigate the view of our key customers and other stakeholders."

"Who are the other stakeholders?" Nicholas interrupted from the head of the table.

"The stakeholders include suppliers, government bodies, and organizations that influence social and economic policy," I answered.

"Why are you bothering to include them?" he asked.

"I think it's important that we obtain a complete perspective of the economy and social shifts, so we have a reliable view of the future."

"I don't think so. Why don't we just stick with customers, as we have always done," he said, phrasing the question like a statement.

"I think it's important to understand not only the market we operate in but also the market that our clients operate in, as well as how that market may change over the next ten years. We can then anticipate the shifts in the market before our competitors do."

"I think Lauren has a good point," said James.

"What's this researcher costing us?" asked Nicholas.

"Around two thousand dollars a day," I answered.

"That's cheap," laughed Nicholas cynically, "too cheap. He's either no good or he's stupid."

"*She* is an outstanding professional, extremely well qualified, and very effective," I said, trying to sound strong. My heart was beating fast, straining under the attack. "Sally Morton is well regarded in her area; in fact, we are lucky to have her. She chose to work with us because of the futuristic nature of the proposal I gave her. She is inexpensive because she works alone and has a low overhead."

By this time, others in the room were again distracted. Hugh and Jeremy were having their own conversation on the side, and Gus was scribbling something on his notepad. Ryan was now sending a text message.

"What's futuristic about it?" quizzed Nicholas.

"Part of the research involves investigating what people in our culture mean by the concept of service," I said, pleased that we were at last getting to the key topic. My optimism was soon cut short.

"What?" grunted Nicholas.

"I'll come back to that," I said, deciding that I would outline the method of research first. I glanced around the room. No one but James was paying attention.

"Let me go on," I said, with as much authority as I could. "We have commenced the research, and the method involves talking to three hundred people."

Jeremy took his lead from Nicholas's aggression and cut in. "Three hundred people! How is that a sensible number? You don't need to talk to that many customers."

"Exactly," agreed Nicholas.

"I don't know much about marketing research," echoed Hugh, arms crossed, "but even I know that that number is too much."

"Can I suggest," interrupted James, rubbing his temples, "that we let Lauren take us through the information and then cover questions at the end?"

I looked to Marcus for help, but he remained stone-faced, impersonating a statue. I soldiered on.

Over the next ten minutes I tried to explain that the three hundred people were a broad section of the community, not just customers. As the purpose of the research was to determine what service meant in our culture, we had to gain the input of a whole spectrum of people. We planned to hold ten workshops of thirty people each.

But the attack got worse, with challenges from every direction being thrown like poisoned darts. It was open season on Lauren, with each person trying to outdo the other.

"Thirty people is too many for a focus group," shouted Jeremy.

"We only need to interview customers," bellowed Hugh.

"We know what *service* means anyway," said Ryan arrogantly.

I was worn down. With the audience so judgmental, so on the attack, they didn't listen long enough to know that Sally and I had already commenced the process. I never got to share the exciting early findings of the study.

"Lauren, we will leave it there," said Nicholas. "I hope the feedback from this meeting will help you."

What could I say?

"There have been a number of questions raised," I said, trying to compose myself, relieved that at least the attack was over. "I will review your questions with Sally Morton and come back to you by the end of the week."

Battle weary, I left the room. I caught just a glimpse of a sympathetic grin from James as he mouthed "Good fight" over Nicholas's shoulder.

33

Poison Pen

AFTER GOING OVER THINGS AGAIN with Sally Morton the next day, I was able to answer the barrage of questions thrown at me by the executives.

To cover their questions promptly, and to reassure them about the reliability of the research, I sent an email on Wednesday, two days after my grilling.

> Hi, Everyone,
>
> I have spoken to Sally Morton and have asked her the questions about the research method that were raised at the SEOM Meeting. Sally has reviewed all of your questions and is confident that the approach being undertaken is an appropriate and reliable method, and within the project budget. Here are the answers to the questions raised:
>
> Question 1: Background on methodology. Answer: Sally is following a proven methodology, validated in other research. Sally has used this method a number of times with good results. A number of leading examples of

archetype, or anthropological, studies have provided unique insights to help companies in industries with products ranging from motor vehicles and ice cream to fresh produce and toys.

Question 2: Is 300 people appropriate? Answer: Yes, that number is appropriate to ensure reliable findings from which decisions can be made.

Question 3: Are groups of 30 appropriate? Answer: Yes, the way the workshops are conducted, 30 people can be easily managed. The approach engages people and gains everyone's input. Larger, and therefore fewer, groups mean a reduction in time and consultant fees, which isn't possible when there are more groups with fewer people in each group.

Question 4: Can the research be reduced from three months? Answer: No. With the sequence of steps, three months is a realistic time frame. To reduce the amount of time would involve additional resources and might not be practical.

Question 5: Is it really possible to do all the stages in one project? Answer: Yes, because the workshops are structured to extract information; whatever views the particular stakeholder has will be captured.

Question 6: Is it necessary to interview people beyond customers? Answer: Yes, to gain a valid understanding of the cultural meaning of any concept, a broad range of the community needs to be included.

I hope this answers the questions raised. Please let me know if you have any other questions or comments.

Regards,
Lauren

When I checked my emails the following morning, only James had replied. He responded that the questions had been well answered and from his point of view, I should carry on with the study. Curiously, by the end of the day, no one else had replied.

On Friday morning, Marcus ordered me to his office—immediately. His tone was ominous. I gave Emily and Sandra a quick signal that I'd been called up to Mission Control.

"Lauren, I want to talk to you about that email," Marcus said aggressively.

He was about to attack, like an enraged pit bull. "People on this floor are talking about that email," he glared. "It was arrogant."

Dumbstruck, I waited to see if there was any more. I needed time to compose myself, and to allow my windpipe to start functioning again.

"What was wrong with it?" I managed.

"I was annoyed." He paused. "And Nicholas was annoyed."

"Annoyed by what, exactly?" I could not believe this!

"Annoyed by the tone."

"What tone?" I exclaimed.

"It was rude and disrespectful to the senior executive team." He was holding onto the edge of his desk.

"I don't see that at all, Marcus," I replied, by now gathering my breath and my wits. "I don't understand what you are saying."

"It is arrogant of you to think that the questions from the executive team were irrelevant."

"But I didn't think that for a moment," I said. "I checked the questions with Sally, and I gave what I thought were reassuring answers. What would you have wanted me to write? There was nothing in my email that should be regarded as disrespectful."

"Well, people on this floor are not happy. Go back to your desk, we'll talk later."

I left, shaken. Dismissed like an insolent schoolgirl, totally thrown by the reaction to what I'd thought was a helpful and reassuring email.

When I got back to my desk, an email had arrived from Nicholas.

> Lauren,
>
> I read your note again this morning, and I have to say, I'm extremely irritated that all the concerns of a group of senior people have been summarily dismissed. I want to quiz Sally Morton more about this. I definitely don't accept that nothing we said added any value to the project. I will leave it to Marcus to discuss this with you and work out what the appropriate next steps are.
>
> Nicholas

My stomach dropped and my intestines went with it. My shoulders drooped. How could my innocent email be so wildly misinterpreted? I reread Nicholas's note several times, feeling more hurt each time.

Nicholas had "replied all," so the entire executive team would read his reply to my note.

Another email arrived. This one was from Jeremy, copied to everyone else as well.

> I would like to see the written proposal and have Sally Morton attend an executive meeting to explain how the research would be structured in order to provide the answers.
>
> Jeremy

Hugh wrote a similar response. Maxine asked for a briefing, due to her absence from the meeting. Ryan offered to assist me in understanding survey methodologies, "if I wished." Thanks a lot! They were like a pack of dogs attacking a wounded animal. My pure intentions to reassure the executive team and respond promptly to their questions had been grossly distorted. Gus didn't reply, which I appreciated.

I had been so keen on maintaining the momentum of the study. The research I had commissioned was fresh and exciting—a whole new approach with profound possibilities. Only a few companies, and none in our sector, had ever embarked on this anthropologically based research. And those companies had seen enormous benefits from their research. I had been excited by the possibilities for us and had assumed that others would share this excitement. But something simple had been turned into something hugely complex. Perhaps they didn't trust me.

James came by my desk and we went into a meeting room together. He tried to comfort and reassure me, tried to convince me that the approach had been misunderstood, and everything would blow over in a few days when people had more important things to worry about. I struggled to accept his confidence.

I agonized for the rest of the day, but before I left for home, I plucked up the courage to respond to Nicholas's email, also copying others on my reply.

> Nicholas, I investigated all the questions to provide reassurance on the matters raised by the executive team. Sally Morton would be pleased to join us at some stage to further explain the topic. Please let me know when that would be suitable.
>
> Regards,
> Lauren

I turned off my computer in a flash and dashed out.

34

A Swann Devoured

OVER THE NEXT FEW WEEKS, I was able to work without interruption on my project. I decided to hold to my course despite the furor over the methods, and Sally and I made good progress on the anthropological research. We were getting highly valuable information that would improve Harlow Kane's services to our clients. And we had a lot of fun working together on something so important.

One afternoon, toward the end of the day, Ben wandered over to me, leaned against my desk, and presented the Aesop book.

"I've finished!" he beamed.

"So, you enjoyed it?"

"Absolutely! It's scary how relevant the fables are to corporate life," he said. "Sorry it's a bit worse for wear."

"That's fine," I said, though I was mildly annoyed that Paul's childhood keepsake had been disrespectfully dog-eared. From the look of it, Ben had put the book to good use. I casually flicked through the pages, refreshing my memory. I smiled at a number of my favorite fables. Ben had left a few marked with labels. I put the book in my bag.

"Gotta run," he said. "Thanks again for sharing the book."

"I'm heading off soon as well," I said as Ben headed to the elevators, his briefcase tucked under his arm. I shut down my computer, pleased with my day's work.

As I reached my car, James Swann walked past me, looking worried. At first he denied that something was wrong, but eventually he admitted he'd had a horrific day. He agreed to go to a coffee shop where we could talk. But he wanted to go farther away than Columbia's. I phoned Paul to let him know and asked him to do the cooking that night.

We drove to a nearby café. The waiters were setting up for dinner, so it was noisy, but it was the only place in the neighborhood open for coffee. After we'd ordered, I asked James what had happened.

"You know how Nicholas wants us to work with an executive coach?" I nodded. "Well, I had my session with Bill Whatman today." James bit his lip. "He had me do some personality tests, and he quizzed me about my family background and stuff." James grimaced. "At the end of the interview, he gave me feedback, and it's really knocked me for a loop."

"What happened?" I asked. I couldn't imagine someone evaluating James as anything but a great leader.

"Well, Bill started the evaluation with, 'I might as well give it to you straight.' I thought that was pretty ominous. He kept me guessing what that was all about, and he kept building up to something."

The coffees arrived. James paused until the waiter had left.

"By his reckoning, I'm a below-average leader."

"No!"

"Part of what he says is okay. He says I'm intelligent and strong at creative thinking. 'That's good,' I said to him. 'I've always thought I had a good imagination.' Do you know what he said to me?" James shook his head. "He said, 'That surprises me, because you don't look imaginative.' Can you believe that?"

I shook my head. "What does imaginative look like?" I asked and sipped my coffee.

"Then he comes to leadership, and that's when he tells me I'm below average."

"In *his* assessment."

James held up his right fist. "It was like being hit in the stomach with a baseball bat." He punched his fist into his other hand. Whack!

James paused. "He says I don't challenge my people to achieve beyond their expectations."

I nearly dropped my cup. "That's not true. Did you tell this so-called coach that your people say they never could've done half the things they've done without you encouraging and supporting them?"

James nodded. "I did. I told him that was exactly what my people say. Thing is, he never asked me that question during the interview. I pointed out to him that I could easily have told him what my people say—if he'd asked me!"

James pushed his cup aside. "Well, anyway, he carried on with lots of crazy stuff about me—I'm not warm, don't get close to people, I—"

"What did you say to that?" I asked, amazed.

"On each point I told him what my people have said, what my staff have said over the years. If he'd asked me about the key topics he was assessing me on at the interview, I could have given him everything. It was like a trick, really." James gazed into space.

"He then said that my relationships with peers will be mixed: close to some and distant with others."

James let out a hearty laugh. No doubt, we were both thinking of Marcus, Jeremy, Maxine, Ryan, Gus, and Hugh!

"I had to agree with him there." James looked tired. "Anyway, for every point he raised, I questioned him and asked for his evidence. I don't think Bill appreciated my debating him."

The waiter cleared our cups and asked if we wanted another. We declined coffee and asked for water. The waiter pointed to a fountain where we could help ourselves. I jumped up and brought back two full glasses.

"Then Bill says I don't like to seek feedback. I asked him how he knows. And then I said, 'I'll tell you what, how about we seek feedback from my staff on what they think of my leadership abilities? Ask them what words they use to describe me to their friends and families?' Then he asked whether I was contesting my report. I said, 'Absolutely. What you're saying is totally different to the actual situation.' He didn't like that."

He closed his notepad and sipped his water. "So, Lauren, that was my day," James concluded.

Early diners were starting to drift in. A dull hum of voices had replaced the table-setting noise.

I stared at James. "Can I just say, James, that this coach's assessment is way off the mark—by a mile. I know what people say about you. They say you're a fine person and a great leader to work for. People always use you as the good example of what bosses ought to do and be."

"My wife said pretty much the same thing," James murmured, without conviction. "She said the report was ridiculous and that he can't be one hundred percent accurate one hundred percent of the time."

"James," I continued, "the evidence is overwhelmingly in favor that you are a good leader. I'd work for you at the drop of a hat. And your people show great results—that's proof."

"He didn't ask me about that," James said.

"What do you mean? Didn't he ask about business results?"

"No, he never even asked me about the output of my division," he said wearily.

I was getting angry at this point. I didn't know who this Bill character was, but I knew for sure I didn't like him. I did my best to ease James's hurt, but not successfully.

Suddenly, a light switched on in my brain. "There's another interpretation," I said with the joy that comes with a new discovery.

"What's that?" he responded, hopefully.

"Maybe a leader with your strengths and ability is unlike anything in his leadership model. Maybe he didn't recognize a great boss when he saw one!"

James brightened, "Thanks, Lauren—great observation!"

"And," I said, "good for you for defending yourself. I know I wouldn't have been able to argue with him. I detest confrontation."

"Well," James said, "I had to. There was no one else to argue for me, and I couldn't just accept what I knew was way off the mark."

I admired his courage. Next time I was in one of those situations where I needed to defend myself, I would try to model myself after James. I told him so.

"Glad to be of service!" he laughed.

"Did you find out about his background? I know Nicholas said at the executive meeting I attended that he and Bill knew each other. Are they friends still?"

"I asked him that. He was evasive until I asked him a direct question: 'When was the last time you and Nicholas were out socially?' He said the football game last weekend. I have a horrible feeling that Nicholas gave him a briefing on me beforehand—from Nicholas's perspective, of course."

I winced. "So what happens now?" I asked.

"Well, Bill acknowledged that I disagreed with part of his assessment. He said I have to do my review with Nicholas next, and then he and I do another session as part of the coaching contract. I don't feel much like doing any more sessions with him."

"Nicholas will expect you to keep going."

"Yeah, he will," James forced a smile, "but I'm not too eager. It's just another predetermined outcome. I get enough of that from Nicholas as it is."

I hit my hand on the table in excitement. "Hey, that reminds me!" I squealed. "Listen to this." I reached into my bag. "Bear with me." I quickly brought out the Aesop book and flicked through it. There it was, marked with a red label. "Okay, this is a book of Aesop's fables," I said, raising the cover to show him. "Let me read this one to you."

> A wolf came upon a lamb straying from the flock and felt some compunction about taking the life of so helpless a creature without some plausible excuse. So he cast about for a grievance and said at last, "Last year, sirrah, you grossly insulted me." "That is impossible, sir," bleated the lamb, "for I wasn't born then." "Well," retorted the wolf, "you feed in my pastures." "That cannot be," replied the lamb, "for I have never tasted grass." "You drank from my spring, then," continued the wolf. "Indeed, sir," said the poor lamb, "I have never yet drunk anything but my mother's milk." "Well, anyhow," said the wolf, "I'm not going without my dinner." And he sprang upon the lamb and devoured it without more ado.

James burst out laughing. "Fantastic. That says it all. Right from the start, he was always going to devour me!"

"I'm starting a movement. I've read the book, Ben has just finished it, Paul's reading it. You're welcome to have this copy if you want. It's a bit worn." I passed it to him.

James took the book and thanked me. He finished his water and insisted on paying the bill.

As we walked back to our cars, he pondered aloud, "I don't know why Nicholas thought this was a good idea—to do executive coaching. And now I have to meet with him to review my first coaching session. That'll be fun."

"When will that be?"

"Next Tuesday."

"Now, James," I teased him, "just don't go changing on us. You're fine the way you are."

The next week, I checked in with James to see how his review with Nicholas had gone.

"It was fine," he said tonelessly. He paused, his face strained. "It was almost an action replay of my session with Bill." I didn't interrupt. "Except, I decided not to be as argumentative with Nicholas as I was with Bill," he grimaced. "He'd just blow his top and say I was being defensive. I did let him know that the chemistry between Bill and me was not good, and we'd be wasting our money if Bill kept working with me. Anyway, the upshot was that Nicholas offered to coach me, to help me improve my leadership—"

"Excuse me!"

"—and my people skills."

It was so ludicrous I had to laugh.

A few days later, I caught up with James again and asked how he was feeling. He was past it, apart from his annoyance at Bill masquerading as a leadership adviser.

"Basically, Lauren, I like myself. I won't let Bill or Nicholas try to turn me into something I'm not."

I smiled. If only I could learn to do that.

35

The Marcus Method of Managing Engagement

NICHOLAS STRANGE WAS ON OUR FLOOR. This was odd. He strutted around, smiling and talking to people in an unnatural, stilted fashion. No one quite knew how to react to his abnormal display of friendliness. Surprise showed on people's faces. A couple of people pointed at Nicholas's back and raised their eyebrows as if to say, What do you make of this?

I tried to remember when I'd ever seen Nicholas on our floor. I couldn't. He always remained bunkered in his own office, rarely surfacing, careful not to be seen with the troops. I guess we made him feel uncomfortable. Meetings with Nicholas were always held in his office—subjects paying homage to the throne.

On the same day Nicholas graced us with his presence, Marcus announced he was recommencing team meetings, starting with an off-site team-building session at the local bowling alley. Oh, goodness no, he even suggested that we do it on a weekend and include our partners. Most people didn't want to cut into their weekend, so it was voted to have it on a weekday. It was left to Marcus to organize.

Marcus also resumed individual review meetings. He had always said these would occur, but up until now, they hadn't.

Whenever patterns of behavior change from the norm, people get suspicious. Sure enough, a few days later, we learned that an employee survey was to be conducted in a month's time. I asked Marcus to explain.

"Marcus," I said, "when I was your delegate and sat in the Senior Executive Operations Meeting, the survey was raised by Grace Reece, but the decision was made not to conduct the survey. What's changed?"

Marcus answered as though reading from a manager's manual. "The senior executive team has decided that conducting a staff survey is a good idea. The vehicle provides an opportunity to gather information on how staff are feeling, what areas of concern exist, and which areas need improvement."

I didn't bother delving any further. Even if Marcus did know the truth, he wouldn't be revealing it to me.

Later that afternoon, I saw Grace Reece from HR in the break room.

"Hey, Grace," I began, "great news about your survey."

"Not so great for me," she replied gloomily. When I asked why, she took a deep breath. "You were there when I first presented the idea. It was a useless waste of time; I wasn't taken seriously. Nicholas saw to that. So I crawled back into my hole. Suddenly, out of left field, the idea becomes a winner!"

"How did that happen?"

"At the last board meeting, apparently one of the external directors raised the issue and recommended that a survey be conducted because he had just done one in his company and found it very useful. It was an old boy network decision."

She paused again and glanced around to confirm that we were alone. "I feel like screaming! I was the one who researched the topic, benchmarked the idea with other companies, and spent all that time thinking about the subject. What happens? Dismissed in a flash. Then, just because of a comment made by some senior person with a male voice, the idea becomes fashionable and it's all systems go."

"I don't blame you for being angry," I conceded, "but at least a survey is being done. That'll be good for our people."

"Yes, I know," Grace sighed. "I'm working on the survey team, but my heart isn't in it. I'll do my job, but I don't have the same energy to give to the task now."

"I know exactly what you mean," I responded. Boy, did I ever. "But a lot of us do know the idea came from you."

Grace thanked me and managed a weak smile as we parted. She lacked the normal bounce in her step as she lumbered back to her desk.

Marcus held a one-to-one review meeting with me the following week, a few weeks before the employee survey was to be conducted. For once, he was punctual. And he reserved the conference room on the fourth floor. He must have thought we were all a bunch of idiots, not able to see straight through his hypocrisy.

"How is work going?" he began, sitting upright in his chair with his back to the door.

"In what way?" I replied. I was extremely guarded.

"Are you enjoying work, finding it motivating and satisfying?" he asked with a foxy smile.

Oh, come on, get to the point. "Do you mean is my morale high?"

"Well, yes, including your morale."

"My morale is fine, Marcus. How's yours?"

"Mine could not be higher. Our department is operating well. We are delivering good results, and I work with a great team of people. Working with people like you, Lauren, is a very satisfying experience."

"That's great to hear, Marcus." My bullshit detector was whirling madly.

"How do you feel about your development and communication?"

"Communication is fine. But I would like to have implemented more from the last seminar I went to," I said.

"Remind me about that," he mumbled.

"You might recall I came back with a range of ideas." I didn't mention the sales rep training proposal that Hugh Worrell had stolen from me.

"Oh, yes," he said with a touch too much enthusiasm, "we should do more with your ideas from that conference. How about preparing a one-page summary, and we can act on your proposals immediately?" I agreed to do so, but I doubted anything would ever come of it.

He coughed and then leaned forward with his elbow on the table and his chin resting in his hand, a thoughtful pose. "How do you feel about your relationship with me?" he asked.

"It works fine, Marcus," I replied hesitantly, glancing away. My bullshit detector was now going berserk.

"Well, hopefully, Lauren, we have the sort of open relationship where you're comfortable to raise any issues of concern with me. You don't need an employee survey to state them," he said, opening his hands to me.

This was repulsive. He was trying to buy my vote, wanting me to say in the survey that he was a good guy and that my morale was high.

"Sure, Marcus," I said flatly, looking down and hoping that was the end of the topic. It wasn't.

"The thing about surveys is that they are not the most effective way to identify issues. I would rather have an open discussion about things and get to the gist of the issue and the fix. That's much more professional, don't you think?" I nodded.

As I looked up, I saw Ben through the glass. Marcus couldn't see him because he had his back to the door. Ben squeezed his lips wide in a forced smile and winked. I choked back a giggle.

"If our survey result is low," Marcus continued, leaning back in his chair, "there'll be a fair amount of focus on the team from the top, and I don't think that will help any of us. We might even find we have fewer funds for training and other things. And if I'm distracted by looking after the executives, I'll be less able to spend time with the team."

My stomach turned in revulsion. "Thank you for letting me know," I said, hiding my disgust. Ben's theory about managing upward was well supported. Marcus's drive to look good to his superiors was utterly shameless.

Marcus leaned forward, his voice dripping with honey. "In terms of my management ability, if there was just one thing I should do better, what would it be?"

This was getting boring. I had a lot to do, and Sally would be waiting for me. What a complete waste of time.

"Gee, Marcus, I think I need to give that some thought. I didn't expect to have this conversation right now, so I need to think very carefully about everything you've said."

"Do that and let me know," he said. "How about we set a time for next week and we can discuss it again?"

Marcus busied himself all week, meeting the members of the team individually. Ben figures he got a pay raise out of it—we'll see!

I dodged the follow-up meeting with Marcus the next week by organizing an off-site meeting with Sally Morton. Answering his question truthfully would have been suicide for me, and completely wasted on him. He was not the sort of person who would listen and take my answer seriously.

The closer the survey date came, the more Marcus showed signs of anxiety. He lost his normal swagger and looked stressed. He went out of his way to be cheery, in a strained sort of way.

The eight of us on the team didn't place the same importance on the survey that Marcus obviously did. Watching him sweat, however, was much more amusing.

A week before the survey was conducted, Marcus called a meeting.

"I have asked you to gather round this morning," he beamed, "to announce that Kylie will be leaving the team and moving to Sales and Services, Western Division, under Maxine Savage. Kylie and I have for some time been discussing her next steps to achieve her career objectives, and as you know, Kylie has been supporting Maxine's marketing activities for a while now. A move to Sales is part of Kylie's plan, and I have been able to organize the move for her. The position in Sales is currently vacant so Kylie will be moving at the end of this week, as Maxine is eager to fill the role immediately." Turning to Kylie, Marcus said, "We wish you well, Kylie, and thank you for your contribution while you've been part of the team. I am pleased that I have been able to help you with your career."

Most of us, with the exception of Kurt Wolfe, were happy to see the back of Kylie. We clapped enthusiastically, and Marcus seemed tempted to bow.

Kylie beamed and thanked Marcus for his support. "Marcus, you have been an inspiration over this last year. I am so fortunate to have had you as a role model, and thank you for supporting me in my career." Oh, please.

"And," she looked at us, "I'd like to thank you, my wonderful team, for being such a joy to work with. I will miss you all."

We murmured our appreciation and were soon back to work.

As the week went by, Marcus seemed recovered from his anxiety about the survey and back to his normal ATC self. The suggested bowling afternoon never happened.

The employee survey started the following Monday and lasted for two weeks. Most of us completed the survey in the first week and shifted our attention to other more important things.

About a month later, Marcus called a meeting to address the results of the survey. We trundled up to the nineteenth floor, even though Marcus could have easily booked a meeting room right where the rest of us worked. Marcus came bouncing down the staircase from Mission Control as we filed into the room.

"Thank you to everyone who completed the survey," he began once we'd settled. "The survey is very important in helping us to understand how people are feeling and to identify priorities for actions. All the managers have been asked to share the overall company results of the survey, and the results for their individual teams."

This will be good, I thought. I was interested in the company results and highly curious about how our team answered the questions about our ATC.

"I'm pleased to say that we had a one hundred percent participation rate, so it's great that everyone took the time to complete the survey." He then shrugged his shoulders and his faced showed disappointment. "Unfortunately, we did not receive a high enough response to get an official result on our team's morale. Managers need at least eight staff reporting directly to them in order to receive a full result. You see, if a team has less than eight people, then the team is considered too small to ensure anonymity of people's answers. We had only seven staff in our team at the time of the survey."

Sensational! Marcus had cleverly organized the hasty transfer of Kylie so our team didn't have the required eight people when the survey was done. And he must have had Kylie's agreement not to complete the survey—I wondered what that had cost him. What a schemer! No wonder Marcus had been so relaxed those few days before the survey.

Sandra coughed loudly. Kurt commented that it was unfortunate for Marcus that he didn't get a result, that he wasn't able to demonstrate the high morale of our team. Oh, yeah, sure! Ben winked at me from across the table. Without a team result, there was no record of how badly most of us thought of Marcus as a boss. I had to hand it to him—he was a clever bastard.

I was so distracted by Marcus's Machiavellian maneuver that I didn't take in much of what was said about the overall company result. I vaguely heard that the general morale of the company was pretty low. People were most concerned about senior management, career development, and pay and benefits. The question that got the lowest score was "How satisfied are you that management will take actions to address any major issues identified in this survey?" Action plans on the survey results were to be developed from each team and sent to senior management.

So we never got to know how Marcus officially rated as a manager. And neither would John Squires nor Nicholas Strange.

Later that day, I went to James Swann's office. He was beaming over his survey results—his division had the highest morale in the company. I asked him if he planned to send the results to Bill Whatman, the executive coach. James said he didn't need Bill's approval, so there was no reason to. He was quietly pleased with the result, and deservedly so. Everyone knew his team was the most satisfied in the company—they were treated well, they felt safe, and they admired their leader.

Over dinner that night, after hearing Annie's and Harry's news of the day, I shared mine. I laughed with Paul about Marcus's management of the survey. Paul congratulated him, cynically, of course. Annie wanted to know what it all meant. We told her it was like a card trick. Harry wanted to leave the table and Annie soon joined him.

Paul pushed his plate away. "Okay," he said firmly, "we know all about Marcus and Nicholas and the rest of them. There has to be a reason why you work with these people," he said, rubbing his forehead. "The reason might be that you learn how to cope. Maybe you can use this as an opportunity to manage yourself."

"Sounds interesting." I got up and moved my chair closer to him. "What did you have in mind?"

"I've finished reading Aesop. I think there are some fables that might suggest how to handle all this, how to become who and what you want to become. You'll need to start in on it the right way, though."

I was intrigued and excited.

Paul tapped his finger on the table. "How about we get a babysitter for Annie and Harry some time this weekend and we'll spend a couple of hours talking this through?"

"That's great! Sandra has offered to look after them any time. We could ask her to babysit Saturday morning, and then she and Tom could have lunch with us," I suggested.

"Sounds like a plan!"

Harry ran into the room. "When's my birthday?"

"Not for about six months."

"How long's that?"

"This long," Paul replied, spreading his hands about a yard apart.

"*That* long!" Harry disappeared out of the room.

36

Wool and Bacon

ON SATURDAY MORNING, Sandra generously drove to our place and picked up the kids. She and Tom would return with them after midday and stay for lunch.

Once the kids had gone, we decided to sit outside for our chat. It was a bright morning and the backyard was comforting. My back was warming nicely from the sun. I passed Paul a muffin and poured the coffee. Paul had the Aesop book in front of him. He'd marked a number of the pages with sticky notes.

"What I thought," Paul said, "was that some of the fables could help you work through your responses to the things that give you such a tough time."

"Yeah, that's great."

"Also, we can talk about how James and Sandra—and Ben for that matter—cope. There may be some lessons you can learn from them as well."

I sipped my coffee.

"So, what do you really want from your job?"

I smiled. "I would like to be able to do my job, which I actually enjoy, and not be distracted by Marcus's behavior and the behavior of other negative people. I just want to make a difference."

"Yeah, that's good. How would you achieve that, specifically?"

I paused in thought. "By not needing their approval, I guess—at least not as much as I do now."

"Anything else?"

"Yeah, not be so put off by conflict," I grimaced. "I need to accept disagreement and confrontation as okay, and not think I need everyone's approval."

He sipped his coffee. I cut my blueberry muffin into four pieces. He opened the book.

"There's a fable here about a mouse who keeps evading a bull by ducking into a hole every time the bull pursues him. The punch line is the mouse calling out in a shrill voice, 'You big fellows don't have it all your own way. You see, sometimes we little ones come off best.'"

I brushed crumbs from my lips. "That's good, but it doesn't tell me how to act."

"Well, I thought it was a good place to start."

"All my life, I've been a good girl. I've pretty much done the right thing, never making waves. Apart from not wanting to get into trouble, I always got too upset with myself if I upset anyone else."

"Well, you admire Sandra and James, and they cope pretty effectively. What do they have that you admire?"

"Mmm . . . I guess it's their strength of character."

"What about it?"

I looked around the garden for inspiration. "They don't need approval. They operate to their own values, and they don't mind if others approve or not."

Paul brushed some dirt from the table. "The fable I think that can really help you is the one about the miller and his son. Do you remember that one?"

"Yeah, I do. I did like that when I read it. Refresh my memory," I asked good-naturedly.

Paul put down his cup and read:

> A miller, accompanied by his young son, was driving his ass to market in hopes of finding a purchaser for him. On the road they met a group of girls, laughing and

talking, who exclaimed, "Did you ever see such a pair of fools? To be trudging along the dusty road when they might be riding!" The miller thought there was sense in what they said, so he made his son mount the ass, and he walked at the side.

Presently they met some of the miller's old cronies, who greeted them and said, "You'll spoil that son of yours, letting him ride while you toil on foot! Make him walk, the young lazybones! It'll do him all the good in the world." The miller followed their advice and took his son's place on the back of the ass, while the boy trudged along behind.

They had not gone far when they overtook a party of women and children, and the miller heard them say, "What a foolish old man! He himself rides in comfort, but he lets his poor little boy follow as best he can on his own legs!" So the miller made his son get up behind him.

Further along the road they met some travelers who asked the miller whether the ass he was riding was his own property or whether the beast was hired for the occasion. The miller replied it was his own, that he was taking it to market to sell. "Good heavens!" said they. "With a load like that the poor beast will be so exhausted by the time he gets there that no one will look at him. Why, you'd do better to carry him!" "Anything to please you," said the old man. "We can try that." So they got off, tied the ass's legs together with a rope and slung him on a pole, and at last reached the town, carrying him between them. This was so absurd a sight that the people ran out in crowds to laugh at it and chaffed the father and son unmercifully, some even calling them lunatics.

The father and son were crossing a bridge over the river when the ass, frightened by the noise and his unusual situation, kicked and struggled till he broke the ropes

> that bound him and fell into the water and drowned. Whereupon the unfortunate miller, vexed and ashamed, made the best of his way home again, convinced that in trying to please all, he had pleased none, and had lost his ass into the bargain.

I finished my muffin and gazed into the garden. A bee was busy at work among the flowers.

"I really don't want to be like the miller."

"Do you think you are right now?"

"I do."

We sat quietly for a moment.

"I'll just have to give it a try," I said, "but I'm not really sure how."

"I'm treating a patient who said something the other day that might help," Paul said brightly. "He said that you visualize a successful outcome by going out past the event that concerns you. Don't dwell on the event and the anxiety the event causes. Go out, say fifteen minutes past the event, and think about the positive outcome you'll achieve and the positive energy you'll feel from that outcome."

"That sounds interesting!"

"Do you want to try—go out past an event that worries you and visualize a successful outcome?"

"It's worth a try. Let's see . . . okay, got it. I've got a scene in my mind."

"What's that?" he grinned.

"Kurt. I can visualize telling him where to go." I smiled, but without much conviction.

"Okay, let's try that. How do you feel about telling him off?"

"I feel horrible. My heart races just thinking about it."

"Okay, so instead of visualizing the event, visualize how you'll feel fifteen minutes after the event." He gave me a moment to ponder it. "Now what?"

I shut my eyes. I thought about confronting Kurt. I felt terrible—nervous as hell.

"Go out past the event," Paul encouraged.

I forced myself to do so, to be fifteen minutes past the confrontation. Suddenly, a wonderful, positive energy surged through my body. My breathing became relaxed and fresh oxygen flowed through me.

I opened my eyes. "That felt wonderful!"

"I could see it in your face!" Paul laughed. "My patient uses this positive thinking to help his recovery, and he does seem to handle stress better and to recover faster than most people."

"Does he have a name for it?"

"I didn't quite catch what he called it, something about a time line thingy."

Paul opened up the book again. "Oh, here's one I marked about Kurt and his gossip. How does this fit?"

> Three bulls were grazing in a meadow and were watched by a lion, who longed to capture and devour them, but who felt that he was no match for the three so long as they kept together. So he began by false whispers and malicious hints to foment jealousies and mistrust among them. This stratagem succeeded so well that ere long the bulls grew cold and unfriendly, and finally avoided each other and fed each one by himself apart. No sooner did the lion see this than he fell upon them one by one and killed them in turn.

I laughed. "Yes, that describes Kurt beautifully. He's a champion at false whispers." I looked at my watch. "It's already half past eleven. Sandra and Tom will be back with the kids soon." I stood up and went around the table. "Thanks, darling." I kissed the back of Paul's neck.

"Just one more." He put his arm around my legs and patted my thigh. "This one's a reminder about how much to give to work."

> A pig found his way into a meadow where a flock of sheep were grazing. The shepherd caught him and was proceeding to carry him off to the butcher's when he

> set up a loud squealing and struggled to get free. The sheep rebuked him for making such a to-do and said to him, "The shepherd catches us regularly and drags us off just like that, and we don't make any fuss." "No, I dare say not," replied the pig, "but my case and yours are altogether different. He only wants you for wool, but he wants me for bacon."

We laughed. "I encourage you," he said as he closed the book, "to try to give bacon to your family but only wool to the people at work!"

We got things ready for lunch. We were having a barbecue, plus some salads, which was easy.

A bit after twelve, Sandra and Tom arrived with the kids. Annie and Harry had had a fun morning at the children's museum. We enjoyed the afternoon together, chatting and joking with our friends. We avoided talking about work. I think we'd all decided to give it a rest.

* * *

The following week, I was thinking about the fable about bacon when Kurt breezed up to me in the parking lot. By now, my skin crawled whenever I was unlucky enough to be in his presence.

"Lauren."

I ignored him and kept walking. Even the sound of his voice made my stomach churn. Unfortunately, he didn't take the hint.

"I understand there is tension between you and Sandra. Do you want to talk about it?"

I snapped. I'd had enough of this creep. Sandra Pearson had become my closest work colleague and one of my dearest friends. I thought of Paul and I quickly visualized the joy I would find in fifteen minutes' time if I fixed this problem once and for all. I stopped, slowly put down my bag, stood tall, and looked Kurt straight in the eye.

"Kurt, you could not be more mistaken. Sandra is one of my closest friends. As a matter of fact, our families spent last Saturday together. You're a wicked person. Now, go and play your cancerous games with someone else. No more with me. That's it. Finito!" I slowly picked up my bag and walked off, leaving him gawking after me.

It was one of the first times in my life I could remember confronting someone destructive. It felt good. The same cleansing emotion I'd felt on Saturday in the backyard flowed through my body, leaving behind a sensation of satisfaction and strength. I had survived the confrontation. The sky had not fallen. And Kurt bothered me no more!

Confronting Kurt and successfully getting him off my back gave me a new lease on life. I was able to work with new enthusiasm on my project. Sally Morton's research was going well and my projections were almost complete. Everything was coming together beautifully.

37

Torture Chamber Revisited

BEFORE I KNEW IT, I was sitting in Marcus's office again, waiting for him to show up for my second performance appraisal. He was late, of course, but plenty had occurred in the last year to keep me lost in thought until he bustled in.

"More drama this morning. Nothing we couldn't resolve," he mumbled. "What are we meeting about, Lauren?"

"My performance appraisal," I said coolly.

"Good answer." He picked up a file from his desk and moved to where I was sitting at his round table. He sat down and pushed the file to one side. He leaned away from me.

"How do you feel this past year has gone?" he invited, picking up his pen.

"I think the year has been very productive. The most important thing is that I am on schedule with the review of marketing strategy and will soon have a final report." I tried to stay focused despite his spinning the pen. "I managed the Sales Managers Meeting and I contributed to a positive team spirit. So, I believe it's been a good year."

"I have some reservations." The pen came to an abrupt stop.

Here we go again. The usual storm was brewing. I started to batten down—becoming quiet and withdrawn. The memory of my successful confrontation with Kurt sprung to mind. And I thought of James and his courage with the executive coach. These thoughts lifted my spirits and gave me strength. I calmly visualized going past this event to how I would like to feel afterward. What I most wanted was not to be pushed around.

"What are they?" I asked sharply, surprising myself with my strength. I braced myself for the rough weather that would surely come.

"I have concerns that we have not made a significant impact on sales and profitability. I have not seen any breakthrough outputs from you on marketing strategy."

"We talked about this last year, Marcus," I responded confidently. "My job has a longer time cycle than twelve months. The project I am working on has a time frame of eighteen to twenty-four months before outcomes are finalized and implemented, and then at least another year before we can determine the impact. I realize sales reps might have a time cycle of one month and product managers maybe six to nine months, but mine is longer."

"My view is that we should show outputs every year," Marcus said sternly. "I find it too hard to assess someone without annual outputs."

"Yes, it is hard. Yes, it is outside the normal system. But there are still activities to be shown for the year."

"But I need to make an assessment of your performance," he objected, again spinning his pen. It was so distracting.

I struggled to maintain my self-confidence, but I was succeeding, slowly. My heart was not racing as much as would normally be the case. I was determined not to succumb to Marcus's attempts to make me feel inadequate.

"I have been doing my job for eighteen months," I said. "I am making significant progress on the marketing strategy project. I am on schedule."

"I would appreciate an update on that."

"I've been trying to do that," I said in an exasperated tone, "but you keep canceling our reviews. I'm ready any time to share with you my thinking and what I will be proposing." I could see he was surprised with the unusual force of my response. I pushed ahead. "There are other things I feel good about regarding this last year. First of all, the Sales Managers Meeting went very well." I waited for acknowledgment.

"Ryan had a big part in making that a success."

I was ready for that. "Actually, Ryan did very little. How could he have done a lot if he got involved only in the last two weeks? Nicole and I did almost everything."

Marcus wasn't convinced. "That's not the way I remember it."

"Well, that's the way it was," I said slowly, glaring into his face. He dropped that point.

My courage was building. "And the marketing strategy is on schedule. I have completed the internal capability reviews and the external research of our competitive positioning and the assessment of our customers' buying motivators. The anthropological study of the meaning of service is almost finished."

Marcus rubbed his neck and opened his mouth to say something.

"Let me finish." I held up my hand. His jaw snapped shut.

"The other thing I feel good about," I continued assertively, "is the assistance I provide to other people in the team. Because of my product marketing background, I'm able to help others in their thinking about their roles and challenges. You don't see that; your office is up here on the top floor, so you don't see a lot of how we actually work."

"This discussion is not about me," he said. "This is about you, Lauren, and I do have some feedback from some of the team who say you're not a team player."

My newfound strength was being tested. "What evidence of that could there possibly be?" I asked forcefully. Only Kylie and Kurt would make up such an accusation. And it was an easy barb to throw. He looked surprised that I would dare say such a thing. "Did you ask for an explanation?" I asked. "Did you ask for evidence?"

"No, I didn't," he answered. "People are entitled to their views." He furrowed his eyebrows at me. "I find it disappointing that you cannot take feedback."

I was about to slip into silence mode again. No, I'd made it this far, I had to fight on. "I think I am very good at accepting feedback when it's accurate and helpful," I said, tiring of his tone. "If you can't point to evidence and facts, you shouldn't say these things."

Okay, I thought, now I am going to throw everything at him. "Another thing I have contributed to," I said, "is the idea for better sales training. That has had a positive impact."

"How can you take credit for that?" he laughed cynically. "That was Hugh's idea!"

Looking him squarely in the eye, sitting straight in my chair, I spoke slowly without even a quiver in my voice. "The idea was actually mine. It was me who gave it to Hugh."

Marcus shook his head. "I don't accept that at all. I remember being in the executive meeting when Hugh presented it." He crossed his arms.

I didn't expect him to believe me, but at least I felt better for releasing my frustration.

"The other thing I'm proud of is that I've worked with the divisional sales and services directors and advised them about their own sales strategies. I have successfully assisted most of them."

"I didn't know that," he said, shifting in his chair.

"Well, you don't know everything I do," I said pointedly. "I don't go around bragging about my achievements. You should get feedback about my contribution from the directors."

"Well, as a matter of fact, I did," he said.

This was news to me. I didn't know Marcus was going to ask the senior people about me, and although I thought it a good idea, it would have been common courtesy for him to let me know.

"How do you think you are getting on with the senior managers?" he asked. A loaded question, if ever I heard one.

"Quite well, I believe," I answered, wondering what he was concealing. "I think I have a productive working relationship with most of them. Why do you ask?"

"Well, I've heard a different story," Marcus said.

"Oh? And what is that?" Again, I braced myself for the onslaught.

Marcus opened his file. "I asked the senior executives for feedback on you and how they find working with you. There are a number of comments that are a concern."

"Such as?" I asked, on edge.

"Well, the first one is from Maxine Savage. She says she does not see much of you."

I rubbed my temple. "I have offered my assistance to Maxine many times and she has declined every time. I have now concentrated my time and energy on other divisions that appreciate my help."

"Nevertheless," he said, "you cannot be selective about who you assist and who you don't. You have to be flexible in your approach to different people."

"Fine," I said impatiently. "Anyone else?"

"Gus Wearing had mixed thoughts. Here's his email."

I read the sheet of paper Marcus handed to me.

> Marcus,
>
> Regarding your email asking for feedback on Lauren Johnson, Lauren has been doing a good job for me and my team. She helped with a challenge we faced through the year of declining sales of some products and worked with my team to help devise a recovery strategy, which worked well. In terms of feedback for Lauren's development, I sometimes hear from others that she can be a bit too hesitant to support her own ideas. I do not find this to be the case. Please let me know if you need anything else or if you need me to explain more.
>
> Regards,
> Gus Wearing

I looked up from the page, confused. "What's negative about that?"

"It says that you have trouble getting on with some people."

I couldn't believe this idiot. In a controlled voice I argued, "How do you read that into it? How can you think Gus was being negative about my performance? He's actually being very complimentary and seems to be pleased with my contribution. Yes, he talks about other people's opinions, but in the context of helping me grow."

"I don't see it that way."

"Well, did you call and ask him? Did you ask him whether he was generally positive?"

"No, I didn't. I don't have time for that, and it is pretty clear to me."

He definitely wanted to give me a hard time. "Who else did you get feedback from?" I asked.

"That's all."

"Did you talk to James Swann? I've been working closely with James and his team for most of the year."

"I did not contact James. I knew his feedback would be positive."

A sensational answer! A surreal moment in the torture chamber. I wondered if he'd heard what he'd said: He didn't talk to James because he didn't want to receive positive feedback on me!

"Lauren, I need to give you an overall rating. In assessing your performance this last twelve months, I rate you a three."

Surprise, surprise! But it was still like a dentist's drill hitting an exposed nerve. The same rating as last year—a three, meeting expectations, average. I decided to argue, to use the confidence I'd found when I'd stood up to Kurt and the inspiration I'd gained from James—the way he'd handled his coach's encounter and the way he held to his values at the executive meeting.

"That's pretty tough, Marcus." No, that was the wrong response. It would appeal to Marcus's tough-guy self-image. But I kept going, this time more carefully. "I think that rating is unfair. I don't think you've taken into account the nature of my role nor the impact I've had."

"Well, sometimes I need to make a call on things," he answered in a measured tone. "I know that won't please everyone."

"I'm asking you to reconsider the rating," I said, proud of myself for arguing.

"No, I won't do that. I think it is accurate," he said, his hands hitting the table. "A three is a good rating."

Rubbish, I thought. Like Ben had said last year, if it was a good rating it wouldn't need to be explained that way.

"I don't see it that way," I said. "In other roles I had in my other company, I always performed well and always scored high ratings. I have never been given an average rating—not before coming to Harlow Kane."

"Well, this might be a higher performing company with more capable staff you're competing with," he declared. What nonsense. So now he was okay with competition among his team. Maybe he should've put those words back in his mouth too.

"Marcus, can you please give me the one-liner explaining the reason for my three rating?"

"The main reason is you have not produced measurable outputs on your key job objective, which is to revise our core marketing strategy, our branding, and our products and services."

"But I have made significant progress. It's just that you haven't been available to hear about it."

"Well, I will make myself available. I will make it a three, which allows you scope for a higher rating when you deliver. It will give you something to strive for next year."

"But I'm on track with outputs."

"Look, Lauren, I'm being criticized by Nicholas over the lack of outputs on our marketing strategy. This is your responsibility. Nicholas doesn't know what you do."

He was wearing me down. Who was doing this appraisal anyway—Marcus or Nicholas? Maybe Marcus was giving me a tough time so he could please Nicholas and get a high rating for himself, if in fact he got appraised by Nicholas. Or was he merely being Nicholas's puppet? It was all too complicated.

Marcus looked at his watch.

"That's all, Lauren. Your rating stands. I will make myself available to review your project. And hopefully, you will achieve a two rating next year."

After leaving Marcus's office, I went for a walk to clear my head. The appraisal was demoralizing, but it wasn't as bad as last time. I'd defended myself and felt less of a victim; the hurt was not as severe. I walked past James's desk. I wanted to tell him that I had confronted Marcus, but he wasn't in.

At home that night, I told Paul about my appraisal. He agreed it sounded like an energy-sapping experience.

"But hey! I'm proud of you. You stuck up for yourself." He hugged me. "Sounds like you held your own."

"I did," I said with a broad smile.

"That's great. Now, let's put it in perspective by planning what we'll do next weekend." He cupped his mouth with his hand and yelled out to Annie and Harry.

They came racing into the room. Paul grabbed Harry. I hugged Annie and tickled her. She giggled.

"Do you want to plan something special for this weekend?" Paul laughed.

"You betcha!"

38

The Money Talk

RUMOR HAD IT that the average pay increase was four and a half percent this year, and with reviews over, we began the waiting game to see if we were slated to get more or less than the average amount.

Marcus phoned and asked me to see him. I gave Sandra and Emily the uppercut signal and went up to the twentieth floor.

"Lauren, I would like to advise you of your pay review," he started. Remembering last year's discussion, I held my breath. "I am pleased to tell you that I have increased your pay by four percent. At your recent appraisal, I said that I consider you are doing a satisfactory job. As we discussed, there are some things that you are doing well, and there are some things that need improvement. I had some concerns about your relationship with some of the team, and feedback from the executive team was mixed."

He'd hit my emotion button. I felt flattened and defensive, fighting his attempt to make me feel worthless. I wanted him to slow down, but I didn't want to show him my feelings. I reminded myself of my last confrontation with him and took heart. I prepared to defend myself. I visualized how strong I would feel after this.

"Can we take that one step at a time please, Marcus?" I asked politely. "First of all, four percent is quite disappointing."

"Four percent is about the average increase," he said.

"As I understand it, guidance to managers is four point five percent, which means I am lower than average. I don't see myself as an average or below-average performer."

"Well, four to four point five is average," he admitted.

"Marcus, was the guidance to managers four or four point five percent? Which is it?"

Marcus must have worked out that he'd been caught and told the truth. "The guidance to managers is four point five, but in our team the average increase is four."

Did he know what he'd just said? He'd just admitted he'd shortchanged the team. He was digging himself into a hole.

"That means you didn't spend all the money you could have on the team's pay raises," I said, joining the dots. "Why would you not spend the budget that you could on our salary reviews?" I quickly calculated he was saving about four thousand dollars on his total annual budget, and probably making himself look good to his boss in the process. Why is it that some managers think they are spending from their own wallets?

"I think, given the overall performance of the team, four percent is about right," Marcus answered.

No, he doesn't know what comes out of his mouth. I threw caution to the wind. "If the performance of a team is really below average, don't you think that would reflect on the manager of the team as much as on the team itself?"

He wasn't fazed. "In my case, no, because I'm still lifting the team's performance from when I took over. I think that we are making improvements in our deliverables and by next year we should be a high-performing team."

It was all about Marcus. He didn't appear to care in the least. For him, calculating salary increases was just a routine transaction. On the radar, off the radar. Did he think we never thought about these things or talked to other people? What did he think I would say to Paul when I got home? Gosh, it probably never crossed his mind that I would talk to my husband about work, and if it did, it wouldn't bother him. Talk about banging my head against a brick wall!

"Matter closed then," I said, taking control and beating him to the punch.

He pulled out my salary review letter and signed it with his extravagant, swirling signature. As I stood, he slowly folded the letter into an envelope, passed it to me, and waited for me to leave.

Standing over Marcus, I said, "I'm not happy about this, Marcus. And I don't understand why you don't get behind me, get me fired up and enthusiastic for the job I'm trying to do. Why do you cut my energy? Why do you treat me as if I'm just a pawn? Remember—I'm on your team."

Not waiting for his response, I turned and walked out, cool as a cucumber, hiding the fact that my legs had just turned to jelly.

Over lunch at our favorite café the following week, some of the team gossiped about their salary review meetings with Marcus.

"What annoys me," Emily began, "is that when new people are employed, they often get paid more than people who have worked at the place for years. Sometimes you wonder if you would be better off leaving and coming back. It's so unfair for people who have been loyal for so long." Emily must have had a disappointing review with Marcus too.

"It's all to do with the system," Ben explained. "The system sets pay grades and ranges for everyone. The paradox is that the system has more control over the salaries of current staff than new staff. When new people come, managers decide the pay grade and the position within the pay range for that grade. But for current staff, any review of grade and pay has to go through a long, drawn-out process. The manager has to submit a case to HR, and then it goes before an executive meeting. The system makes it very difficult for a current staff member to have their grade changed, and it's difficult for any pay raise to be granted other than the annual increase."

Everyone started swapping review stories. Ben told us he'd missed out on a pay review one year. He had no idea if his name fell off the spreadsheet or if it was a deliberate zero increase. "Even if it wasn't changing, I should have at least been told!"

I shared a story about Deadly Di Ashman. "She never met with people face-to-face to hand them their salary review letters. She would make sure they'd gone to lunch or were in a meeting, throw the letters on their desks, and then run away."

"I once received a recognition award like that," said Sandra Pearson. "I'd done a really good job on a project. I got an award for my efforts and for the great feedback we received from clients. I got a lovely letter from my boss, but, same as you, Lauren, it was just dropped on my desk!"

"This same manager," I continued, laughing, relieved to be able to find humor in any discussion about Di Ashman, "couldn't give compliments. She would always add 'but' if she fell into giving one. Once, she came by my desk and said that she had received some good feedback on a presentation I'd given. You could see her mind working—*'Hold on, I've just given a compliment'*—because then she added, 'But we'll have to wait and see if we get any business out of it.' That was pretty mean, I thought."

"I think it's all about the manager's own insecurities," said Ben. "Some don't want to pass on good news or give compliments. Some think if you're doing well, then that means they're not. They see the world as a ledger system that has to balance out." I could identify with that, thanks to Deadly Di *and* Marcus Pomfrey.

"Meg Montgomery was great at giving recognition," said Sandra. "She would pick her moment and present an award in front of the whole team. She was always very sincere with her words. And what was really special is that she would then follow up afterward by calling the person into a room and having a quiet word of appreciation. She'd point out specifically what she appreciated. The other thing we valued is that she wouldn't necessarily wait for a project to be completed before it was recognized. If it was well on track and heading toward success, she wouldn't hesitate to acknowledge you. It was always assumed that you would finish the task successfully, and you made sure you did! It was very motivating. If your manager believes in you, it's much easier to believe in yourself."

What a pity I'd worked for Meg only one day.

"James Swann is like that. He's good at showing appreciation," said Emily. "Once, not long after I came back from maternity leave, I was working on a project for James that took me away from home for two weeks. It was a tough time for my husband and me, but I really wanted to do the assignment. Well, James sent a letter of appreciation home to Jack, acknowledging the impact my business trip was having on us, and offering any help he could. Jack and I really appreciated that."

Wow, I thought, *it was a simple act of appreciation, but how powerful—good for you, James.* I would love to have a manager like that!

Time was running out and we quickly finished up our lunches.

Ben had the last word. "Just remember this. A salary review reveals lots about a manager. It's like a personality test—about them, not us. If managers are generous, it's a reflection of their generous spirit and their satisfaction with themselves. If managers use complex formulae to calculate increases, it shows their preoccupation with detail and the comfort they get from hiding behind figures. When managers blame HR for having to decide things in a certain way, they're showing their own lack of courage. Some managers think they're spending their own money, which shows they're stingy. Some use salary reviews as a tool of power, which shows their need for exercising power. Don't take it too seriously. It's about them, not us."

We paid for lunch and went back to work. For me, that meant the final parts of my Strategic Marketing Review. I felt slightly better after the lunchtime banter with my colleagues. Obviously, I was just one of many who'd suffered through another lousy salary review. There was some weird sense of relief in that.

On our way back to the office, I caught up with Ben and asked him more about his views on bosses.

"Ben, you know what you were saying about bosses' actions being a reflection of their personality? Why do you think so many bosses are so tough to work for?"

He smiled. "Well, my theory is that there are two causes of this problem. First, what you see in many managers are the things that served them really well early in their careers—you know, behavior that is competitive, arrogant, and aggressive. For one reason or another, they progress and keep getting promoted. They rely more and more on that behavior, which—in their minds—earned them those promotions. When they get into management, they use the same behavior repeatedly to get what they want."

"And the second thing?" I asked.

"Power." He rubbed his chin. "It goes to some people's heads when they get it."

"I have a hard time with that kind of attitude," I responded.

"That's because you're not driven by power and competitiveness. You're no match, I'm afraid, Lauren."

"Yes," I agreed. "I guess that's a good thing."

We walked comfortably in silence for a few moments.

"You know," said Ben, "the system's also pretty tough on bosses. In the end, they find out that they are either on the way up or on the way out!"

I burst into laughter. "Thank you, Ben!"

39

Trying for First Base

DESPITE MORE OBSTACLES THAN A STEEPLECHASE, I made terrific progress in my review of Harlow Kane's marketing and branding strategy. I had a good idea of the nature of products and services that could position the company well for the next ten years. Especially exciting was the anthropological review. Sally and I had uncovered insights both simple and profound. This gave us interesting new ideas for our strategy to the market and our competitive positioning.

I was tremendously excited about how it had all come together and the breakthrough approach contained in my report. I was sure it fulfilled Meg's original vision. The new strategy was substantial, with millions of dollars at stake. If it worked, our revenue, market share, and profit would improve significantly.

The time had come to win executive support, but based on past experience, I knew I would need to tread carefully.

Because he was my boss, I needed Marcus to be familiar with the proposal and to be supportive of it. But trying to arrange a meeting with him that he'd keep was a hopeless endeavor.

In response to a desperate email I sent, Marcus suggested I go ahead and meet with the other executives. He would review their input with me after my round of meetings. This was risky, but I had to push on, so I went ahead.

Unfortunately, James Swann was away on an extended vacation. I would've liked to have gone through the presentation with him, but he was not due back for several more weeks.

I decided it was best to review the proposal with the executives individually. This would take more time, but I also knew from past experience that a review at one of their team meetings could well be the kiss of death for my ideas. It would take only one negative comment from someone to cause a whole chain of abuse. The idea could be accepted or rejected on a whim, or sabotaged by just one careless remark.

John Squires had made it clear that he looked to Nicholas Strange as the decision maker. Meanwhile, Nicholas relied on little but his friendships to guide his decisions. Still, if I had the support of the four sales and services directors by the time I was to meet with Nicholas, I would have a much better shot at getting him to agree to my plan. So I put a good deal of thought into the best sequence for individual meetings.

Because Jeremy and Maxine were so picky, they would be the hardest to convert. Picky and very, very nasty. James was away, and Ryan Gunn was at an executive development program.

I decided, then, that Gus Wearing would be the first person I should meet. He wasn't well thought of by the other executives, but he'd given me positive feedback when Marcus asked. He might listen to what I had to say without trying to cut me down on principle, and having one positive assessment would help me start the process on the right foot.

Although I knew Gus reasonably well, I had never presented an idea to him, so I needed advice from someone who had. I arranged to meet one of his sales reps, Veronica Baker. I'd become friendly enough with Veronica to ask her for any inside information she had on Gus.

"Well, it will be best if you meet with Gus on your own," she started. "He prefers one-on-ones rather than groups."

"Why is that?"

"He doesn't like things to get complicated. He wants to be in control."

"Okay. What else?"

"He won't want to go into any detail. Gus gets lost in detail, so keep it simple. Don't use more than five slides to explain yourself."

"Oh, you've got to be kidding!"

"Nope, I'm deadly serious. All of us who work closely with Gus know that more than five slides is pushing the limit of his attention."

I hadn't anticipated this. "That'll be hard," I told her. "This is probably one of the most important proposals Harlow Kane has dealt with in the last few years, and it doesn't lend itself to being explained in five slides!"

"Well, then, keep it simple and straightforward," she warned.

In the end, I had twenty-two slides with a file stacked full of backup information, if needed. The slides covered everything—market and social trends, the breakthrough anthropological research, competitor analysis, sales projections, sales incentives, product details, advertising and launch information, investment proposals, and financial returns—the complete package.

I practiced my presentation with Sandra and Ben the day prior to my meeting with Gus, and the next morning, I boldly headed up to Mission Control for my ten o'clock appointment.

Gus invited me into his office. I sat among the plants and photos of his golf trips. As usual, his table was covered in files. He looked puzzled at the sight of my stack of papers, but he obligingly cleared space so I could put everything down. Thank goodness he was wearing a white shirt so I wouldn't be distracted by his dandruff. I forced myself not to check out his shoes.

Following my plan, I put my detailed file to one side and placed my slide pack on the table in front of Gus. I sat on his right-hand side so I could flick through the slides with him. Deliberately, I hesitated before opening it up.

I told him about the proposal, how it was a comprehensive review that required a significant capital investment and therefore risk, yet it had the potential to propel the company forward in the market. I said that I was asking him, as sales and services director, for his support in helping to implement the strategy. I thought I detected a slight swelling of Gus's chest when I used the words "sales and services director," and he seemed to sit more upright in his chair.

As I covered the background, not yet opening my slide pack, he listened quietly. He fiddled with his pen, then absentmindedly put the blunt end of it first in one ear, then the other, cleaning each thoroughly.

I opened my folder of slides. He leaned across and flicked through the slides to see how many pages there were. I was about five slides into the presentation, at the point of summarizing the financial projection, when he stood up and began to walk out.

"Carry on without me," he said over his shoulder. And with that, he left.

I couldn't believe what was happening. I looked around. There had only been him and me, and now there was just me! How could I carry on? I sat, stunned and glued to my chair. I would have been speechless—if there'd been anyone there. Perhaps the plants had ears, or maybe the photos. Perhaps they were interested in my proposal.

Maybe Gus was in the bathroom. I checked with his assistant. No, she said he'd left, saying he was heading downstairs. I waited another five minutes, but he didn't return, so I packed up and left.

By twenty past ten, I was back at my desk, in a total daze over what had just happened.

"So, how'd it go?" Ben asked. He looked at my face, which must have been as white as snow judging from his reaction.

"What happened, Lauren?" he repeated. "Is everything okay?"

I looked at him and slowly shook my head, not quite ready to speak.

"Lauren, are you okay?"

Again, there was an anxious pause.

"I'm fine," I said, coming into the present. "Nothing drastic."

Ben waited. Within a few minutes, I was back on planet Earth and in the right time zone.

"I've just come out of the most amazing business meeting I have ever had," I began, shaking my head. "I was five slides into my presentation, just getting into some of the nitty-gritty, when Gus got up and left the room. He told me to carry on without him!"

Ben stared, open-mouthed.

"What did he expect me to do?" I continued. "Convince myself?"

"But . . . surely he'd been called out of the office by—"

"No, he hadn't," I insisted. "And he didn't come back, either. He didn't want to know the details, didn't want to have to make a decision . . . 'Carry on without me!'"

By this stage, Ben was starting to see the funny side. His lips curled to a grin, then his eyes sparkled, and finally he broke out into a huge belly laugh. Other people looked over.

Theatrically, Ben repeated, "Carry on without me" and moved away.

Ben's performance infected me. I started to giggle, then laughed uncontrollably as tears streamed down my cheeks.

I couldn't believe the story I would have for Paul that night.

I never heard back from Gus, so I turned my mind to the next executive on my list—Maxine "Wicked Witch of the West" Savage. And after her, Marcus, if I could manage to nail him to a time.

And I'd just been invited to the company's Strategic Planning Conference, which was only three weeks away. If I could speed things up and complete my presentations to the executives, I might be able to take the proposal to the conference.

40

Presenting to the Witch

TWO DAYS AFTER WASTING MY TIME WITH GUS, I was on my way to the nineteenth floor to meet with Maxine. She was now going to be the first executive to see my proposal—not what I'd planned, exactly.

I placed my files on one side of the conference table and waited patiently for Maxine to arrive, which wasn't too long.

Her walk hadn't changed—a wavering gait caused by heels too narrow for her shape. She had her hair tightly pulled back, and she was dressed in another tight suit that showed off every unflattering curve. She was her normal grumpy self.

I sat facing the glass window so Maxine would not be admiring her reflection. That way, I'd have just one Maxine to deal with!

"Hi, Maxine," I said confidently when she sat down. "Thank you for making the time to talk. I want to review with you the marketing strategy and branding proposal I've prepared. Before we start, would you like a drink—tea, coffee, water?"

"No, thank you." She folded her arms. "Let's get this over with. I have a meeting shortly, so let's just get into it."

"Sure," I responded, no longer surprised by her rudeness. I reached for my presentation pack. I glanced up and caught Maxine rolling her eyes. I was not, however, going to let her derail me.

"This review is the result of more than eighteen months' work and has involved a number of internal people and external stakeholders."

"Yes, I know. Can we get to the point?"

"I will get there shortly," I said forcefully.

I started with an explanation of the compelling reasons for the review. I quickly established the case for conducting the review of strategy, demonstrating that sales had flattened in the last three years and market share was static. During that same time frame, two of our key competitors had increased their market share at the expense of several smaller firms. Some smaller industry firms had failed in the last few years and were being consolidated into the larger firms. The need for change was obvious, even to Maxine.

She leaned forward in her chair, focusing on the information, her eyes locked on my charts. Good, I had her attention.

I moved to the external context in which we were operating. From the outstanding research conducted by Sally Morton, I painted a clear picture of the current social environment, of the trends causing changes in the social and political climate, and the predicted effect of those changes on consumer and business sentiment over the next ten years.

Maxine actually opened her pad and made a note!

Next, I talked specifically about marketing trends and quoted leading examples of companies in other industries that were responding successfully to the forces in the market.

Maxine questioned some of the examples, more for clarification than contention. She nodded thoughtfully.

I explained the anthropological research and the discovery of the meaning of service in our country.

"Was this like an archetype study?" she asked. Wow, she was speaking to me!

"That's right," I said, conscious that she had not been at the fateful executive meeting where I had presented the concept.

She made more notes.

I then moved to the implications and opportunities for Harlow Kane. Currently, none of our competitors had taken any breakthrough actions that had fundamentally altered their strategy.

I moved on to the options and explained the exciting recommendations—recommendations that had profound implications for our business and, if successful, would set us apart from our competitors. Part of the power of the breakthrough ideas was their simplicity.

Looking up from the page, I caught a glimpse of a subtle smile moving fleetingly across Maxine's face. Quickly, her face resumed its normal impassive expression.

"Now for the financial analysis," I said, turning the page. I included only the high-level summary. The business case was impressive and, provided the assumptions were valid, would generate an early positive cash flow. She tested me on a number of the assumptions but could find no flaw.

I moved to the proposed action plan to implement the idea. Again, she listened quietly.

Finally, I explained what might happen if we didn't take action: We would maintain our position in the short term, but our competitors would not be silent. We could expect to be in an increasingly weakened position, and if one of our competitors discovered ideas similar to the ones I was proposing, then we would seriously suffer. Doing nothing was not an option.

"So, that's it, that's my proposal," I concluded, turning the last page.

Silence. She checked her notes. She reached over, dragged my file closer to her, and flicked back three slides to the breakthrough actions.

"Is that it?"

"What do you mean, 'Is that it?'" I asked, confused.

"Is that the proposal?" she repeated.

"Yes."

"Just these recommendations?"

"Well, calling it "just these recommendations" diminishes their significance. These recommendations could alter the way we do business. It alters the go-to-market model we use and the value proposition that our clients see from us. It also alters our overall brand and what we want to be famous for."

"Frankly, Lauren," she said shifting in her chair and patting her hair, "it's a very flimsy proposition. In fact, I think it's a rather disappointing result from such a long project. I can see some value in the idea, but it's shallow."

My jaw clamped shut; I was speechless. Yes, she still had the power to shock me. I'd thought I had her convinced.

"Have you shown this to any of the other executives?" she frowned.

"No, not yet," I said weakly. "I've tried to review it with Marcus and Gus but haven't been able to."

"Tell you what," she said in an unusually friendly tone, "I'm prepared to help you. There are a few things I can do that I know will fix it. Do you want to leave the file with me and I'll think about it? In a week or two, we'll meet again and go over my improvements."

I smelled a rat. Why was she being so helpful all of a sudden? I couldn't work out her angle.

"What do you have in mind?" I asked, uncertain.

"I'm in a bit of a rush now, and I want to give myself plenty of time to think about it," she said and closed her pad.

"I don't know," I said, undecided. "Actually, I'm quite pleased with the proposal as it is. I believe it all holds together pretty well."

She waved her index finger at me. "Thing is, Lauren, I know the jury is still out on you," she said in a cutting tone. "I know for a fact that some of the senior executives don't like you. They doubt that you are adding any value at all. Some even wonder why you're here." She threw up her hands. "You need my help. If you miss the mark on this, then the future will be bleak for you." She finished with a squinting glare.

I panicked. I knew from Kurt's rumormongering that some negative things had been said about me, but I didn't know it was this bad! I tried to think quickly.

I was in a bind. On the one hand, I had to be open to suggestions. I had to make this proposal work: I knew it deserved to be successful; it was a world-class solution, one that would be the envy of our competitors. If Maxine had improvements to make, then shouldn't I listen? This was what reviews were all about—taking comments from the executives so the proposal would more likely gain support at the executive meeting. I didn't want to run into a problem like I'd had with the email. I knew what the gossip would be: Lauren didn't want anyone's help.

On the other hand, I definitely did not want to lose control of the proposal. This was my work, my blood, sweat, and tears gone into every tiny detail. What if it got stolen, like my sales rep training idea? No, I couldn't let that happen again. This was mine!

I quickly decided, however, that there was a middle ground.

"Look, Maxine, I would really appreciate your ideas, but I won't leave the pack with you. I need it in a few days to take Nicholas through the proposal, and I still need to review it all with Marcus too. Perhaps we could meet in a couple of weeks to go through any suggestions you have."

"How about emailing me a soft copy?" She had the friendly tone switched on again.

"No, it's still a draft," I answered. Maybe I was being paranoid, but I had been bitten before.

"Okay," she said, "then just let me make a few notes from some of the key slides." She opened her pad again and quickly flicked the pages back to the beginning and made a few notes on the key topics. When she'd finished, she looked up. "It's a good start."

A good start! How patronizing—a good start. She was the total package!

"Yes . . . a good start," she repeated, to make sure I'd heard her insult. "But it does need more work. I'll see what I can do. I'm sure I can add value to it and make it a really good proposal. It will be a challenge, but I have extensive experience in these things and I'm sure, with some thought, I can solve everything."

What could I say?

"Thank you, Maxine," I lied. "I appreciate it. I will contact you in about two weeks and talk about it with you then."

"I'll be at the Strategic Planning Conference in three weeks," she said. "We could meet after that."

"Yes," I said, "I'm going too. Could we—"

"Are you?" she interrupted, eyebrows raised.

"Yes. I'm going as the second Marketing representative and also because of my role in strategy."

"Fair enough," she said, shaking her head.

What was that for? She was probably thinking that all sorts of undesirables were being let into the planning meetings these days.

"Okay," she said, standing on her unsteady heels. "I'll see you later. I will do what I can to help you get it to a stage where you can be proud of it."

She left the room, steadying herself with the door frame in her rush.

I stayed behind, my energy sapped, just as it had been in every other interaction I'd had with Maxine. Once again depressed and battle scarred, I dragged myself back to my desk.

41
Driving Mr. Marcus

OKAY—THIS HAD TO BE THE DAY. By eight-fifteen in the morning, I was at my desk checking my emails and going over my presentation pack once more.

After five failed attempts to meet with Marcus to take him through my final proposal, I'd become increasingly frustrated and annoyed. I wanted—no, needed—the marketing director, *my boss*, to be fully informed and supportive.

Despite Gus Wearing's disinterest and Maxine Savage's patronizing response, I was incredibly proud of my idea and excited by the impact it should have on the business. I hoped others would also see it that way, but I needed my boss's support. It was critical that I see him.

In the back of my mind, I was terrified that a competitor would develop similar ideas and we would lose our advantage. But the whole proposal was being stalled by my inability to nail Marcus to a chair long enough for him to listen. Hopefully, this would be the day.

My meeting with Marcus was to start at ten-thirty. Just as I was wrapping up a discussion with Ben Bowser at ten-twenty, my cell phone flashed Marcus's number on the display screen. Great, I thought, here we go again; yet another cancellation. Expecting another lame excuse from Marcus, I apologized to Ben and answered the phone.

No, this time it was only a change of venue. Marcus wanted us to meet in the company car while he was being driven to an appointment across the city.

After finishing the call, I exclaimed to Ben, "How do you ever succeed in nailing Marcus to a meeting?"

"I catch him at the urinal," answered Ben, deadpan.

Five minutes later, I was greeting Albert, the chauffeur of one of the Harlow Kane company cars. Albert was in his late fifties and was a little paunchy, probably from sitting around in cars too much. As usual, he wore a white shirt, bow tie, and a chauffeur's cap. The car, a sleek late model black Mercedes, was made available exclusively to the top executives. Albert spent his days delivering our busy executives to their various meetings in and around the city.

I decided to sit in the back so I could be next to Marcus, who hadn't yet arrived.

"Hi, Albert," I greeted him as I settled into the soft leather seat. "How's your day going?"

"Great, thanks, Lauren. I'm looking forward to my grandson's birthday party this evening. How's everything with you?"

"Very good, thank you. I really need some time with Marcus, so I hope we're going a decent distance from here." I had decided to bring only one file with me—the summary charts. I put them on the seat next to me and placed my handbag on the floor near my legs.

"You should have about twenty minutes or so, depending on traffic."

"Mmm, maybe not quite enough," I said, thinking it was still better than a cancellation. "Perhaps you could drive slowly," I quipped. Albert laughed.

"Or you could talk really fast!" he joked back.

"Hey, so what did you get your grandson for his birthday?"

"You know what, Lauren, he gets so excited every year, I don't actually give him a present. He and I play this birthday game where I let him search my pockets until he finds the ten-dollar bill I hide. Only trick is, I have to make sure I take my wallet out of my pocket first, in case he thinks I've turned supergenerous!"

Marcus jumped into the car. "Hi, Lauren. Good morning, Albert. Let's get going. I'm a bit late." On no, he'd got into the front seat next to Albert. I had to say something.

"Marcus, would you mind sitting in the back with me, so I can discuss the Strategic Marketing Review?" He hesitated. I tried another line to convince him. "This is the review you committed to do at my performance appraisal."

"Oh, yes, Lauren," he said happily and skipped around the side of the car and got in next to me.

"Are we going across town to Peach Hills?" asked Albert as we drew away from the curb.

"Yep," mumbled Marcus, smoothing his hair into place and flattening his tie under the seatbelt.

"So, Marcus," I ventured, "there is so much to cover. Do you have a preference for what comes first?"

"No, Lauren—shoot from the top. Hey, speaking of which," Marcus shouted to Albert, "Albert, did I tell you about my basketball game last week?" I hadn't heard so much excitement in Marcus's voice for a while, maybe ever.

"No, you didn't, sir," answered Albert, glancing in the rearview mirror at me. I shook my head and looked out the window.

"What a triumph!" continued Marcus. "I was in top form—you should've seen me. We were tied at halftime, going basket for basket in the second half."

Marcus then gave a blow-by-blow description of the entire second half. I drifted in and out of the conversation. Albert was slightly more engaged.

"We were down by one point with ten—no, seven—seconds to go," said Marcus like an overexcited child. "The opposition was in a forward press, hoping to seal the game, when I intercepted a pass." He grabbed an imaginary ball from my hands. "I beat one player," he faked in his seat one way, "then beat another," he faked the other way, almost throwing his head on my shoulder, "and had an open path to the basket, scoring the winning point with two seconds to go—two seconds, Albert!" He dunked the make-believe ball into the front seat. "What a win!"

"Wow, that's fantastic," said Albert. "But don't mind me if you and Lauren want to talk work."

"How about you, Lauren," said Marcus, appearing not to hear Albert, "are you into sports?"

"My family and I do like sports. We used to do a fair bit of sailing before the children were born," I answered, deliberately keeping it short.

"And anything else?" asked Marcus.

"Oh, some basketball."

Marcus didn't respond. Perhaps he didn't hear me. I may have mumbled.

"Last year," he said, "I went to the open tennis championship. Got invited into a corporate box by one of our consultants. Now, that's the way to see tennis."

This was hopeless.

"Watching the sport played at such a high standard really brings back a lot of memories of my own career," continued Marcus.

"I didn't realize you had an athletic career, Marcus," I interrupted, panicking. "I would love to hear more about it when we have more time. Let me show you—" I reached for my file on the seat.

"I was there for the classic match of the championship last year." Oh, joy. I switched off for the next few minutes. ". . . and after the match, all the players got mobbed by the fans."

"They must get tired of the constant exposure," I said, coming back to the present.

"Can't imagine that!" Marcus laughed. "Who could ever get tired of all that admiration? You know, Nicholas was there with me last year."

"That's great, Marcus," I jumped in, wondering how he linked admiration with Nicholas. "Speaking of Nicholas, I'm sure he will be very eager to know how we're progressing with this project, and it would be great to brief him soon. Let's go through the key parts of my presentation so we can make any adjustments before my meeting with him next week."

"Sure," said Marcus, "but you'd better hurry up. We have only a few minutes left—the traffic is unusually light today."

I wanted to scream. Instead, I reversed the usual order of the presentation and rushed through the key numbers first, to try to capture his attention with the potential of the idea before I got to the concept itself. I could see a total lack of interest as he snuck the occasional glance out the car window.

"Okay, Lauren," said Marcus as we pulled up beside the curb, "are we nearly done?"

"Well, Marcus, we've really only started. I haven't even gotten to the key concept yet. Can we just stay in the car another ten minutes and we could almost cover it, at least in summary?" I wanted to beg, I was that desperate.

"No, sorry, Lauren. I'm running late as it is. I don't like keeping people waiting. Let's talk back at the office."

I wanted to shout. "It's really important we make the time so I can keep going on the project."

"Definitely, Lauren—catch you later."

Marcus jumped out of the car and was gone.

"So, where to next for you?" asked Albert, smiling at me in the rearview mirror.

Where next indeed, I pondered. With my project review and Marcus? I didn't have the slightest idea!

"Back to the office, thanks, Albert."

"Okay," he said, steering the car back into traffic.

Another failed attempt at trying to brief Marcus.

I didn't want to be angry with Albert. "Thank you, Albert. We're really lucky to have this chauffeur service. It must save incredible amounts of time for our senior people, helping them stay focused on their jobs and not having to worry about driving themselves around."

"Y . . . yes," hesitated Albert, "it certainly helps them."

"By the way, what was Marcus's appointment?" I asked.

Albert gave me a smirk in the rearview mirror. "He's getting his hair cut."

42

Fate

EXECUTIVE SUPPORT OR NOT, I still wanted to share my idea with Nicholas. I strongly believed that the proposal provided a breakthrough for Harlow Kane. I knew that somewhere in the company I would eventually find a champion who could see the possibilities and support me.

Ultimately, it was Nicholas Strange who would decide whether the idea was a winner and whether it would be accepted. Ultimately, I would need to review it with him. Maybe fate was playing a hand and I was destined to review it with Nicholas before most of the others—so better sooner than later.

Then Nicholas's assistant called to cancel my appointment with him. Something urgent had come up. So much for fate. I had hoped to share my proposal with him before the following week's Strategic Planning Conference. Nicholas's next available time wouldn't be until the week after the conference. For the time being, I could do nothing more to win support. I would just have to wait.

The reason for Nicholas being unable to meet me soon spread like wildfire throughout the company.

"Have you heard the news?" Ben Bowser whispered over my shoulder as I returned to my desk. "Jeremy Hyde has resigned!"

"What?! When?"

"Just now."

"Trust you to be the first with the news. Why has he resigned?"

"Don't know," said Ben. "But I'll find out. Sexual harassment or something, I'll bet. I'll get back to you when I know more."

Within a few hours, John Squires sent a brief email to all staff saying that, unfortunately, Jeremy Hyde had resigned for personal reasons. John went on to explain how much he had enjoyed working with Jeremy and what a strong contribution Jeremy had made to the growth of Harlow Kane. I'd thought when John sent the note about Meg that it had been sweet and sincere, but perhaps he did this for everyone who left—who could sincerely have enjoyed Jeremy?

The situation ignited the gossip fires. Everyone knows senior people don't just resign "for personal reasons." Only the truth would extinguish the flames.

Everyone had a theory. One was that Jeremy had been found in a compromising position with another staff member. Another was that he had bullied people once too often. Another was that there were illegal financial practices that had been exposed. Another was that Jeremy's elderly mother had become seriously ill and Jeremy had resigned to provide her with full-time care. That last rumor fizzled quickly.

Ben hung around the corridors for a few days and came back with what he guaranteed was the undeniable truth. He took a few of his trusted buddies out to coffee to fill us in.

"Okay," he began, after coffees had been ordered, "what happened was that Jeremy had been accused of bullying by a person in accounting who recently resigned."

"Did the person resign because of that?" asked Emily.

"That's only part of it," Ben insisted. He was not going to be denied telling the story his way. "Mary Spelling resigned a few weeks ago. Soon after, her lawyer wrote to John Squires alleging that Mary had been bullied by Jeremy over an extended period of time. The bullying had such a traumatic impact on Mary that she was unable to work." Ben looked at me. "Mary and John go back a long way together in the company, so John really paid attention to what Mary was saying." Ben looked back to the others. "John met with her. No doubt he got the real story from Mary about how Jeremy operates and the effect he has. There was no doubting Mary's sincerity and the extent of her trauma. And at the end of the day, John is a decent person."

Ben glanced around to see if anyone else was in earshot. "When Jeremy found out about the letter from Mary's lawyer, he exploded. He went looking for Mary's close friends here at work and tore into them about what Mary had done."

"Goodness," Emily said, "he dug a big hole for himself, stupid idiot. But certainly true to form." Our coffees arrived.

"Well, in John's meeting with Mary it got very interesting. Mary spilled the beans to John about a scandalous business practice that has emerged in the company over the last year," continued Ben. "Jeremy, and presumably Nicholas, have been misrepresenting our financial performance." A waiter came to see if we wanted anything else. We waved him away.

"What's the business practice?" I asked, concerned about any illegal or questionable practice.

"I'll bet it was the overstating of revenue at the end of each quarter," Sandra said.

"What do you mean?" I asked, intrigued.

"How it works," Ben jumped in, "is that on the last day of the quarter, trucks are loaded with product and shipped out of the warehouse to real customers. Once the product leaves the warehouse, it's recorded as a sale. The only problem is that the customers haven't ordered the product. So the trucks sit overnight, the product is recorded as a sale in the quarter just closed, and then it's returned to the warehouse the next day and recorded as a credit."

"That's disgusting!" I exclaimed. I would not have believed a reputable company like Harlow Kane would deliberately falsify the books. "But wait, wouldn't the next quarter start with negative revenue, then?" I asked.

"That's the game, really. You're betting that the next quarter's revenue will be growing strongly enough to cover the negative start. It works while the market is growing. If the market drops, then it backfires and comes crashing down," said Ben. "It's been going on for at least a year."

"And everyone knows about this?" I asked, floored. "How could the executives be so blatantly dishonest and throw their credibility out the window? And what about other staff at the warehouse and in accounting? They would have to be in on it too. How could so many people look the other way?"

Emily shrugged her shoulders. "It happens in suppressive dictatorships—people turning a blind eye," she observed nonchalantly.

"But surely Nicholas and John would have to know," I said.

"Well, probably in the case of Nicholas. Only possibly in John's case—he misses a lot. The scheme has only recently emerged, so most likely it's Nicholas's doing. Anyway, it's not provable. Nicholas is smart, and he's clever enough to have a fall guy in Jeremy to protect himself."

Sandra added, "Yep, I heard about it at the end of last quarter."

Yuck. I felt tainted just knowing about it.

"So, anyway, John had had enough and told Jeremy that it was the end of the road. He let him resign with so-called dignity. The reaction in Finance has been ecstatic. They're all going out for a victory dinner on Friday night."

"And now," I reached down for my bag and my wallet, "having been motivated by all of that, Ben, we are supposed to go back to work and slave away for the company?" I put my money on the table. "Who's coming?"

On the way back to the office, I walked with Emily and asked her how she was doing.

She moved closer to me and whispered, "I'm pregnant!" She put her finger to her lips to signal it was a secret.

"That's great! Congratulations," I whispered.

"I'm telling only a few people at the moment. I don't want Marcus to know until I'm showing. I can't predict how he'll react."

I touched her elbow. "I'll hug you when we're on our own. I'm so happy for you!"

43

The Luv-In, Not

I HUGGED ANNIE AND HARRY and kissed Paul good-bye as I set off early on the morning of the Strategic Planning Conference. Even though I would be back the next night, I was still going to miss them.

The conference was being held at a vineyard resort, about a three-hour drive from the city—an ideal setting for two days of reflection and planning. Having worked at the company less than two years, I was delighted to be included in setting the future direction of the business. I looked forward to the whole experience.

As I drove, I listened to my favorite music—a mix of symphonic works and songs from musicals. The conference was due to start at ten-thirty, after brunch. I arrived at the vineyard at ten o'clock, checked in, and was shown to my room by a bellhop who pointed out the conference room we'd be using. When we got to my room, he made a great show of opening the curtains, proudly revealing a private terrace overlooking the vineyard. In the bright sunshine, the vineyard looked picture-perfect. I would've loved to have been enjoying this with Paul especially. Maybe it was time to start looking into a big family trip.

When the bellhop had gone, I unpacked my few clothes, gathered up my conference file, and went down to brunch.

The heads of each department would be at the event, plus a number of other Harlow Kane people of different roles, ages, and lengths of service. I knew about half of them. Ryan Gunn was back from his development program. John Squires and Nicholas Strange, as well as Hugh Worrell, Maxine Savage, and Gus Wearing, would all attend. I knew James would be back from his vacation by now; I would keep my eye out for him. Marcus, as marketing director, obviously had to attend. Jeremy, of course, was missing. I didn't know who had taken his place.

I popped into the conference room, put my files on the nearest table, and then went to find the coffee. The breakout area was spacious, with luxurious lounge and reading areas. I knew that twenty-five people, plus an external facilitator, were attending the conference. It looked like most everyone had arrived; the room was noisy with the din of chatter. Ryan was talking earnestly with John. Maxine, Hugh, and Marcus were laughing together. Nicholas was sitting alone in one of the leather chairs with a newspaper spread out in front of him, a cell phone to his ear.

I served myself coffee and a scone and looked around for a friendly face. Oh, wonderful, James was over at the glass doors opening out to the vineyard.

As I made my way over to him, Maxine cut away from Hugh and Marcus and waved her hand at me to stop. She bustled over, teetering on her dangerously narrow high heels.

"Hi, Lauren," she smiled, trying to sound friendly. "It's good to see you." We made polite conversation about our travel to the retreat. I wanted to join James.

"By the way," she asked nonchalantly, "did you get to review your strategic marketing presentation with Nicholas and Marcus, like you planned?"

"No, I didn't. We're planning to catch up in the next week or so. You're the only one who's seen it properly so far." Maxine nodded and said she was going for coffee.

I moved over to James, who was talking to someone I didn't know. James smiled broadly, clearly pleased to see me. He introduced me to George Banks from Finance, who was attending in Jeremy's place. George and I shook hands. James looked tanned and relaxed. He asked me about my project, and as an aside, quickly explained to George what I was working on. I told James I'd love to review it with him, but we'd have to wait until after the retreat. I also wanted to hear all about his vacation, but the conference was about to start and we separated to find our seats.

I collected my files from the table where I'd left them and found my seat—between Gus on my right and Hugh on my left. I wondered how I was unlucky enough to get this seat. The only clue I could think of was that someone wanted the few women in the room to be evenly spaced apart. Oh, and people from the same departments had been separated from each other. Well, at least I didn't have to sit next to Marcus.

There wasn't much room as I squeezed in between the two men, who were already seated. Hugh grunted hello and occupied himself with text messages on his phone. Gus greeted me brightly and sat back with his hands behind his head, underarms in close proximity to my nose. I hoped we wouldn't be doing any outdoor activities! I hadn't seen Gus since the absurd "carry on" meeting. He didn't appear to be feeling embarrassed about it, though.

Alison Weeks, the organizer, called everyone to attention and opened the meeting. She greeted us and gave a special welcome to our facilitator, Christopher Robertson. She then asked us to take a couple of minutes to introduce ourselves to the rest of the room and describe our roles at Harlow Kane. Most people spoke briefly, but a few droned on—Ryan, Hugh, and Marcus being the main culprits.

The introductions completed, Alison moved to a flip chart and revealed a prepared list on the pad of paper. She stood back from the board and clapped her hands.

"There are seven rules at this conference," she said firmly. "Rule number one, we will not defend past decisions. Rule number two, we will not use our positions to intimidate others to agree with us. Rule three, we will be open to new ideas. Rule four, we will respect the dignity of others by listening to what they have to say. Rule five, we will not kill ideas. Rule six, we will believe in the process. And Rule seven, we will encourage maximum participation." She tore off the paper and stuck it to the nearest wall.

She then switched to an "icebreaker." Each of us was asked to draw an animal that we felt represented the nature of Harlow Kane currently. I thought about a few different animals, but my explanation for choosing some of them would get me into hot water. Gus whispered to me that he chose a camel. "Because it's relatively self-sufficient, stores up resources that are needed, carries its load, and always gets there." Hugh kept his head down and didn't say anything.

I laughed to Gus, "Mine's an ape. We work in a community, there are social norms, we have leaders, we are under threat, and we need to adapt to survive."

When it was clear from the increasing level of noise that everyone had decided on an animal, Alison walked over to one side of the room and invited people to show their sketches.

The room suddenly grew quiet and tense. People snuck sideways glances at Nicholas, no doubt trying to assess his mood, evaluating whether it was safe to contribute.

From the other side of the room, John saved the day. "I've chosen a cow!" He held up his picture and laughed at himself. "Although it looks nothing like a cow."

"We agree with everything you've said!" laughed James. Glad to have the tension broken, everybody else laughed as well.

John explained, "I've chosen a cow because a cow is solid, harmless, and dependable, and cows produce the goods."

Alison thanked John for going first. She asked for another volunteer.

Ryan's hand shot up. "When I was at Harvard, I spent time thinking about where we are as a business. I think of us as a cheetah—sleek, efficient, fast, able to change course quickly, and up and about early for food." He smiled in his smug way.

I glanced over to Nicholas, who was nodding approvingly at Ryan.

Gus shared his camel and I contributed my ape. One of the younger members of the group, whom I hadn't met before, said he thought the company was an elephant ". . . because we are top-heavy, driven by older people with experience but who aren't out for challenges, aren't very focused on work, and aren't that hungry."

Nicholas changed visibly—a red shade crossed his face. He whacked his hand on the table, clenched his teeth, and snarled to Alison, "Where's all this taking us?" He dismissively waved his hand. "Let's move on."

Alison remained composed. "Okay, that's where we might be right now. Let's turn to where we want to be." We had to draw an animal that represented the desired future state of Harlow Kane.

Within minutes, zoological pictures flowed easily and safely. This time I chose a penguin—fast, flexible, adaptable, streamlined, an effective feeder who nurtures its young and looks smart.

Hugh suggested, "We'll be a leopard—nimble, strong, fast moving, and powerful—not that we aren't already."

One of the young participants was about to say something when Maxine spoke over her, "We'll continue our evolution and be even more of a thoroughbred racehorse: We win races, we are well-disciplined, we are agile, fast, and focused. But we are vulnerable to injury." She laughed at her own joke.

After a few more ideas were shared, Alison brought the exercise to a close. "Thank you, everyone, that was excellent!" She bowed slightly.

"I'll now hand you over to John, who will formally open the conference and set the scene for what we hope to gain over the next two days."

John extracted his long body from his chair and moved to the front of the room.

"Good morning all, and welcome! Here at Harlow Kane, we have had an excellent few years," he began. "We have righted the ship. We have achieved the targets we have set out to achieve. We have good revenue and profits, and we have a reasonable degree of customer satisfaction. We have a lot to be thankful for. But we cannot be complacent. The world around us is changing, and we need to change too, if we're to continue to be successful. The challenge for the next two days is to plan where we need to be in five years' time and what the key steps will be over the next twelve months to achieve our five-year plan. The future is in our hands, and it is up to us to create that future."

John moved to the other side of the room. "I have invited the heads of departments to prepare a summary of performance for the last year. We'll go through each of these in turn." He looked at Nicholas. "Nicholas, would you like to present the update on the Operations group, please?"

Nicholas stood up, and as he moved to the front, Alison started up a slide presentation.

He gave a glowing summary of revenue, profit, and customer satisfaction at a company level. He then moved on to the divisional picture. A slide was shown of revenue by division.

"The only problem division we have is the Eastern Division . . ." There was an audible sigh from Gus. I felt sorry for him. ". . . and we must address the issue in the east or face changes." There was no doubt what Nicholas meant by that—Gus would either be moved or sacked.

Nicholas moved on to the profit result by division with a similar message and then to customer satisfaction. The customer satisfaction result showed that Gus's division performed reasonably well, while Maxine's Western Division was lowest.

Nicholas waved his hand. "I don't put much faith in these results." He looked at Marcus. "Marcus, we really need to make a better attempt at measuring customer satisfaction more reliably."

Marcus nodded thoughtfully. "I agree," he said, easily removing himself from the problem. "I'll be giving it to a better member of my team to manage."

Nicholas carried on and gave Operations an overall performance score of exceptional.

John invited George Banks to give Finance's report. George did so efficiently, covering cash flow, accounts receivable, treasury functions, and administration. He was candid about strengths and weaknesses and identified the main issues for improvement as managing cash and collecting money faster.

Marcus was invited to give Marketing's report. He wore tight jeans that rode high on his waist and a tight T-shirt with short sleeves—an athletic look for a nonathletic, paunchy body. I had to admit, though, he did speak well, even if he was a bit light on the details. He spoke about product releases, the sales commission plan, the Web site, and the customer satisfaction survey. He spoke about new directions for the department—they were news to me. He even referred to a major review "we" were completing.

"Any other questions for Marcus?" invited John.

"I'm interested in the client satisfaction survey results," said Janice Waters, the senior representative from IT. "I know Nicholas mentioned it earlier, but I'm interested in the process we used to select the customers in each division. I'm wondering if the clients surveyed were nominated by the division or if they were randomly selected."

Nicholas Strange jumped in. "That's a detail, Janice. Don't let's waste time on that."

Janice's head, with eyebrows raised, did a double take. No one else moved. Momentary silence.

"You have a good point, Janice," said John. He turned to Alison, "Let's put that on the flip chart and we can come back to it."

John turned to Marcus. "Thanks, Marcus, good report." Marcus beamed, adjusted his pants, and sat down.

"Okay, Hugh." John looked at Hugh who was still sitting next to me. He was playing with his phone and looked up in surprise. "Would you like to share your HR report?" John beckoned.

I shuffled my chair to one side so Hugh could extract himself. He updated the audience on the employee survey results from several months before. The results he shared were more positive than I vaguely recalled from Marcus's presentation at the time.

"Okay," John said, "thank you, everyone. We're in good shape but need to be conscious of the challenges for the future. After lunch, we'll be thinking about our future."

Alison jumped up from her seat near the front. "Okay, we have an hour break for lunch. Be back here at two. Thanks, everyone!"

When I arrived at the lunchroom, most seats were already taken. There were two options—either a spare seat next to Maxine, or a spot at Nicholas's table. A tough choice. I chose Nicholas, who waved a hand, welcoming me to take a seat.

Nicholas, on my left, was in deep conversation with the external facilitator on the other side of him and with Hugh opposite. I was at the end of the table so there was no one on my right to talk to. The seat opposite me was vacant. I ate in silence, as if alone.

Soon, Alison appeared and ushered us back into the main room. All the younger people had arrived, but a number of the executives were missing. John was already in his seat.

Shortly thereafter, Nicholas bustled in, followed by Ryan and Maxine. Hugh arrived, and then Gus.

"We've been for a walk," Gus explained as he plopped himself next to me. Not for too long, I hoped. I didn't want a sweaty Gus in my face all afternoon.

Finally, everyone was present. Alison clapped her hands for our attention. "I now want to formally introduce you to our facilitator, Christopher Robertson, who has worked with Harlow Kane for many years. Christopher is going to help us with a key objective of this retreat, which is to plan our vision and actions for the next five years. Please join me in giving Christopher a warm welcome."

Christopher rose to his feet, which took some time. He was a large man, balding and untidy. When he spoke, his cultured voice didn't match his messy appearance.

He paced slowly to the front of the room and planted his feet. "I've been involved in facilitating Harlow Kane's strategic planning conferences for six years now." His booming voice shook the room as he continued. "We should be proud of the gains we have made as a company."

I wondered whether he should be claiming to be part of the Harlow Kane "we."

"In this next session," bellowed Christopher, "we're going to brainstorm where we want the company to be in five years' time. Take a piece of paper, and for the next six minutes, write down where you believe Harlow Kane will be in five years. What are the forces shaping our future? What is the environment we need to respond to?"

After six minutes, Christopher called us to attention and asked us to share our thoughts.

A rush of good ideas flowed—about future society, about the economy, about global power shifts, about technology and communication, about employment and education, about ethics and corporate governance.

Every now and then, Gus piped in a shallow contribution: "In five years' time, we will be truly client focused." "In five years' time, all employees will live our vision."

One of the quiet young professionals offered, "In five years, we need to be good at knowing our market segments."

Nicholas ridiculed the idea with a cynical laugh. "We need to know that by yesterday!" The young woman looked embarrassed and maintained silence after that.

Christopher wrote all our ideas on the flip chart in small, scratchy writing. Finally, he called an end to the five-year horizon session. "I'll write this up tonight. Let's move on." He turned the flip chart to the next blank page.

For the next three grueling hours, it was open season on what was good, bad, or otherwise about our current vision. Most of the debate raged among eight or so people. Everyone else declined to fight for airtime. Because the discussion was allowed to run wild, in order to enter the debate and be heard, you had to start talking just as the current person was finishing. If you waited politely for the speaker to finish, someone else jumped in ahead of you. I had no hope. I looked over at Alison's seven rules and mentally ticked them off—yep, we'd broken almost all of them.

After hours of pointless babble, only pre-dinner drinks saved us from further agony.

"Okay," commanded Christopher, "if no one's got anything else to say, we'll finish it there. Any other comments? No? Well, that's decided—going, going, gone!" He punched his right-hand fist into his open left hand to end the discussion.

Alison looked up in amazement.

"The current vision stays," Christopher announced.

Alison raised her eyebrows and dropped her mouth in surprise.

Drinks were served on the terrace. People complained that the whole session had been a complete waste of time.

Just before I thought we'd be heading into the dining room for dinner, I made sure I was near James.

"Can I sit next to you?" I whispered.

"Of course!" he smiled.

"You can fill me in on your vacation."

Dinner was enjoyable—great company, food, and wine. James told us all about his African safari.

I felt another twinge of guilt about resisting Paul's begging for a vacation. Soon, we could have a good long trip. It wouldn't be long before I would have my project reviewed. Then we could have a break before I began to implement the recommendations.

44
The Way Ahead

THE NEXT MORNING AFTER BREAKFAST, we gathered afresh outside the conference room.

We ambled into the room for the scheduled eight-thirty start. I said hello to Gus and sat down. Hugh was no longer sitting next to me. He was now sitting next to Nicholas, and Janice Waters was next to me. That was an improvement.

Alison looked anxiously at her watch, waiting for stragglers to arrive. She went to the door to check for latecomers. There didn't seem to be any. She shrugged, shut the door, and walked to the front of the room.

"Okay," she clapped her hands lightly, "let's—"

The door swung open and in walked Maxine and Ryan. "Good morning," they sang happily. No apology.

Alison smiled and continued, "Let's get started. I received feedback last night on yesterday afternoon's session, and we'll revisit the vision later in the day." There was a rumbling of approval.

"Now," she said, "I want to pass you straight over to Christopher who will lead the next session on priorities for the coming year."

"Thank you," boomed Christopher, tucking his shirt into his pants as he stood. "We are now going to move into teams. Team One will consider the subject of clients. Team Two will look at suppliers. Team Three, your topic is people, and Team Four will be considering new products and services. Please break off into your teams now and be back in thirty minutes with your key recommendations. You can use the rooms along the corridor," he said, pointing.

He turned a flip chart to show who was in which team. I was in Team Three—people. That's a pity, I thought. My skills and interests would have been much more suited to the new products and services team.

We obeyed his instructions and left the conference room in search of our team rooms. My group found ours, and we gathered around the table. There were six of us, but chairs for only five. I volunteered to go out and search for an extra chair. Gus, who was on my team and standing near the door, waved that he would find a chair. He left and never returned.

"What does Christopher want us to do?" we asked each other. Everyone was confused. My team consisted of George from Finance, Clive from Sales, Jodie, a young sales rep, Alan, an experienced sales rep, and Gus, who'd gone missing. I introduced myself to Jodie, Clive, and Alan.

"He wants us to do an analysis of our strengths, weaknesses, opportunities, and threats," George answered.

"Do you think we should do that?" I smiled at George. "We only have thirty minutes; there's no time to do a complete SWOT analysis."

"But we can't get to recommended actions until we consider our current situation," Clive said. He was sitting at the head of the table.

"I'm going to get clarification," I said.

I started to walk back to the main room when I saw Christopher come out of another room. He was a daunting figure, this bear of a man.

"Christopher," I said, "our team needs clarification on our assignment."

"Okay," he said. "I've just been helping Team One as well."

As we walked to our room, Hugh cornered us from the opposite direction with the same request. Christopher rolled his eyes, sighed, and said he would join him in a moment, after he'd helped our group.

We were now down to twenty-five minutes to complete our exercise. Christopher said we could have another five.

He stood at the front of the room with his hands on his hips. "Your exercise," he explained very slowly, as if we were kindergarteners, "is to identify the top three things that the company should do to make the most progress on being an employer of choice, where employees want to join you, stay with you, and are motivated to contribute enthusiastically."

"Oh! We can do *that*!" everyone chorused with childlike enthusiasm.

"Why didn't you say that in the first place?" Clive said. It had to be what we were all thinking.

"It was clear enough—for smart people," waved Christopher as he left us to join Hugh's team.

For another ten minutes, we argued. It was Clive who broke the deadlock. "I'm going to find Hugh and see if he can set us straight on what information HR has." He was back in a few minutes.

"Hugh says the top three issues are career plans, first-line supervisors, and flexible work policies. Let's go with those."

"It's all we've got," Jodie said. "I agree."

Clive quickly wrote the three items on a flip chart. I wondered why, if Hugh already knew the answers, we were going through this process.

Christopher put his head in the door and asked us to make our way back to the main room. Clive volunteered to present our report. No one objected.

As we resumed our seats, Christopher was herding everyone back, including the stragglers who were grabbing coffee.

He stood at the front of the room, waiting, as the noise level escalated.

"Will everyone shut up!" he hollered.

Instant silence.

"Okay," he smiled approvingly, "Team One, could you please present your views on the subject of clients."

Ryan Gunn, as the spokesperson for his team, walked to the front of the room.

"At Harvard, this topic received a great deal of focus. If we accept that client relationships are important—"

"Can I interrupt you there?" interjected Christopher. "Why if?"

We'd had enough. Christopher was himself interrupted by twenty people demanding "Let him speak!" Ryan and Christopher glared at each other. Finally, Christopher waved for him to go on.

"*If*," Ryan continued, heavily emphasizing the word, "we accept that client relationships are important, there are three recommendations that we suggest. The first is that we need to improve our client surveying methods. Currently, each division nominates the clients they would like to have surveyed. We should select clients randomly so that the surveys are more reliable."

I glanced at Janice Waters. This was at least an acknowledgment that her idea from the previous day had been worthy after all. She looked blank, giving nothing away.

"The second thing is that we should nominate a key group of large clients we want to become particularly close to and strategize our specific approach to each of those clients. And the third thing is that we need to appoint and train a client manager for each of these key clients."

"Well done, Ryan," said Christopher. "That is excellent direction."

Ryan beamed. I felt all of Team One deserved the credit, not just Ryan.

Team Two went next on the subject of suppliers. Hugh Worrell spoke. He covered seven steps before Christopher interrupted.

"The group has done a thorough job." Christopher gestured to the chart. "If you had to nominate just three actions, what would they be?"

Hugh started to nominate three topics, but others in his team had other ideas. Christopher suggested that during one of the breaks the team regroup and decide the three most important actions.

Christopher applauded Team Two and invited our team, Team Three, to share our report. Clive presented the three proposed subjects: career plans, first-line supervisors, and flexible work policies. Hugh and Nicholas signaled agreement. We were asked what we proposed to do about the issues.

"We were about to get to the fixes, but we ran out of time," Clive answered.

"What you should do then," said Christopher, "is to have Hugh work with the group following the conference to develop action plans on the three topics."

"Team Four," said Christopher, "please present your report."

Maxine jumped to her feet and almost ran to the flip chart. Thank goodness she was wearing low heels for a change. I could relax.

Janice leaned over to me. "I think we came up with some really good ideas. This session was wonderful—Maxine was our inspiration!"

As Maxine proceeded to turn the blank cover page over to reveal her team's presentation, my breath instantly left me. In the next second, I was suffocating, my air suddenly cut off, my throat knotted. I felt ill. This couldn't be happening. I was having a nightmare. No, I wasn't. This was real. It was there, right in front of me, in front of everyone—*my* presentation!

The following fifteen minutes are still a blank for me. I was out of my body, floating elsewhere, not concentrating or focusing. I struggled, successfully, to hold back tears. I was too angry to cry.

Without shame, Maxine Savage went through, exactly, the key aspects of the presentation I'd explained to her two weeks earlier. The market assessment. The competitor analysis. The social trends. The financial projections. The capital investment. The anthropological conclusion. The key breakthrough ideas. Abbreviated, but still my work. The deceitful cat! She'd liked my ideas after all. More than liked them, she'd loved them, stolen them, and taken the credit. And she claimed to have come up with it in twenty-five minutes!

Vaguely, I heard her finish and the applause in the room brought me back to the present. Group Four looked as pleased as punch.

"Maxine!" John stood, clapped, and beamed. "It's fantastic! This has every potential to revolutionize Harlow Kane. I am really excited about this. We'll be so far ahead of the competition; we'll be first to the future! It will take them so long to catch us, and in the meantime, we'll have enjoyed a honeymoon of market share growth and increased profits. But we need to keep this top secret. We should all re-sign our confidentiality agreements—today. I can only begin to dream of where our business will go." He was out from behind the table, shaking Maxine's hand. Maxine was beside herself with glory.

"How did you get all that done in such a short time?" he asked. "Who else was in the group?" The group proudly waved their hands.

"Well done, everyone!" said John excitedly.

"To be fair," Janice spoke up next to me, "it was really Maxine's work. She had all the ideas and seemed to have it all worked out in no time. All we really did was confirm that her ideas were brilliant."

John turned to Christopher. "Christopher, thanks for helping us get ideas like this. I think we should change the rest of the program and use what time we have together today to develop Maxine's ideas into a specific action plan. That way, we can leave here with a final plan and begin to implement it immediately. I'm absolutely taken with this idea. It's so clever, yet so simple, and so damn practical!"

John turned to me. "Lauren, can you please work closely with Maxine for the rest of the day and pick up what you can?"

Words would not come, my throat still in a knot. Surely, this was not happening.

"Let's break for five minutes," John said, still smiling, "and when we return, Christopher will have organized teams for the rest of the day to fast-track Maxine's ideas to finality. We're going to leave here with the future painted very bright. And it's a beautiful picture."

Everyone stood and clapped. Maxine raised a hand slightly in acknowledgment. She stood by the door and received handshakes and praise as people left the room. I waited, stuck to my chair, until Maxine had left the room. Then I could leave.

I had to get outside—had to escape. I went for a walk. I'd left my phone in the room, so I couldn't call Paul. I was on my own. I tried to think through the situation logically, but my thoughts were jumping all over the place, emotions flowing between anger and shock, always coming back to the same unanswerable question—what now? Do I expose Maxine? Who would believe me?

The only other senior person I had shared my presentation with was Gus, and he had only sat through the first few slides. He was hardly a reliable source of support. I would talk to James, but not yet. This was neither the place nor the time.

By now, I was out of the vineyard on a gravel road leading nowhere. Hot tears flowed, streaming down my face. I stopped to wipe my eyes and tried to focus. I desperately needed Paul and Annie and Harry, needed them right now. I walked aimlessly for hours.

By late afternoon, I was composed enough to return to the scene of the crime. No one seemed to have missed me. Their work had been absorbing, and final presentations were already under way.

I sat dumbstruck in the conference room as each group presented an aspect of the initiative. Within only half a day, it had gathered a pace and a life of its own.

How would I ever be able to expose the scam? I would be called a liar and a thief if I tried to set the record straight. I packed my bag and drove home.

Finally, finally, I returned to my refuge, my home, my family.

"Hi, honey!" shouted Paul as I slammed the front door. "How was the retreat?"

I flew into his arms and sobbed my heart out.

45

Fork in the Road

AS I POURED MY STORY OUT TO PAUL, the whole time I'd spent at Harlow Kane was flashing through my head. The way I'd said nothing when Hugh stole my sales training idea and my chance for an early win. The way I'd struggled to show my strategic marketing proposal to people who hadn't had the time to see ideas that were now so electrifying as the product of a twenty-five-minute brainstorm. The way my contributions had been scoffed at and my value questioned from the start. I'd never be able to recover from the theft of eighteen months' work.

Paul kissed me on the forehead and gathered me into his arms, shocked. "I can't believe it. And they weren't even suspicious?" He took a step back and looked me in the eye. "They're not good enough for you. They don't deserve you. You should leave the bastards."

"You're right." I heard the words come out of my mouth, and suddenly they seemed like a real option.

"Don't be the victim anymore! You don't have to accept it." He was getting angry. I sat glumly, wondering what to do. We were silent for a few minutes, absorbing the enormity of it.

Paul's tone turned sympathetic. "But you are the only one who can decide how you choose to respond. It's as much a question of your character as it is of hers. What are you going to do?"

"I know what I would like the answer to be!" I said.

Annie came into the room.

"Well," Paul said, touching my shoulder, "you need to do something, so you can at least sleep at night. Let's talk later."

"Are you talking about your boss again, Mom?" asked Annie.

"Yes, darling," I answered, emotionally drained.

It was Friday, so at least I had a few days to think about my response. I had had enough for one day. After settling the kids in bed that night, I went straight to bed myself, telling Paul we'd talk in the morning. I hardly slept.

* * *

The next day, Paul asked what my thoughts were on the things we talked about.

"Well, first of all," I said, "I agree that I need to do something. I can't go on like this. I'm exhausted, and that doesn't help you or the kids. I have no energy to devote to myself, to my family, let alone do my work properly."

"So, what are you going to do?"

"Well, one option is to look for another job. Another is to leave work and be a full-time mom. Another is to set up my own business as a consultant. Or, of course, I could try to stay at Harlow Kane."

"I like option one," he laughed. "And it's good you've got choices. You'll be successful at whatever you do."

We talked for a long time. I kept circling back to two key thoughts. First, I really liked the challenges of a corporate job and felt I still had more to offer. Second, a serious wrong had been inflicted on me. As tempting as it was, I had to think carefully before running away. I had run from Deadly Di Ashman and straight into Marcus, Maxine, and Nicholas. I couldn't keep running. I had to stop being the victim.

I drew a deep breath. "I think I should expose Maxine!" The instant the words left my mouth, I felt stronger. Yes, this was right.

Paul looked up at the ceiling and then at me.

"Are you sure?"

"No. I'm not sure," I said, "but I prefer that option."

"I'm with you if you want to do it. But I wouldn't think less of you if you just wanted to walk away."

"All my life I've walked away," I said with growing confidence. "I've let people walk over me because I didn't want to fight, didn't want to be the bad girl. But it's time for me to grow up and stand up for myself." It was good to say it, to acknowledge it out loud.

I stood up. "I'm going to tell them what she did!"

"What will you do?"

"Well, I know James will back me up," I said, sitting back down, "so I'll get his advice. Also, Sandra and Ben know the work I did, and I'm sure they'll back me too. And there's Sally Morton. The key person will be John Squires. If Nicholas Strange was the CEO, it would be hopeless. He wouldn't be the slightest bit interested or worried about it. John is at least ethical. He doesn't like conflict, but he's prepared to face issues when he has to, like when he sacked Jeremy Hyde."

Paul came over and knelt in front of me. "I'm proud of you, darling."

46

Grasp Firmly

BY MONDAY MORNING, I was having second thoughts. Doubt had set in. Taking on the Wicked Witch was going to be rough. I worried that people wouldn't believe me. And I had no idea how dirty Maxine would fight. When it came to dealing with people like her, I was a babe in the woods. But I knew I had to expose her actions. If I didn't, then I would be crushed forever.

I stayed home that morning until I'd gained fresh courage about my decision. At about ten o'clock, I drove to work.

The first thing to do was see James Swann. He said he could see me early afternoon. When I sat down with him in a meeting room, I explained how Maxine had stolen my proposal. He said he'd known something serious had occurred, that Maxine's presentation was so much more substantial than anyone would expect from a single thirty-minute team session.

"Show me your presentation," he said. I took him through my files. He saw clearly the material that Maxine had stolen.

"And," I said with a forced smile, "I couldn't have developed this in the few days since the conference." He nodded his understanding.

James stared out the window for a few minutes, reflecting. "And you say that Sandra, Ben, and Sally know about this? Are they familiar with the work you've done?"

"Oh, for sure. They were very much involved."

"Will they support you?"

"I'm sure they will. I haven't asked them yet, but I have no doubt they will stick up for me."

"I think the best step is for you to talk with John Squires. I'm happy to come with you, or do anything to help."

"Thanks, James," I said, suddenly teary. "I will see John on my own, but I appreciate the support."

"You know," he said, "it might get pretty tough. You're doing the right thing, but Maxine is a hell of a fighter. I don't know how she'll react or how dirty she'll play. I wouldn't be a friend if I didn't say this to you. But I'm with you all the way."

After leaving James's office, I grabbed Sandra and Ben and explained everything. They were totally disgusted; they couldn't believe the stunt Maxine had pulled. They agreed to support me wholeheartedly. Next, I went to the top floor, Mission Control, and made an appointment with John Squires. He couldn't see me until the next day at eleven o'clock.

I tossed and turned that night and even came close to changing my mind. Maybe I wouldn't be supported. Maybe I would come out the loser. Maybe I would be the one who suffered. But I had to be able to look myself in the mirror, knowing I had done the right thing and not been a coward.

I decided to go in late again, just in time to see John. I spent a quiet hour at home on my own, made a second cup of coffee, and sat outside. I went through the fable book for inspiration.

> A boy was gathering berries from a hedge when his hand was stung by a nettle. Smarting with the pain, he ran to tell his mother and said to her between his sobs, "I only touched it ever so lightly, mother." "That's just why you got stung, my son," said she. "If you had grasped it firmly it would not have hurt you in the least."

I thought about the outcome I wanted. I thought about the meeting with John, and I visualized the relieved, confident feeling I would have fifteen minutes later. I urged myself to hold on to that uplifting sensation, that cleaning surge.

I had a wonderful feeling of calm as I drove to work.

47

The Judge and Jury

THE CALM FEELING DIDN'T LAST, of course. My hands shook and my heart pounded as I made my way up to Mission Control for my appointment with John Squires.

At first, it was hard to breathe, and I could speak only in short, sharp sentences. John—being the gentle and considerate man that he is—tried to help me relax.

He listened impassively, not giving anything away. This didn't concern me; I could see he was being impartial. The main thing was that he listened intently.

I told him what had happened: how I'd worked on the whole proposal, part of which he knew from the meeting Sally and I had had with him, and about the discussion that I'd had with Maxine and her subsequent stealing of my work at the conference. I showed him my presentation and the support files.

"I am sorry to bring this to you, John," I concluded, breathing a big sigh of relief.

For what seemed like ages, he said nothing. He thumbed through my proposal and looked deep in thought. I waited for his verdict. Finally, he spoke.

"You're right to bring this to me, Lauren. I'm not giving any judgment on the matter at this point. I have heard only your side of the story. I now need to see what Maxine says about this. I'll also need to speak to Sandra and Ben, and I'll talk to Sally Morton as well. I'll confine my investigation to just a few people, only those who are critical to finding out the truth."

"That's all I want—the truth," I said, reassured by John's fair approach to the matter.

"Now, just let me double-check that I understand the situation correctly. You did not share your presentation with any other executive member?"

"That's correct," I said. "I tried to share it with Marcus and Gus and Nicholas, but for different reasons, I couldn't do so. Those meetings were either canceled or, if the meetings did take place, a different subject was covered." I didn't bother to tell him about the difficulties I'd had trying to be heard in the first place.

"Did you leave a copy of your presentation with Maxine?" he asked. I knew now it would've been helpful if I had. It would prove Maxine had specific knowledge of the material.

"No, I didn't. She asked for a copy, but I didn't give her one." What irony—I hadn't given or sent her a copy because I was worried that she would steal my ideas! "But she did take notes," I emphasized. "When I declined to give her a copy, she went back through my presentation and made notes, right in front of me."

"Okay," John said, "I will ask for those notes." He leaned back in his chair, a look of concern on his face. "Thank you for bringing this matter to my attention, Lauren, but I do find it hard to believe that Maxine would do such a thing. Maybe it's a misunderstanding. I'll talk with her, and with Sandra, Ben, and Sally. I'll get back to you within the week."

I thanked John again for his time, left, and waited nervously for his response.

I was due to take Nicholas Strange through my marketing strategy presentation. I canceled the meeting.

48

Hare versus Tiger

SANDRA PEARSON AND BEN BOWSER saw John separately the following day. Sally Morton called and said that John had been in touch. I told Sally I didn't want to know what she had said to John. I didn't want to say or do anything inappropriate during the investigation.

"Don't worry," she said, "I just told him the truth."

Ben found out that Maxine had been in John's office the next day. I kept well away from places where I thought she might be. But the very day that John and Maxine met, she caught me in the parking lot. Luckily, James Swann was with me. Maxine was a few yards away from us as we walked to our cars. I ignored her, but she began walking menacingly toward me, wobbling on her narrow heels.

"Lauren," she barked, "I have just been hauled up to John Squires's office and was given a proper grilling. You're a liar. Why have you laid this shit against me? You're a nasty, wicked woman!"

I was astonished, rooted to the concrete. I didn't want to, but I had to face her. I slowly put down my bags. She and I being about the same height, she held my stare. Oh, God, she was angry. Her face was on fire. I took a deep, slow breath and quickly visualized the wonderful feeling I would have driving home after I successfully confronted this woman.

That beautiful cleansing feeling surged through my body. My strength returned.

"You're the culprit here, Maxine. You stole my presentation. You used my research. Those recommendations were mine. It's unethical and has to be exposed." I felt stronger. "I'm not going to stand by and be a victim, Maxine. Do you understand?"

Without saying another word, she stormed off—as best she could in her wobbling heels.

I began to shake. My legs felt weak and I held onto James's arm for support.

"Good for you, Lauren," he said.

After a few moments, I'd recovered enough strength to resume walking to my car.

"If it makes you feel any better," said James, "you know that by her actions just now, Maxine has severely harmed her case. And what's more, she's now involved me. I'm going to call John tonight at home and tell him what just happened."

I sat in my car for a moment before starting the engine. I was pleased with myself. I had confronted Maxine and not taken a backward step. I had not faltered at the critical moment. I felt stronger now—once my legs stopped shaking,

I turned the car on and drove out of the parking lot for home. I had that wonderful feeling I'd visualized.

That night, while Paul put the kids to bed, I relaxed and listened to Mozart. I opened the fable book for reassurance. I knew them well by now and thumbed through the pages. One caught my eye—I must have read it several times before—but now perhaps it had much more relevance.

> When the lion reigned over the beasts of the earth he was never cruel or tyrannical but as gentle and just as a king ought to be. During his reign he called a general assembly of the beasts and drew up a code of laws under which all were to live in perfect equality and harmony. The wolf and the lamb, the tiger and the stag, the leopard and the kid, the dog and the hare all should dwell side

> by side in unbroken peace and friendship. The hare said, "Oh! How I have longed for this day when the weak take their place without fear by the side of the strong!"

I hoped John would be seeing things this way.

Paul came into our room after tucking the kids into bed and he rubbed my shoulders.

"How do you feel?" he asked.

"Surprisingly, fine. I know I'm doing the right thing, Paul. I've had enough of being pushed around." He stopped massaging. "Keep going!" I urged.

49

The Verdict

THE FOLLOWING MORNING, as I finished checking my email and was wondering what to start on next, my phone buzzed. It was John Squires. He told me he'd completed his investigation and asked me up to his office, immediately if possible. What a relief—he'd come to his conclusion in only three days. I whispered to Sandra that I was going to meet John. Kurt was sitting dangerously close to Ben so I didn't say anything to him.

In the elevator up to Mission Control, I suddenly got nervous. I was about to hear the judge's verdict. I made a quick detour to the bathroom, looked at myself in the mirror, and gave myself a good talking to—"Get a grip, Lauren." I shut my eyes for a moment and visualized a successful outcome. I took a deep breath and left.

"Thanks for coming up," John said, inviting me to sit down.

"First of all, Lauren, I want to thank you for being prepared to raise your complaint with me. That took courage. I also appreciate your obvious trust in me." He had his notepad open and I could read, upside down, that he had half a dozen points listed.

"I have spoken with Sandra, Ben, and Sally. And I have spoken with Maxine. I also had a call from James last night. He told me about the confrontation in the parking lot. The bottom line, Lauren"—I squeezed my hands together and held my breath—"is that I know what you said to me is the truth. Maxine has acted unethically and inappropriately."

Utter relief surged through my body. Tears welled in my eyes.

"When I met with Maxine," he continued, "she denied the allegations. She was also not particularly forthcoming with the notes she made at the meeting with you. I had to insist on seeing her notepad. I could see that her notes and her presentation at the planning conference too closely matched your presentation to be a coincidence. And Sandra, Ben, and Sally corroborated your evidence entirely. At home last night I started to contemplate what punishment suited Maxine's crime. I sought Nicholas's advice.

"He spoke in support of Maxine. He said she is a high performer and her division is performing well. Nicholas disagreed with me that a person's impact should be measured by how much their values and behavior match our culture. He thinks only in terms of their performance."

John stopped speaking for a minute, then went on slowly. "I don't agree. It's not enough for our people to be high performers. They also need to comply with our culture and they must behave appropriately."

John glanced down at his notes. "Given that Nicholas, as Maxine's manager, supports her, I was prepared to give her the benefit of the doubt and give her a formal warning and reprimand. However, when James called and told me about the episode in the parking lot, well, I'm afraid that tipped the scales. I will be talking to Maxine shortly and will advise her that she will be leaving Harlow Kane. I'll allow her to leave with dignity by requesting her resignation, but if she doesn't cooperate, she will be leaving anyway. We cannot condone such behavior."

I felt drained. The emotion of the last weeks was catching up with me. "Thank you, John," I said quietly.

"I will be talking to Maxine in about . . ." he checked his watch ". . . ten minutes. Please do not mention this to anyone. Maxine's leaving is strictly confidential until you see an announcement." He closed his book. "One last thing," he added with a smile. "I stand by what I said at the planning workshop. The strategy ideas—*your* strategy ideas—are fantastic. Congratulations! Could you please make a time to take me through the whole presentation, and then I hope that you will lead the implementation for us. I will be your project champion if you wish, to make sure you have the right level of support. I will communicate to the people who were at the meeting that you are the true leader on this effort."

"Thank you, John," I said, beaming. "That sounds fabulous. I would very much like that!" I stood to leave.

"Thank you, Lauren, for your courage and your professionalism. We need people like you."

"Thank you, thank you very much," I nearly stammered, and left his office.

I floated to the elevators as though walking on air. Mixed emotions struggled for supremacy—I smiled and cried all at once.

The elevator light flicked on, and I moved to the big steel doors as they slid open. Who should pop out but Maxine Savage. She was early for her meeting with John. She stormed past me, tilting on her rocky platforms and hissing over her shoulder, "Your presentation was crap anyway!" Sour grapes.

50

The Beginning

IT'S BEEN A MONTH since Maxine Savage announced her resignation. She left immediately, quietly.

Marcus has been icy to me ever since, but not openly vindictive. He must know what happened, but I think John must have warned him not to punish me. Perhaps Marcus knows which boss is really in control after all. Maybe Marcus respects me more now because of the courage I showed with Maxine. Or maybe Marcus is just more guarded.

Kurt keeps out of my way.

Ben's planning his retirement party, even though it's in two years' time.

I'm driving home and thinking about the role of a boss. It can't be that hard, can it—creating the sort of environment that people find secure and motivating? As a boss, how silly are you if you don't want your people to do their best?

I've decided that if I ever become a manager, I will help anyone who reports to me to be competent and confident. I will treat them as a priority. I will be a boss people can trust because I will trust my people. Above all, I will care.

At this point, I plan to stay at Harlow Kane to see my project through. The company isn't perfect. Nicholas is still a tyrant, and Marcus will never be my ideal boss. But it's also up to me to manage my own responses to situations.

I drop my bags at the front door and head to the kitchen for a glass of wine. Paul sits at the kitchen table poring over a bunch of brochures. Annie and Harry are playing on the floor. As I arrive Annie jumps onto her favorite stool. Harry tries to shove her off, quarreling and insisting that he had the stool first. She ignores him.

"What have you got there?" I ask happily, gesturing to the brochures.

Paul turns to me. "Our next vacation, that's what!"

"Is that right!" I laugh, and go to the cabinet. "Want some wine?"

"Yes, please, love," answers Annie cheekily. I smile mockingly. Harry keeps yanking at Annie's stool.

"I'll have a beer, thanks," says Paul. "How about it. Can we have a decent vacation now?"

"Please, Mom," beg Annie and Harry. They've sorted out the issue of who gets the stool—Annie has conceded.

"Sure!" I shout. "Where do you have in mind?"

"We need to work that out," says Paul. "I've got stacks to choose from. We can have a family discussion and decide."

"Okay! And Annie and Harry . . ." I point to the stool. I don't want Annie growing up giving in to anyone who gets angry, or Harry thinking he can shove people around. "If that stool is so important to you both, you can share it—five minutes each—okay?"

The Boss Reading Group Guide

1. *The Boss* shows some reasons why work negatively impacts people's spirit. In what way does Lauren's experience help you take a fresh perspective with your own work experience?
2. What was your emotional connection to Lauren? Did your connection with Lauren change as the story unfolded? Why?
3. *The Boss* highlights various dynamics of office politics. Which incidents and characters did you most identify with from your experience? Which incidents most amazed or disturbed you?
4. Why does the author use fables to draw parallels to office situations? What fables can you relate to your own work experiences? How might thinking of work situations in terms of fables help you deal with these situations?
5. James Swann encourages Lauren to record her first impressions of the executive staff. What are the advantages and disadvantages to Lauren of this advice?
6. When Hugh Worrell, the HR director, steals Lauren's sales rep training proposal, Lauren feels she has no recourse against such a high-

level executive. Do you agree with Lauren, or is there some kind of action Lauren could have taken?

7. In chapter 39, it seems ridiculous when Gus Wearing says, "Carry on without me," and walks out of the one-on-one meeting with Lauren, but this incident, like all in the book, is based on an actual experience. What may have caused Gus to retreat from the meeting? What would you do if you were Lauren?
8. Sandra and Ben seem to have an easier time than Lauren does in dealing with the difficult personalities at work. What can Lauren learn from her coworkers that might help her in the future?
9. Marcus Pomfrey is known as the Air Traffic Controller. What incidents in the book reveal Marcus's behavior of focusing only on things of immediate, personal interest? What could Lauren have done to better manage her boss?
10. Lauren and her husband, Paul, work on a technique to help Lauren combat stressful work situations. What solution do they come up with? How does Lauren use this to deflect Kurt Wolfe? What other techniques could she use?
11. At the beginning of the novel, Lauren is a victim, suffering under Di Ashman. How does Lauren mature in her ability to deal with bosses?

One way to learn from *The Boss* is to take care in knowing what sort of boss you might be working for when you are interviewed for a job. At www.hardwiredhumans.com you can find ideas and a set of questions to consider when you are preparing for your next interview.

The Boss Workplace Guide for Developing Leaders

UNDERPINNING THE EVENTS IN *THE BOSS* is a serious message about leadership and the impact leaders have on the energy and output of their people. Also underpinning the plot and characters are two key leadership concepts.

The first is the Human Synergistics leadership framework. This model is based on the premise that leaders rely predominantly on one of three styles: constructive, passive, or aggressive. The boss characters in *The Boss* each demonstrate one of these styles.

The second key leadership concept is hardwired human instincts. Courtesy of authorities such as Professor Nigel Nicholson at London Business School, instincts are those behaviors that come as part of the package of being human. Readers associate with demonstrations in *The Boss* of hierarchy and status, contest and display, gossip, coalitions and politics, the power of first impressions, processing information based on emotions or feelings, confidence before realism, aversion to loss and the unfamiliar, empathy and mind reading, and the importance of a family-sized work group. For more on human instincts and the value to leadership practice, visit our Web site: www.hardwiredhumans.com.

Discussion questions and facilitator's guide

The author's motivation in writing *The Boss* is to help grow good leaders and constructive workplaces. There are a number of ways *The Boss* can be used for this purpose. The following discussion questions assist managers in learning from the events of *The Boss*. The questions primarily relate to six chapters in the book. We have selected these six chapters as they are universal leadership subjects and also ones where managers can demonstrate their expertise or their inadequacies.

A free facilitator's guide with suggested answers to the questions is available at www.hardwiredhumans.com.

The Boss and the discussion questions are being used in a number of ways by organizations:

For HR practitioners, trainers, and coaches

Use *The Boss* as a resource for developing effective leaders.

- Management workshops—using chapters as training scenarios with debriefings based on the facilitator's guide
- Lunchtime briefings—small group discussions with you as the facilitator
- Executive coaching—one-on-one coaching to explore the behavioral choices and impact of leaders
- Graduation gift—a gift at the conclusion of your leadership program through which leaders understand their impact on staff energy and output

For leaders

Use *The Boss* as a resource for developing leaders who report to you.

- Mentoring—senior managers can use *The Boss* as a conversation aid with their managers
- Training new appointments—upper management can establish the behaviors they expect of leaders by having them read *The Boss* and then explaining their expectations
- Developing future leaders—executives can illustrate behaviors to model and those to avoid

General Questions About the Leaders in *The Boss*

1. Which character in *The Boss* reminds you most of yourself? What aspects of that character serve you well as a manager, and what aspects might be causing interference?
2. What is the key management style of CEO John Squires? What are the advantages of this style in a CEO, and what are the disadvantages of this style? What could John do differently?
3. How would you describe the leadership style of Nicholas Strange? What are the advantages and disadvantages of his behavior? What are the implications of his behavior for other managers and for Harlow Kane team members?
4. How about Marcus Pomfrey? How would you describe his management style? What are the implications of his style? What should he do differently?
5. What insight do you have into James Swann's leadership style? What actions does James take that endear him to Lauren and her colleagues?
6. If you were featured in a novel, what would you like to have written about you? Write down five words that you would like your team members to say about you. What specific actions are you going to take over the next twelve months to live up to these five words and be an effective leader for your team?

Interviewing Potential Employees

Chapter 2: The Search

On page 9, Lauren arrives at Harlow Kane for her initial interview with Meg.

1. What is your overall impression of the interview?
2. What is your overall impression of the way Meg conducts the interview? What does Meg do well? What does she not do well?

3. Through her behavior, what messages does Meg send Lauren? Are these messages positive or negative? Does Meg's behavior assist her overall goal of hiring a strong candidate?
4. List five words that describe your impression of Meg. Are you left with a feeling that you would like to work for Meg?
5. Describe the key interview technique Meg uses. Does she gain useful information to make an informed hiring decision?
6. Think about the people you have hired. Of the people you have employed, how many would you employ again? Is there information you learned about the people after they were employed that you would like to have known before you employed them? What questions could you have asked at the interview?
7. Learning from *The Boss*, what are you going to do to be more effective in using the job interview as a key management responsibility and your first interaction with a potential new team member?

First Impressions

Chapter 11: The ATC

From page 56 Lauren meets Marcus for the first time.

1. What is Lauren's first impression of Marcus? Write down five words that describe Marcus from Lauren's perspective. What is it about Marcus's words and actions that create this impression?
2. What does Marcus do on his first day? What impact do Marcus's actions have on his authority to lead?
3. Given Lauren's and Marcus's different personalities, Marcus has challenges in being Lauren's manager. How could Marcus have used his first meeting with Lauren to better understand her and how to most effectively be her manager? What management style do you consider would allow Marcus to get the best out of Lauren?
4. What are the possible consequences for Marcus in having Lauren leave Marcus's office dissatisfied with their first meeting?

5. Imagine that you are Marcus and you are planning your first day. Write down your plan for the day:
    a. What is your objective for the day?
    b. What do you want your team members to say about you at the end of the day?
    c. What are your first actions?
    d. What is your approach in a first meeting with individual team members?
6. The next time a new person joins your team, what are you going to do to create a positive first impression? Please name any specific examples of things you currently do or have seen others do to create a positive first impression.

Performance Appraisals

Chapter 20: Torture Chamber

From page 98 Lauren has her first performance review with Marcus.

1. What are at least five attributes of a productive appraisal review?
2. How does the appraisal in this chapter rate on your list of attributes? In your view, what are the aspects of Lauren's review that represent good practice, and what aspects represent poor practice?
3. What is it about appraisals that cause concern to team members?
4. What is it about appraisals that cause concern to managers?
5. How did Lauren feel that night when she went home and over the weekend? What is likely to unfold in Lauren and Marcus's relationship if nothing changes?
6. Imagine that you are Marcus and are preparing for Lauren's appraisal. Write down your plan for the review:
    a. What is your objective for the review? What outcome do you want?
    b. How do you plan for the review?

   c. How do you start the review?
   d. How do you point out any concerns you have? Write the first sentence you will use to point out concerns.
   e. How do you cover the sensitive subject of the appraisal rating? Write down the words you will say to Lauren.
   f. What words do you want Lauren to use to describe her appraisal to Paul when she goes home that night?

7. What will you do differently in the future based on your learning from this chapter?

Salary Review

Chapter 22: Oh, to Feel Valued

From page 108 Lauren has her first salary review with Marcus.

1. Why does Lauren feel the way she feels?
2. What has Marcus done well during the review? What has he done poorly?
3. What are the factors that a manager takes into account when reviewing salaries? How can you incorporate these factors into your conversation with a team member informing them of their salary review?
4. What are the aspects of salary that most impact a team member's satisfaction or frustration with their salary raise? What are the likely aspects of a salary review discussion that can cause concern to a team member? What can you do to avoid these potential negatives?
5. Imagine that you are Marcus and you are about to conduct Lauren's salary review. Write down your plan for the review:
   a. How do you start the review? What words do you use?
   b. What explanation do you give for Lauren's salary review?
   c. How do you want Lauren to feel when she leaves your office?
   d. What words do you want Lauren to use to describe her salary review when she goes home that night?

6. What will you do differently in conducting future salary reviews based on your learning from this chapter?

Developing Employees

Chapter 23: Feeding the Horses

From page 114 Lauren meets with Marcus to discuss her career development.

1. Lauren was angry after the meeting. What was it about Marcus's behavior that provoked her response?
2. What are the desired outcomes of an effective development discussion between a manager and a team member?
3. What questions might managers use to help their team members think through their development and career options?
4. What are some strategies and tools that managers can use to assist others in planning and developing their career?
5. If a team member has *not* identified a development point that you considered to be important, how would you raise this?
6. Imagine that you are Marcus and are planning the career development discussion with Lauren. Write down your plan for the meeting:
    a. What do you do in preparation for the meeting?
    b. How do you start the discussion? What words do you use?
    c. What outcome do you want to achieve?
    d. What words do you want Lauren to use to describe her career discussion and you when she goes home that night?
7. Compared to career discussions you have done in the past, what will you do differently in the future based on your learning from this chapter?

Review with the Senior Leader

Chapter 29: First Looks

From page 141, Lauren has a project review with Nicholas Strange. Marcus is also present.

1. Explain the events in this meeting from the perspective of each of the characters: Lauren, Marcus, and Nicholas.
2. What are the likely implications of Nicholas's response to Lauren? How did Lauren feel that night when she went home?
3. Knowing that each interaction with a person influences the relationship (positive or negative or both), in your opinion what impact would this review have on
    - Future interactions between Lauren and Nicholas?
    - Future interactions between Lauren and Marcus?
    - Future interactions between Marcus and Nicholas?
4. Why does Marcus not support Lauren? What motivates Marcus to make the choice that he makes? What are the advantages and disadvantages of his choice? What would you have done, specifically, if you were Marcus?
5. With the benefit of hindsight, what should Nicholas have done at the point where he began to doubt the value of Lauren's proposal?

www.ingramcontent.com/pod-product-compliance
Lightning Source LLC
Chambersburg PA
CBHW030825310726
48980CB00006B/640/J
* 9 7 8 1 9 2 9 7 7 4 8 9 0 *